CW00420806

GRAVE

MATTERS

An anthology of dark fiction and verse
selected by W.A. Grüppe

Contents

Foreword

Dear Reader,

Over a year has past since my last collection of darkness was brought to your attention.

And now, with dank chills running through the putrescent molluscs of my desiccated heart, I bring you my latest tome — Grave Matters — a masterpiece of pure malice for you to feast your eyes upon and duly wither at the darkest thoughts and mindscapes conveyed within.

Sincerely yours,

W.A. Grüppe

Grave Matters

Grave Matters

By Colin Butler

On a grey Hallowe'en Evening,
The graveyard shrouded in mist,
Cold enough to freeze your bones,
Just the place for a ghostly tryst.

Ominous shapes start to appear
As darkness overcomes the light,
Shambling out of the gloom
To relish the kingdom of the night.

A grave splits open with an eerie creak,
A decomposing corpse clambers out.
The graveyard is filled with rotting corpses
Enjoying their annual walkabout.

The bells toll their funereal dirge
In the belfry of the church tower.
The graveyard a mass of eerie shapes,
The clock strikes midnight – the bewitching hour.

The zombies are on the move
Shambling forward in a parody of ballet.
The stench of corruption fills the air,
Beware anyone who obstructs their way.

Reborn

By Paul Bunn

Chapter 1

The vagrant sat on the cool ground, back propped against the gravestone, and gave a ragged sigh. The bottle of red wine he held in his grubby hand was half empty, his eyes like slits as he fought against the drunken stupor that was gradually overcoming him. He lifted the bottle unsteadily to his cracked lips. "Come to papa," he said with barely a whisper.

The liquor burned the back of his throat, with some of it spilling out onto his grizzled, unshaven chin, soaking the threadbare, grey jacket he wore and mixing with the other unmentionable stains it carried. It had been a long time since he had worried about his appearance.

He tried to remember when he did care; there had been a beautiful woman and a child, a boy he thought. An unfamiliar yearning came over him at that moment and for the first time in a long time he felt warm, salty tears roll down his cheek.

Not wanting to feel the hurt anymore he took a large swig of wine and the memory quickly washed away like water through his fingers. He tilted his head back and finished the bottle in two or three gulps before throwing the empty away.

"Time for another one," he slurred, getting unsteadily to his feet. He had a stash around somewhere he was sure.

He hardly noticed a gnarled hand shoot up from the soft ground beneath his feet and grab his leg tightly, pulling him down. He didn't have time even to register a scream.

Chapter 2

"Where am I?" My voice sounded flat in the darkness.

Slowly, I raised my hand until I touched some sort of surface inches above my face... it was slimy and wet, yielding slightly to my touch as I tried to gauge how much space I had to manoeuvre in.

It was cold; a bone chilling numbness encompassing me causing a shiver to run up my spine. Still, I was confused, unable to think of what had happened to me, memories of my life were vague and distant. I raised my legs until my knees touched this same material that my hands had reached. A sense of alarm rose within me as I could still not see anything and a claustrophobic blanket of fear spread itself rapidly across my mind.

Pushing hard at the surface above me, it gave way with a soft crack releasing what felt like soil over my face. It poured into my nostrils, mouth and ears and I began to choke, having no luck at stemming the flow with my hands. Frantically, I started to push my way up, thinking it was all I could do. A sudden surge of strength forced my way through the dirt until my hand reached through into the coolness of the air above.

Chapter 3

Somehow, I got out, looking down on the hole which had been my prison. Had I been buried by mistake or was there something more sinister going on?

It was still pitch black with distant street lighting having very little impact in the gloom surrounding me so I had no idea where I was, except it was a graveyard.

There was one thought though that nagged at me; no matter how much I tried I couldn't remember my name. In fact, not a thing about my life. It was as if I had been born in the coffin just moments ago into a completely new existence.

Looking around I tried to see if anyone was about, although what they would make of someone covered in dirt having emerged from their last resting place I didn't know. I just needed to get out of there, and sooner rather than later. Perhaps if I could get to a police station then maybe they could help out, piece together my life for me. I just needed to start somewhere.

I stood up but my legs were stiff, unwilling to move themselves at first so I stood there, swaying slightly, hoping they would regain some sort of momentum shortly. Frustrated, I plunged my hands into my earth clogged pockets and was surprised to find something metallic amongst the detritus. Retrieving it carefully, I picked as much dirt off as I could but was unable to see it properly in the gloom. The limited light however did give it a faint glint of gold; it was some sort of ring, quite chunky and with some weight to it.

Intrigued, and with the sudden hope that I had something to identify myself I forced my legs to move themselves, which reluctantly they did, although still very inflexible.

"I bet I look like a zombie," I said, suddenly breaking out into a fit of giggles as the sudden thought of a blood thirsty ghoul crossed my mind.

Recovering my composure, I moved towards the nearest shaft of light so I could get a better look at the ring I carried. After approximately 50 yards of tortuous walking with my legs squealing in protest, I stood under the orange glow of a sodium streetlight and peered closely at the ring for the first time.

It was a gold initial ring with the letters "GW" on it, and was, as I thought, quite chunky. I turned it over to see if there was an engraving on it but the mud was too encrusted to see properly.

"Damn," I said under my breath and tried to find a stick or something to pick it off but a quick search found nothing. On the point of giving up and waiting until daylight, I saw a stand pipe just feet away with water dripping from it in a slow splatting sound onto the footpath. Forcing my legs to move once more I reached it and, turning it on, allowed the gush of cold water to flow over the ring, rubbing it hard at the same time with my fingers.

Gradually the mud washed away and I saw there was a small engraving along the inside. It was elaborately written but read:

To Graham, all my love L x

"Graham," I said out loud in the hope of it ringing a bell. "Is that me?"

For the first time I felt a connection with something, a thought that perhaps I did have an identity, that there was someone out there who knew me, loved me even.

Turning the tap off I sat down on the ground and stared at the ring once again, rolling it over and over in my fingers. Still, my mind was a blank page, nothing came back to me, not even a hint of anything tangible.

A noise like a breaking twig brought me out of my reverie and I looked up. I could not see much beyond a few feet but there had been movement I was sure, a deeper shadow amongst the shadows had sped past. It could have been an animal but some instinct told me it was something else. I couldn't put my finger on it though. Crawling slowly over towards the area I thought it had come from, I felt a frisson of fear worm its way into my mind. Had someone been watching me?

I shook my head, pushing the thought away. "Stupid idiot," I scolded myself as I reached and then peered over the stone. There was something lying on the ground but it was too dark to make out exactly what it was. Gingerly, I reached down and picked the object up, it was soft and sticky as I brought it up until a shaft of light caught it. It was a human hand.

The fingers were half closed with blood covering most of them and the wrist area looked as if it had been torn off as it was a jagged mess. It was also still warm.

I expected myself to be running away in terror at this find but I didn't, morbid fascination being my main reaction. Although there was some sympathy for whoever the appendage belonged to, my thoughts turned to who or what had done it and why?

Placing it back to where I had found it I stood up, looking around carefully to see if I could find the culprit. No movement caught my eye this time so I returned to my original position, trying to make sense of everything that had gone on so far that night.

Chapter 4

Among the deep shadows he hid, the hungry eyes looking at the figure as it searched for him. There would come a time when they would meet but not now, there were things to be done first. Yes, he nodded his head in self-agreement, much to do. Turning without looking back he made his way silently off into the gloom.

Chapter 5

As sunlight peeked its head over the horizon, it touched the leaves on the trees in such a way that they glistened as it caught the early morning dew. A myriad of colours reflected from them dancing in front of my eyes.

I raised myself from the ground having slept peacefully the whole night. My mouth felt dry as if I'd swallowed sandpaper and getting a good look at myself for the first time in daylight I could see what a state I was in.

I had on what could only be described as tattered jeans, with tears in the knees and the material around the ankles in ribbons. My brown (?) shoes were covered in mould with the upper and lower parts beginning to separate in places, showing worn socks with my toes poking out of the side and ends. I had a T-shirt on with some sort of logo which was illegible due to ground-in dirt. In short, I was a mess.

"Christ, you look like Worzel Gummidge," I said only half-jokingly.

It was early but I had an idea, making my way carefully out of the cemetery, wary in case anyone was about. The streets were silent, too early even for the commuters into town who would normally be scuttling their way to the train station.

Following a row of terraced houses along, I dashed down a side street hoping to find what I had been looking for. I needed to get out of this clothing and into something a little more inconspicuous, otherwise I wouldn't pass unnoticed for long. Fifty yards further down I came to an alleyway running along the back of the houses, hoping against hope I would find what I wanted.

Most of the back gardens were empty of anything useful but then I saw something about halfway down which I hoped would help. Sneaking into the yard I reached up, pulling a pair of trousers and a shirt from the washing line and sneaking off with them.

Quickly changing I felt a little better with clean clothes, dumping the old stuff into a wheelie bin. Ensuring I still had the ring I made my way along the road, not really sure where I was heading.

Chapter 6

Lynn Blundell was a tall woman, almost six feet even without her heels. Her body was slim and toned from the thrice weekly gym visits. Her brunette hair cascaded into loose waves onto her shoulders, with a face set with large dark brown eyes and full lips. The only blemish was her nose which had a slight twist at its centre, giving her a nasal twang when she spoke.

The white blouse and knee length grey skirt perfectly complimented her figure, which she was never slow in showing off in her male dominated office environment.

Today, she was in one of her black moods which her colleagues knew was as good as "do not disturb" as she could have a vile temper, something she never used to have.

The thought of her ex and what had happened still encroached on her mind even after the last year since they split up. She had loved him, giving her all but then something had changed, something she still couldn't put her finger on, and then tragedy had struck...

A knock at the door snapped her back into the present and she looked up from her laptop. "Yes?" she said rather too abruptly. The Office Junior, Mike, hesitantly opened the door, craning his head around, reluctant to enter the office further.

"What is it, Mike?" The eighteen year old visibly winced at the sharpness of her voice, his mop of dark brown hair sliding off his shoulders as he cleared his throat.

She didn't want to be abrupt but when the mood took her she was sucked in and couldn't change her demeanour. "Well?" she said, arching her right eyebrow questioningly.

"Sorry to interrupt, Lynn but there's a call for you and it's urgent," he pulled nervously at his shirt collar as he spoke. "The police."

Lynn's heart quickened, what could they want after all this time? She had painful memories of the last time she had had to meet them which now seemed in another lifetime.

"Put them through now please," she said hastily. Mike's head disappeared from the door without further bidding.

Lynn looked at the phone as if it were some unclean object when it began to ring. "Come on, just answer it," she said to herself. She saw Mike out of the corner of her eye looking over, receiver in hand waiting to transfer the call.

"Shit," she said finally as she grabbed the handset and put it to her ear. As the person on the other end gave her the information, her face changed from a look of incredulity, to confusion and finally to despair.

"I'm coming over," she finally said when the voice finally stopped talking. "I'll be there in about fifteen minutes."

Chapter 7

For the rest of the day I hid from view, not wanting to be seen by anyone. I'd bumped into a couple of young lads as I made my way through an alleyway and had nearly got beaten up.

"Hey, scarecrow man," one had called, who'd had a grey hoodie covering most of his face. "Give us some money."

I'd tried to ignore them both, but the other one grabbed me by the shirt. "Didn't you hear him?"

Again, I shrugged the boy off dismissively but then one of them tripped me up and I collapsed into a heap, hitting the ground hard. It didn't hurt me but I was suddenly very, very angry. "Hey man, are you drunk or something?" Grey hoodie man laughed at his own joke. They both stood over me, looking at me with mocking eyes, "You should cut down, and it's bad for you."

Suddenly, one of them pulled a knife and held it firmly, just inches from my throat.

"Wrong move," I said before my arm shot out and grabbed grey hoodie by the throat.

What happened next seemed like a dream, as if someone else had taken over my body, knocking the two lads out of action in seconds. I stood in front of both of them, surprised and a little scared of my handiwork as they lay on the ground bloodied and moaning in pain. My hands were covered in their blood and I began to shake. I had to get away from this scene before someone came along.

Looking around furtively I strode away, getting as much space as possible between us; eventually I broke into a run until I reached this hiding place. It was in a small area of woodland, not one hundred yards from the housing estate I had been walking through earlier. I was concealed within a tight knot of small oak trees where the foliage was thick and low to the ground.

What had come over me? The strength I had exhibited against the two thugs was both frightening and exhilarating at the same time, I felt invincible. I heard the faint sound of emergency services vehicles gradually getting louder, someone had obviously called them out after my exertions from a while ago. I went to put my head in my hands but stopped as I noticed marks on them. On each palm small black spots had appeared, I was certain they were not there when I looked at them last. Initially, I thought they were spots of dirt but after spending a few seconds scrubbing them together and seeing no difference I took a closer look. The spots appeared to be under the skin not on the surface and for some reason filled me with dread. I had the strangest feeling a clock had started ticking and time was short, no time for dithering.

Letting out a deep breath I peered out of thicket to see if anyone was around; there was a man walking his dog and a couple arm in arm strolling slowly towards the far end of the road opposite. I was going to have to wait until darkness again but that was alright, I had no clue what to do next.

Chapter 8

He had eaten well the previous night so was not hungry. His thoughts now turned to recruiting volunteers and he had heard on the grapevine there were two candidates that would be ideal. He needed some eyes and ears to keep him informed of what was going on over the coming days.

Finding them wasn't a problem as he sneaked his way through the various hospital wards until he found them. His senses were keen and he knew these two would be of help, their minds were weak and controllable.

They were sedated but he still managed to wake them with a touch from his cold, leathery hand although not enough to startle them with his appearance.

Focusing on each one in turn he gazed into their eyes steadily, his pale green eyes strangely hypnotic, "I know who did this to you and can help you in gaining revenge, as long as you help me." He smiled at their affirmative responses and claimed them both as his own.

"Time for the pace to quicken," he said gleefully.

He left without being seen, hiding in the shadows as he moved silently along the street.

Chapter 9

Lynn waited for the detective at the police station, pacing up and down unable to relax, all the old emotions simmering beneath the surface. She ran through the conversation she had had on the phone over and over in her mind and still it didn't make sense. How could anyone do this? The door opened next to the reception desk with a loud squeak and she saw Detective Inspector Chivers standing in front of her. He was about the same height as Lynn but carried quite a lot of weight, especially around his stomach. His face was chubby with small blue eyes and a large bulbous nose that always seemed to have a red tip, as if he had a cold. The lips as he spoke were thin with uneven yellowed teeth caused by his heavy smoking.

"Miss Blundell, please come through," he held the door open for her and indicated with a wave of his arm that she should go first.

The interview room was cold and windowless as she sat herself down opposite Chivers and studied him carefully. "So, what the hell is going on?" Lynn's face hid her feelings well as she waited impatiently for more details.

Chivers sat back and folded his hands on his lap, pursing his lips, uncertainty clouding his face.

"Well?"

Nodding slightly as he came to a decision he leant forward, gazing steadily at Lynn as if looking for answers. "We reckon he was dug up sometime during the night and his body taken away in some sort of transport, a van maybe, but we are still making house to house inquiries."

Lynn looked confused, "Is that it? Haven't you got anything else?" The incredulity in her voice was evident as she stood up suddenly, a hot flash of temper slamming through her body.

Chivers raised his hand, indicating for her to retake her seat, "I haven't finished yet," he said firmly. "Sit back down please."

She stood for a moment or two more before reluctantly taking her seat again. "Graham's wasn't the only body stolen, another was taken not one hundred yards from his grave," he shook his head slowly, his short silvery grey hair shining in the reflection of the room's single light bulb. "The horrible things some people do," he sighed, letting his heavy shoulders sag. "It's very puzzling."

"If you haven't got any answers then what am I doing here?" Lynn felt her anger rising again, but held it in check.

Chivers was a ditherer, one thing she hated in a person and not an ideal trait for a police officer when decisions needed to be made. "I need to ask you where you were last night," he said finally.

Lynn gave him an incredulous look, not believing what she had just heard. "You think I dug Graham up, just for the hell of it," her voice rose sharply. "Are you mad?"

Chivers raised his palm, trying to placate her, "I know it's difficult but I have to ask this question as you were closest to him before he died."

She rose to her feet again, hot tears stinging her eyes, "How dare you ask me that," she said storming out of the room without a second glance.

Chivers did not bother stopping her, he thought he knew from her response that she had no involvement with the events of the previous night.

Chapter 10

I slept fitfully within my hiding place, ignorant of the world around me until woken by the sound of a car horn. My back felt stiff from lying in an awkward position as I sat up and looked around. It was almost dark now, the streetlights just starting to switch on in the gloom. The rest had not made me feel any better, in fact, I felt drained.

"Are you OK, mate," the softly spoken voice came out of nowhere and I turned startled in the direction it had come from. I nearly turned and fled, not wanting to get involved in another altercation that could end up messily.

I could just make out a man of medium build and long shoulder length hair, all other features were hidden from me but he walked with a severe limp in his right leg.

"Who are you?" I took a step back, ready to bolt if need be.

"Don't panic," he said giving a short laugh. "I'm not here to hurt you, was just passing this neck of the woods is all."

He moved closer and I began to make out some of his features, his face had a few days growth of beard and was lean and angular. The nose was small and his eyes were dark, a deep brown that seemed to shine in the limited light available.

"You look lost," his smile was friendly and he seemed concerned. "Do you live around here?"

I was unsure how to respond to this approach, I knew nothing of this man but needed help in finding out who I was; still no memories came to mind when trying to recollect my past.

My hand went to my pocket, fingering the ring that sat heavily there, my only link to a previous existence.

"I seem to have had a bit of a memory lapse," I said falteringly. I didn't know what else to say.

"Why don't you come with me, I only live a five minute walk away and you can tell me over a cup of tea." The man held out his hand, "I'm Colin by the way."

I looked at the hand and hesitated, I wasn't sure what to do. He seemed kind enough but I didn't know him, but what else was I going to do?

I took the hand and shook it, searching the Colin's eyes for answers I knew he didn't have.

"Pleased to meet you," I said with little conviction, "I might be called Graham but I can't guarantee it."

"Graham it is then," he said with a broad smile. "Follow me."

He lived in a small one bedroom flat, which at one time had been part of a bigger house that had been converted. He was on the top floor which meant climbing two flights of steep, narrow stairs.

Placing his key into what looked like a very flimsy door, it opened with a squeak from the hinges and he entered the room. Following him in, my first impressions were not great; we had walked into a small lounge area with just one brown sofa and a small flat screen TV on a table in the corner. The carpet was well worn, almost completely threadbare in some places although reasonably clean. There was a window looking out onto the street below with black curtains hanging loosely at each end.

"Sorry it's a bit cramped but please take a seat," he indicated towards the sofa and headed for the kitchen. "My mum always said that having a cuppa was the best pick me up of the day and she wasn't wrong." How d'you like it?"

"White without," I said without thinking.

"See you know something about yourself," Colin said with a smile. "Even if it is only how you like your tea."

For a moment I was stunned, where had that come from? Was it just the first thing that had come into my head or something more significant? I wasn't sure but it felt like the first crumb of something tangible had happened to me.

Chapter 11

The place he was to use as a base was ideal. There were many dilapidated buildings on this disused industrial estate and this was the largest of the warehouses by quite some distance. The remoteness of the site was also perfect, with no traffic and no people coming anywhere near the place. The one calling himself Pitch was aware of its existence and quickly led them here after absconding from the hospital.

"You have done well," he said with a thin smile.

Pitch shifted uncomfortably from one foot to the other in embarrassment, staring at the floor. "It's no problem, me and

Smudger come here all the time if we need to get away for a bit."

The one called Smudger was three or four inches taller than Pitch and looked at his friend knowingly, "Yeah, when we need to keep our head down." They both giggled at their attempt at humour.

The cold stare he gave the two of them stopped their merriment in its tracks. "By the way, what do we call you?" Pitch said, with a slight tremor in his voice.

In response he clasped his hands together as if about to pray, gazing steadily at his two recruits. "I regard myself as the first of my kind so call me Adam; that will suffice."

"Adam," they said in unison.

With that Adam turned away knowing they would do anything for him should he ask, and that time would be soon.

Chapter 12

She looked into the grave intently, Lynn sensed something didn't seem quite right about it, a wrongness she couldn't quite put her finger on. She had slipped through the police cordon and now stood with the rain steadily falling around her. Her long hair, in which she took particular pride, now hung loosely in wet strands around her neck and across her face. This conveniently hid the tears that had started falling down her cheeks. She shivered but not from the cold; from distant memories that now came back to haunt her, images that brought pain and some anger.

Kicking subconsciously at loose soil at the edge of the grave she realised what it was that had been nagging at the back of her mind. The loose soil was thrown haphazardly all around the grave but that wasn't it, although you would expect maybe one or two piles of shovelled dirt and no more. The hole was round and of reasonably large size but she felt there would be no way of jumping into it and dragging a body out in the space there was. There was something else though, tufts of grass lay all around and on top of the loose dirt; she shuddered. It was as if someone had been digging from the inside to get out.

She felt tingles of fear run up her spine and looked around anxiously, "Pull yourself together woman," she admonished. A cool breeze blew across the cemetery and the leaves rustled like dry bones rubbing together. She no longer wanted to be there and turned, walking hurriedly away. She told herself it was just a silly thought and that dead people didn't come back to life like in some old Hammer horror film.

Getting into her car she turned the ignition key and the engine fired up straight away. She sat there, the car idling, wondering at her sudden insight into what had happened at the grave. Resting her head on the wheel she felt suddenly tired, wanting to rest more than anything else in the world.

A tap on her window caused her to yelp, startled at the intrusion on her thoughts. Detective Inspector Chivers peered in, a grimace across his podgy face. Opening her window she quickly wiped away any tears and gave him a questioning look.

"Can I sit with you a minute, I've got one or two things to ask you and I am getting soaked here."

"Sure," she said indicating the front passenger seat. "Jump in."

Waddling around the car he climbed in, his large frame swallowing up the seat next to her. He took off his trilby hat and placed it on his lap.

Something was troubling Chivers, she could see from his pursed lips that he was chewing things over. "What caused the split between you and Graham?" he said casually, suddenly focusing his full attention on her.

Lynn stared at Chivers for a moment, taken aback by the question and trying to understand its relevance. "What has that got to do with anything," she said, her voice rising.

He raised his hand, trying to stem her obvious anger at his question. "I'm just trying to fill in some gaps; anything that can help me with my investigation, that's all."

Lynn studied Chivers for a moment, pursing her lips, not wanting to re-live a painful time in her life all over again.

Finally, her shoulders sagged, the bold, forthright woman disappearing into an emotional quagmire. She remembered Graham's face, the strong features he had and that wonderful smile that lit up her life whenever he produced it.

"He changed," she said recalling his sudden mood swings which had never been a part of him from the time they originally met. Chivers said nothing, knowing it was best not to interrupt when possibly vital evidence was being divulged.

"We were young, happy, and carefree, all those things a couple can be when they are in love." She took a tissue from her coat pocket and used it to gently dab at her eyes. "I've known many men inspector but Graham was the only one, who made me feel..." her forehead creased as she tried to find the right words. "Special," she said, nodding slightly, happy with her choice.

"You said he changed, in what way?" Chivers coaxed.

Lynn's face almost crumpled but she held it together – just; detaching herself from the memories of the man Graham had become.

"It started about eighteen months after we first met," her hands gripped the steering wheel tightly, knuckles whitening as she remembered their first fight. "I'd got home from work early and wanted to surprise him by making dinner, ready for when he came in."

For about a minute she said no more, staring fixedly out of the windscreen, seeing nothing. Chivers kept his patience.

"He didn't come in when I expected, in fact it was another two hours before I saw him. The dinner was just cold slop in the bin by now," she said in a matter of fact manner, just wanting to relay the cold, hard facts. It was easier that way.

"I could tell something was wrong straight away, even taking into account his lateness. He was agitated, not making eye contact with me, not even giving me a hug as he had done every night." Her voice cracked with emotion but she willed herself to continue. "He took his coat off, tossing it carelessly onto the floor, barely acknowledging my presence. I assumed it had been a particularly bad day at the office, but it just wasn't him!" She looked over to Chivers as if he might understand better the change that had come over Graham but only saw an inscrutable face staring back at her.

"Did he become violent?" Chivers didn't want to push Lynn too hard but was eager to find out how the relationship ended.

"Not the first time, no," she said. "I asked him why he was late, that was all," Chivers could see her neck muscles tighten as she fought to keep her emotions in check.

"He stared at me for a few seconds and I will never forget that look, it was as if I was a piece of shit on the bottom of his shoe." This time she could not prevent herself from sobbing and buried her head in her hands. Chivers passed her a tissue from his pocket and tried to comfort her, although he felt uncomfortable when it came to this sort of situation. He said nothing though, waiting for Lynn to recover so he could get the full picture.

Chapter 13

We sat in silence for a few minutes, lost in our own thoughts just drinking our tea and staring into space. Colin's right leg was stretched out straight and I saw the discomfort in his face as he tried to get it comfortable, "I fell off a climbing frame in my local park as a kid," he said by way of explanation. "The bloody hospital never did set it properly but my parents, bless 'em, never complained," I saw the hurt in his face at the memory, "didn't want to cause a fuss."

"Do you want something to eat? I've got some sausages and oven chips that I can rustle up for you if you like?" He quickly changed the subject and started to lift himself out of the chair but I stopped him with a hand on his arm, "Don't worry I don't feel very hungry, I just want to find out who I am," I pleaded.

Colin sat back down and gave me a quick smile, "Well, I haven't got anything better to fill my days with so I'd be happy to help if I can."

I felt a sense of relief and trepidation at the same time; relief that I wouldn't have to do this on my own and trepidation at what I might find at the end of my journey.

"All I have to link me to my past is this," I said passing Colin the ring I had found in my pocket.

"Umm," he said turning it over slowly in his hand, "just a minute." Giving the ring back to me he gingerly got out of the chair and went into the kitchen where I heard him routing around in some drawers. Returning he sat back down and held up a jeweller's eye glass, "Something I kept from a previous life," he said, taking the ring back and placing the eye glass under his left eye. He studied it for a few minutes, continually turning it over in his hand, taking particular note of the inscription on the inside.

Finally, he finished and looked at me, a satisfied glint in his eye, "I think I know who made this; can I borrow it for an hour or two?"

My heart leapt at his announcement, a sudden flicker of hope igniting within me. "Do you really know who made it?" I hesitated, feeling a certain reluctance to let the ring out of my sight. I had barely known Colin five minutes so how could I be certain he wouldn't just flog it?

He saw my uncertainty and came over to me, taking something from his breast pocket. "Here," he said, placing the object in my hand firmly, "hold onto this until I get back."

It was a black and white photo of a woman faded with age but clearly a striking beauty with long, flowing, possibly blonde hair and soft dark eyes that had a smile all of their own. "Who's this?" I said.

"It's my only link with the past," he said with a distant look in his eyes. "The only thing I ever cared for and it's all I have left of her." He turned and headed for the door, "Keep good care of her," he said with his voice cracking, "I'll need her back."

Before I could say anything else he was gone, the door closing with a gentle click, his unique footsteps disappearing out of earshot.

I was left in silence, staring at the photo and hoping Colin would come back with my ring intact. As I pondered the day's events I knew I had little choice but to believe he would return.

There was no doubt in my mind that I needed help, I would get nowhere on my own, especially the state I was in.

I looked at my hands, noticing how the spots were now becoming more widespread, some even merging together forming a black mass. I shuddered, wondering what kind of disease this could be. Getting up, I searched for the bathroom and found it just off the kitchen, comprising a toilet, small sink and shower cubicle. Tearing off my clothes I got in the shower, allowing the hot water to wash me over, using the soap I found to scrub every part of me as clean as I could manage. When I finished I found a towel next to the sink and dried myself off before traipsing back to the lounge with the towel around my waist. I still felt dirty, as if no amount of washing would cleanse me. All over my skin these strange spots had appeared, covering about a quarter of my body and for the first time I felt truly terrified.

What was happening to me?

Sitting with my head in my hands I waited for Colin's return, hoping against hope that he would have some answers for me.

Chapter 14

Adam knew he had to confront Graham if he wanted to live, something he had felt unable to do when he saw him in the graveyard. He hadn't felt strong enough then but his strength was building gradually, particularly with the sustenance being provided by his henchmen.

The latest victim had just been delivered and Adam watched the tied up and bloodied bundle in front of him.

"I hope she's suitable for you," Pitch said a little nervously.

The young woman was still alive, faint screeching noises coming from her cloth tied mouth as she struggled against the bindings on her hands and feet. Adam circled her slowly, seeing her panic stricken eyes following him around, not daring to let him out of her sight.

"Perfect," he said smiling. "Now leave us in peace."

Pitch and Smudger needed no second invitation having inadvertently seen him in action before and hurriedly left the room. Adam knelt in front of the girl and began to stroke her flowing locks of brown hair, "Don't worry my sweet, you are about to go to Paradise."

He grabbed her neck in his vice like grip and gave it a violent twist. "There," he said as the life disappeared from her eyes, "now it is time to feed."

Standing outside, Pitch looked at his long-time friend and shivered; they had had a close shave today with the latest catch and he was nervous. "We were lucky tonight mate, bloody lucky."

Smudger shrugged, "We got away with it and at least he's happy." He nodded with his head to the room they had just left.

They had laid in wait for her for over an hour, just off a path in the local park, not too far out in the open but near the gates for a quick exit. Previous "hits" had gone like clockwork, with the victim quickly overcome and bundled away ready for "processing" as Adam liked to call it.

The initial grab had been ok, catching the girl completely by surprise and putting his hand around her mouth, but then she had bit him hard on the index finger, which had been too close to her mouth, and she had squealed like a pig.

Hearing shouts nearby they had, under cover of darkness, carried her quickly to their waiting van, throwing her in back and driving off at speed. Pitch was still unsure whether anyone had seen them and it had been praying on his mind.

"Should we tell him?" Pitch suggested.

"Not if we don't want to end up like her," Smudger replied, fear etched on his face.

Pitch was going to say something else but stopped himself, knowing Smudger's response had been true. "Besides, with the chance of revenge against that bastard in the offing, I'm happy to do whatever he wants."

Chapter 15

"His personality changed completely and over such a short period of time." Lynn sat in the coffee shop opposite Chivers, feeling drained but wanting to explain the end of her relationship with Graham.

At one point Chivers hadn't been sure he would get the full story from Lynn and had suggested a coffee to give her time to calm down. He knew of this particular coffee shop a few minutes' drive away and suggested it to Lynn, who accepted.

Now she was in full flow, "Do you know what caused him to change?"

Lynn looked at him perplexed, "Absolutely no idea, it was as if a switch had been turned off in his head," she swirled the remnants of her drink in the plastic cup, staring into it intently. "God knows I tried to work out what his problem was."

She finished her drink in one gulp, "He became physically violent the one time with me," she stated a little too loudly, "slapping me around the face after going on a night out with some friends," she placed the cup firmly down on the table, "and that's where I ended it."

Chivers leant forward, "Just like that?"

Her gaze dropped to the table in front of her, "Well, from my side it was anyway, but he kept hanging around in the shadows," she shivered, her face a maelstrom of confusion, "But he never approached, just watched and I never understood that. I tried to approach him on numerous occasions but he melted away before I could catch up with him."

"Why didn't you call the police?" Chivers slurped noisily at his still hot coffee, enjoying the slightly bitter taste.

"And tell them what exactly? I didn't feel threatened, just confused as to why things changed so suddenly." She closed her eyes, remembering, "I wanted...still want answers, that's all."

Chivers leant back, his stomach flopping over the front of his trousers, picturing a man who had had some sort of mental breakdown. Was this what led to his death? The image was still unclear and he felt frustrated at not knowing more than he actually did.

"OK, that's all for now, unless you've got anything else to tell me," Chivers hesitated as he rose from his chair, "something that may shed more light on the matter?"

Lynn shook her head, "Find who did this," her voice was almost a whisper, "that's all I ask."

Placing his hat on his head and pushing it firmly into position he left the café, shoulders hunched and made his way to the car.

Chapter 16

I heard Colin before the key was put into the door, whistling tunelessly but obviously happy. Striding through to the lounge he looked at me in surprise and then laughed.

"Sorry, I used your shower because I felt so…dirty," I shifted in my seat embarrassed at the liberty I had taken.

Colin raised his hand, merriment still dancing in his eyes, "Don't worry, it's not often I come into my flat to be faced with a half-naked man," he laughed again, slumping down into the settee.

"I'll get you something to wear in a minute, but first the good news!" Colin rubbed his hands together before retrieving the ring and tossing it back to me. "I thought I recognised the handiwork and I was right, it was made by my old colleague Ron, who owns the jewellers just along from where I used to have a shop."

I forced myself to keep calm at this sudden revelation, not wanting to raise my hopes in case they were dashed on further investigation. "Well, don't keep me on tenterhooks, tell me what you've found."

Colin's face turned serious for a moment and he held his hand out, "The photo…please?"

I had completely forgot about it and quickly retrieved it from the back of the sofa where I had left it. "Sorry, it slipped my mind."

Colin took it, a look of relief on his face and placed it back into the breast pocket of his shirt. "Thank you," he said gratefully.

"Anyway, where was I? Ah yes, the ring," he warmed to his task, placing his hands onto his knees, rubbing his palms gently on them. "It was purchased by a Lynn Blundell and she lives only a few miles from here."

The name rang no bells with me, and I felt disappointed. I thought that perhaps a name would break down the mental block so that I would remember the life I used to have.

Colin saw my dejection but refused to be downbeat himself, looking at me with a steely determination he hadn't shown before. "I suggest we go and see this Lynn woman now and see what reaction we get," he got up from his seat, "but let's get you some clothes first, you look about my size so I'm sure there will be something for you."

I watched him limp from the room, admiring his attitude to my predicament, pleased now that I had someone to guide me through this.

The clothing Colin supplied was not a perfect fit but adequate; the trousers were a little tight for me and the sleeves on the jacket ran a couple of inches over the wrist. Still, at least I looked better than I did earlier in the day and I wouldn't feel quite as conscious of my appearance as I had. Almost human.

Colin ordered a cab and we waited for it to arrive. "You don't have to come along with me, this is something I need to deal with."

He shook his head slowly, a smile crossing his thin lips. "What and miss out on all the fun, you must be joking. Besides, you don't know what sort of reaction you'll get from her." He looked at me steadily and put his hand on my shoulder, squeezing it gently. "Let me tag along, just in case you need my help, we don't really know what we will find."

I knew he was right and appreciated his loyalty to me; despite the fact we had only just met, I already regarded him as a friend.

The cab tooted outside so Colin grabbed his front door key. "Once more into the breach," he joked and we both left the flat in good spirits.

Chapter 17

"It is time," Adam studied his two assistants carefully, seeing the thirst for revenge in their eyes, matching his own desire. He had dreamt, during his own short periods of rest that Graham had found the woman with the help of another. Although it had happened quicker than he had thought, he was glad. "You will need to move now," he said clasping his spindly but powerful hands behind his back. "Have you still got the address details I gave you?"

They both nodded almost imperceptibly and left without saying a word, knowing what was expected of them.

Chapter 18

Stopping outside their destination, Colin paid the taxi and, with some difficulty, got out of the car. I followed with some trepidation, my mouth dry and hands, even though the day was cool.

"Are you sure this is the place," I said, suddenly having the urge to run away and forget the whole thing. Colin looked at me and gave an encouraging smile but said nothing, just making his way to the front door.

"What if she's not in?" I said, almost wishing that would be the case.

"Then we wait," Colin said firmly.

Reaching up, Colin pressed the doorbell and we waited, no sound came from within. Colin tried again, after a few seconds this time there was movement and someone behind the door fiddled with lock and eventually opened it just a crack.

"Yes?" Came a woman's irritated voice.

"Hello, my name's Colin and I have someone out here who is interested in meeting you."

At this point, I was standing behind Colin so the woman couldn't see me and I felt reluctant to show myself, unsure of her reaction.

Colin stepped back and I saw the partially hidden woman's eye turn from confusion to recognition before she gasped and fainted. The door swung open as she fell back and after initial hesitancy we rushed in, closing the door behind us.

"Is she alright?" I could not hide the concern in my voice as Colin examined her carefully. "Yes, she'll come around in a minute, just fainted is all."

We lifted her gently and walked through to a small lounge with a white leather settee in one corner. Laying her down gently onto it we both took up the two other single seats but with the same white leather upholstery.

After a minute or two the woman who I assumed was Lynn Blundell began to stir, moaning softly as she slowly raised her head.

"Whaa?..."

"It's OK my dear, we're not here to hurt you," Colin soothed. "We're just a couple of blokes looking for some answers."

Lynn opened her eyes and focused her attention on me. The same befuddled expression crossed her face as when she had first seen me at the door, but this time she studied me closely for some time before speaking.

"Who are you?" Her voice was more measured, her mind appearing to work overtime, trying to make sense of the situation.

The question flummoxed me as the truth was I hadn't a clue. Was I this "Graham" person as Colin appeared to think or someone else entirely?

"I...don't...know," I stuttered feeling alone and lost.

On the point of tears I looked around for a tissue to wipe my eyes. "Here," Colin handed me his handkerchief and I quickly used it before handing it back.

Colin cleared his throat and re-counted with Lynn how we had met and what he had found out from his visit to the jewellers about the ring.

"What ring is this?" Lynn said sharply, her questioning eyes focused on me. I fiddled around in my pocket feeling like a naughty school boy and fished the ring out.

When I passed it to her she turned it over in her hand until she saw the inscription on it, and took a sudden intake of breath. "Where did you get this?" she said.

"I found it in my pocket when I..." I couldn't bring myself to say what my first memory was, it felt too painful and weird.

"What?" she said, arching her eyebrows.

"I just found it," I said without much conviction.

Lynn approached me cautiously, a flicker of uncertainty crossing her face. "Who are you?" she said lifting her hand to my face and brushing the back of her hand against my cheek. "Really."

I forced myself to gaze in to her eyes, searching for answers that wouldn't come to me even now. Should I know this woman? Was she someone from my recent past? I was getting a headache just thinking about it.

"You look so much like him," she said wistfully and sighed, "but he's dead." She stepped back and sat down opposite.

Reborn

Colin eased himself from the chair, standing unsteadily on his bad leg. "Now I don't know much about relationships but one thing I have noticed," he stretched his back and stifled a yawn. "You two know each other whether you realise it or not and that's a fact."

I looked at Colin questioningly, his assertion hitting me like a hammer blow. I felt a faint stirring inside my mind, like a cobweb being blown by a gentle breeze. A fragment of memory came back to me but I couldn't quite grasp it and it fell from my grip like so many grains of sand.

"I'll keep hold of this," Lynn said holding the ring up to the light, "it is mine after all."

I nodded almost imperceptibly, having no fight in me to want to keep it.

Colin puffed his cheeks and sighed, made as if to head for the door but stopped in his tracks, turning back and addressing Lynn directly.

"This man needs your help," he said exasperated, "I found him tired and alone on some piece of wasteland in some dirty clothes, not knowing what to do with himself."

"So what do you expect from me?" she appealed, shrugging her shoulders.

Approaching he took her gently by the hands and held them firmly in his grip. "Come over and take another close look at him and tell me what you see."

Lynn went to say something, opening her mouth, but stopped herself, agreeing to Colin's request with a nod.

This time when our eyes locked a spark flew between us and a cloud seemed to lift, memories poured through.

Chapter 19

Adam moved restlessly amongst the shadows in the warehouse, awaiting the return of his henchmen. He had his concerns about their usefulness but at least they did as they were told without question, which is all he wanted from them.

Tonight he would get what he needed to lure Graham to this place and then he would get from him what he needed. An ugly smile crossed his face and he gave a little skip of delight in anticipation. "Oh what fun I'll have," he said.

Chapter 20

Pitch and Smudger watched the two men leave, seeing the hug given by Graham to Lynn on the doorstep.

"Ah sweet," said Pitch grimacing as they sat in the car a hundred yards away, "all lovey dovey."

Smudger focused his piggy eyes on the scene, itching to get some action.

"Wait," Pitch said sensing his friend's impatience, "just a few more minutes and then we can make our move."

Smudger was still smarting from the beating Graham had given them and wanted his revenge, just to squeeze the life out of him with his bare hands. No one had given him a pasting before and he wanted to make sure there was going to be payback – big time.

"Can't we just go and grab them all and save time?" Smudger was on the verge of leaving the car, his shoulder already at the door. Pitch grabbed him.

"Wait I said." This time there was menace in his voice. "Screw this up and that will be it for us." Pitch drew his index finger across his neck.

Smudger reluctantly sat back and did as he was told, giving Pitch a cold stare. "OK, we'll do it your way."

Finally Graham and Colin departed, leaving the road quiet again with just an occasional passer-by. "Right, pull up outside," Pitch pointed towards the outside of Lynn's house. Climbing out, he took a quick look around before approaching the front door, gripping the cold steel tightly in his pocket.

When the door opened he pulled out the gun and pointed it at Lynn. "Get in the car – now," he said indicating the idling car by the kerb.

Chapter 21

I had never felt so euphoric, although still confused as to exactly what happened. I decided we should get the bus home being low on funds but it didn't bother me. Lynn and I had had a "connection," a shared memory of a day out we had had in our early days together, we both felt the occasion, the smells, sights and sounds and we began telling each other what we saw, eyes still locked together, like a mental lover's embrace.

The sound of screeching tyres brought me out of my reverie and I turned to see a car whizz past dangerously near the kerb. Stepping back I looked up and saw a frightened face peering out of the rear window, before being forcibly pulled down out of sight.

"Lynn," my shocked voice came out in a whisper.

The vehicle disappeared around the corner, just missing a pedestrian crossing the road. I sprinted to the corner but it had already gone from view.

Colin was still walking as fast as he could towards me, concern etched on his face.

"They've kidnapped her, let's go back to the house and call the police."

With panic rising inside of me I sprinted back, and saw the front door still hanging open. Storming through I noticed a white card on the floor which I was certain hadn't been there before. Picking it up I turned it over and saw a scrawled message along with an address:

"*Come and get her you piece of shit.*"

I read it again and again, anger building up inside of me. "Noooo," I bellowed in anguish, lifting my face to the sky.

Colin appeared, his face composed and eyes clear, after reading the note.

"Come, we have work to do," he said.

Chapter 22

"It's a couple of miles outside the town," Colin said matter of factly. "The estate hasn't been in operation for years."

I didn't respond, my only thoughts were to find Lynn and get to know her again, no matter what our past was.

After what seemed forever, the taxi came to a halt in what could only be described as a wilderness. A number of buildings stood around, all empty and abandoned with broken windows and doors.

"Are you sure this is the place you want to be?" The cab driver sounded uncertain.

"Yes, this is it." Colin paid the man and stood watching him drive off.

We both looked around, trying to see any signs of life in any of the warehouses but saw nothing at first. With anxiety rising,

I started walking towards the nearest one, thinking I had to start somewhere.

"Wait...look," Colin pointed to one corner where two buildings stood side by side. Just visible, was the rear bumper of a car that had a familiar look about it. "That's the one we saw," I said. "Definitely."

Colin gripped me on the shoulder, "Be careful, don't rush, they will be waiting for you."

"Yes I know," I said curtly, shrugging off Colin's hand. "Let's just find Lynn."

We made our way across the expanse of concrete that had once been a car park, dodging pieces of rubbish left strewn everywhere by the wind. The only sound was Colin's laboured breathing as he tried to keep up with my fast pace.

As we got closer I noticed a door had been wedged open by an old oil drum, the entrance was cloaked in darkness.

"Come on in as the spider said to the fly," Colin whispered nervously.

Peering through the door I could make out very little except some yellow stained windows high up towards the roof along the far wall. As my foot crossed the threshold it crunched on broken glass which echoed around the empty warehouse.

"Welcome," said a gruff, leathery voice as banks of lights were gradually switched on, creating an almost antiseptic effect with their white brightness. What I saw almost broke my heart: in the middle of the room in a small metal cage sat Lynn, her beautiful hair now limp and lifeless down the sides of her frightened face.

"Graham?" she said in hope and expectation.

I headed towards her wretched form yearning to hold her again so didn't see the club crash down on my head, knocking me unconscious.

When I awoke, I felt numb, at first unsure where I was or what was happening. The first thing I noticed was that my hands were tied above my head, on ropes that seemed to stretch towards the ceiling. Trying to clear my head, two men approached me and I immediately recognised who they were.

"Well, well, well, who's going to take the pasting now," one of them said, nudging his partner in crime.

"I don't know Smudger, do you?" They both laughed and lifted their clubs menacingly towards me. "Let's see how he likes this."

"Stop!" that same voice I had heard earlier, interrupted them before they could beat me.

The two henchman hesitated before standing back to let their master through. The man was small, only about five feet tall, with a bony, angular frame and claw like hands. His face was pale with small light blue eyes. There was no compassion in them.

"At last we meet again Graham," he chirped.

There was something unsettling about this man, not just his appearance that I couldn't put my finger on.

"Oh, before I introduce myself I think we can say hello to some of your old friends. " From the far side of the warehouse two cages were wheeled over on trolleys with two unmoving figures in them.

"I believe this one is a policeman," he said pointing at a well-built man, wearing a dark suit. In one corner lay a hat.

"He will be particularly tasty," the man said licking his lips.

"And this one, I believe is Colin, your new best friend." Although in a state, with blood trickling from the corner of his mouth, there was colour in his cheeks at least.

The slow burn of fury started to eat at me, and I pulled on the ropes uselessly.

"And now for the main event," he bowed theatrically, "I am your twin brother, a twin with no name, but you can call me Adam."

Chapter 23

I looked at the man dumfounded, trying to digest the words I had just thought I'd heard.

"Twins?"

It didn't make any sense, what was he talking about?

He saw the puzzlement in my eyes and gave an amused smirk, enjoying the fact he knew something I didn't. "Ah, but of course you don't remember much at all do you?"

He gave a quick snigger before continuing. "That was just a bit of fun."

"What are you trying to tell me?" I shouted, already tiring of this game he appeared to be playing.

Adam looked at me coldly, annoyed at my interruption, wanting to reveal more at his own pace, after all he had been waiting for this moment to arrive for quite some time.

"All in good time," he said holding my gaze to ensure I got the message.

A groan from one of the cages interrupted Adam and he turned to the one that had the policeman huddled inside. "The big guy awakens," said Adam with a smile that didn't spread to his eyes.

"Poor soul he must be hungry," Adam circled the cage, sizing up the man within.

"Leave him alone," Lynn whined, her voice breaking with emotion. "He's done nothing to you."

Adam spun around and nodded to one of his henchman, Smudger, who approached the cage menacingly. Carefully he unlocked the cage and reached in, grabbing Lynn by the hair and pulling her out in one movement. Her piercing scream was cut short as she hit the floor with a dull thud.

I looked at her crumpled form helplessly, not knowing what I was going to do to get out of this predicament. I felt tears sting my eyes and looked to the floor, not wanting anyone to see this weakness in me. After a few moments where I almost fell into a black pit of despair, I forced myself to focus on the here and now. There were people I cared about here and I at least had to try and do something, even if I didn't know what.

"Buy some time," I thought.

I raised my head and stared directly at Adam. One thing I did need to know is what he wanted me for and why.

"Why am I here?" I was surprised at the strength of my voice and thought I saw a flicker of uncertainty in Adam's eyes but couldn't be sure.

Adam came closer until he was just a couple of feet in front of me. I sensed his hatred for me but still didn't understand why.

"Before I kill you I should give an explanation I suppose," he teased licking his lips. He drew closer still and I smelled his fetid breath and felt it brush my face in noxious waves.

"We are twins," he repeated. "We shared the same mother's womb but something went wrong and it was all your fault!" His voice rose steeply until the last word was shouted out with venom.

Adam suddenly turned his back but I still caught a glimpse of fear on his face as he recollected what he remembered.

"Where you grew as a normal child I shrunk and became weak and helpless, starting to wither away into nothingness." Adam's shoulders hunched and he shuddered. "But I would not accept my fate; could not."

He turned back to me, a smile dancing on his lips. "As you got bigger I held firm and let you envelop me, swallow me whole," he let his mouth imitate someone eating. "And then it was my turn once you, or should I say we, were born."

Adam's eyes sparkled as he recounted his tale, eager to tell all. "I became the parasite who fed off your personality, slowly as the years passed taking control of your mind until you became me."

I watched him with growing contempt, feeling my hands ball into ever tighter fists. What right did he have for holding me here? I knew nothing of this man or what he was achieving by keeping us all in this God forsaken place.

"Why don't you just let us go," I said trying to sound reasonable.

He ignored me as he paced up and down, clasping his arms behind his back. "And then, just as I began to impose my personality on you, you go and die," he threw his arms up in the air in frustration before coming to a halt in front of me.

His words hit me like a sledgehammer and I felt suddenly numb all over. Die? But I was alive? Then I remembered the first memory I had in the cemetery; of digging my way out of the grave and feeling the fresh air on my face. Reality took me in its grip and I shivered despite not feeling cold – I should be dead.

Chapter 24

The first thing Colin felt was the thumping inside his head as he stirred on what felt like a cold, unforgiving surface. Where was he? What had happened? Were his first two thoughts as his brain tried to re-engage him back into consciousness. Raising himself he saw pinpricks of light in front of his eyes and almost fell to the floor again before levering his body into a sitting position. Peering out of what he now knew was a cage he saw this strange little man who appeared to be talking, although his ears had yet to pick up much in the way of sound except for a ringing noise which only slowly began to dissipate. His heart sank when he saw the predicament they were all in; with Graham tied up and Lynn lying on the floor. He didn't recognise the motionless male figure in the other cage though and wondered what his involvement was.

He then saw two other men move towards him, with one of them opening his cage and gripping him roughly by the arm.

"Hey, what's all this about?"

He didn't get an answer as he was unceremoniously pulled out and held in a standing position by each arm. Colin felt dizzy and was sure he would have collapsed if he hadn't had any support.

"So Graham, this is your knight in shining armour - Colin," the little man said with a wicked grin. "The man who helped you re-discover yourself."

Colin watched as the man began to circle him like some sort of vulture, gradually moving closer until he could smell his fetid breath. And then a pain like he'd never felt before exploded inside his stomach and his legs turned to jelly. Looking down he saw the hilt end of a knife being slowly pulled upwards and he watched disbelievingly as a roll of intestines flopped onto the floor.

"Who are you going to rescue now, my friend?"

The last thing Colin saw was the stunned look on Graham's face...and then there was nothing.

Chapter 25

Adam ogled Colin's innards with hungry eyes, saliva dripping from the corner of his mouth and it took all his willpower not to gorge himself on this meal he had created. "Save it for later," he said, a thin smile crossing his lips.

"Now for the main event, you are all about to see something truly wondrous." He gave a theatrical bow in front of me and withdrew the bloodied knife he had just used on Colin from his jacket. He approached me, a burning malevolence in his eyes and held the knife up to my face. "When you died the first time my plan fell apart," he held the knife up to my neck and sighed. "My intention was to take your mind and body over, take your strength just as you did mine in the womb."

I stared back at Adam, trying to keep my emotions in check as he continued his rant. Something was happening to me that I didn't understand, I felt energised and strong, a buzz flowing through my body like an electric current.

"Your death separated us, physically and mentally, but I knew we would come back," Adam eyes shone with excitement, the hand holding the knife shaking briefly. "You see separately we are normal, living humdrum lives but together we are special," this time a tear ran down his cheek.

"Special? Well how did I die in the first place?" I said with a sarcastic tone to my voice. Adam shook his head and tutted.

"That was my fault, pushing your mind and body too far as I tried to manipulate you into my way of thinking and being," he shrugged. "So I had to bring you back to life so that your death was at my choosing, not yours." I sensed his grip tighten on the blade against my throat. "Revenge will be so sweet," he whispered in my ear before slashing my throat.

Chapter 26

I felt nothing at this but watched him do it like an interested bystander. The power I had been feeling grew exponentially and I pulled at the ropes holding my hands which snapped like twigs. Adam recoiled as if I'd hit him and staggered back, for the first time fear and uncertainty appearing in his eyes.

"Get him!" he screamed at his two henchmen who strode purposely forward eager to get a piece of the action with their clubs in hand. In no time they both had been dealt with, broken and bloodied on the floor; I felt invincible but knew instinctively this feeling wouldn't last for long. I saw the black patches that had been growing all over my body now accelerating over the remainder of my skin. Adam made a run for the door, eager now to make a getaway but I stopped him just short of the exit. He squirmed in my vice like grip trying to bite at any part of me within reach like some sort of rabid dog. I had to act quickly as the supernatural power was already ebbing away; pulling him to me a sudden flash of blinding white light engulfed us both and we were joined together for one last time before disappearing into nothingness.

Chapter 27

Lynn came around and sat up, gently feeling the bump that felt like an egg on her forehead and wincing in pain. Looking around she saw the disembowelled body of Colin and immediately felt nauseous, trying hard not to vomit on the spot and succeeding. The two bodies of Adam's henchmen were a few yards further on but Lynn didn't want to look too closely at them, preferring to see if she could see Graham.

"He's not here is he?" The voice of Chivers came to her as he crawled ungainly out of his cage, hat back on his head.

Lynn took a deep breath and stood, meaning to have a look around but suddenly feeling light headed. "He was here a few minutes ago, and where's Adam?"

She was still confused by the feelings that had begun to stir for Graham all over again and still could not quite believe he could come back to life but was willing to see where these new urges took her.

A glint of light on the floor in front of her caught her eye and she walked over to pick the object up. Turning it over she saw it was Graham's watch that she had bought him in what seemed a lifetime ago. Curling her fingers around it she held back the tears and raised her face to the ceiling. "Goodbye my love," she said. "Until we meet again."

With that she took Chivers by the arm and walked out of the warehouse without turning back.

Chapter 28

We were floating together, my brother and I in a place of light and shadows, figures flitted in and out of view but never quite materialised into recognisable form. A strange but safe place, free from harm. Our "second" lives were a mistake brought on by my brother's thirst for vengeance. I held onto him now and no longer felt anger or pity, but understanding that he wanted his own life to live but fate had conspired against him. After all, isn't that what we all want?

The Deserted Ballroom

By Colin Butler

The old ballroom is deserted,
With doors all boarded up,
Windows shuttered or broken,
Layers of dust on all the fittings.

The flowers have all faded,
Gone are the shrinking violets,
And the sad, lonely wallflowers,
Romances that flowered now long past.

The dancers have all waltzed away,
And the bands have all departed.
The bandstand stands silent as a tomb,
Yet the mirrorball still shimmers in the misty light.

Through the dim light, I see ghosts
Of myriad dancers of yesteryear,
Ladies elegant in long flowing gowns
And men suave in tails and suits.

The ballroom could tell so many tales,
So much happiness and so much heartache,
Do I hear the ghostly sounds of music?
Or is it just my vivid imagination?

A Mother's Revenge

By Sandra Maynard

Chapter 1 - Matt

It was two o'clock in the morning. Matt Bellman let out a long, low, guttural groan as the seizure took hold of his young body. He was totally powerless to control the spasms that convulsed through him causing his jaw to lock tight and his azure eyes to roll backwards into their sockets. A small trickle of bloodied spittle dribbled out of his lips which were beginning to turn blue from lack of oxygen getting to his brain. His leg and arm muscles jerked sporadically and his head banged into his headboard. Hearing the crashing and banging, his parents, Maureen and Pete rushed in to his room. "Quick, get him on his side, Pete, to stop him choking!" Maureen's voice was urgent. Despite being used to Matt's fits now, she still wished the helplessness, she always felt, would disappear. It never did.

Together, they managed to turn their son then, mission accomplished; they fell back exhausted, onto his bed, and waited for the electric storm in his brain to stop its raging.

"That's the third one this week," Maureen's voice was harsh. "Obviously the incident in Science last week, involving that bloody Danny Ward, is still stressing him out. The College are doing absolutely nothing, as usual!" For a mother, it was truly exasperating and she was powerless to do anything about it.

Pete Bellman sighed. "I just don't know what we can do next? They say they've spoken to his mother but she can't control him."

"I could control him but it wouldn't be pleasant! That damn boy is ruining Matt's chances of getting a decent education. I wish he'd leave him alone." Her shaking hands pulled the duvet up to her eyes and wiped away the salty tears that had fallen onto her cheeks.

Pete put his arm around his sobbing wife and felt her chest heaving against him. It was all too much. Danny had been a thorn in their sides for the last three years, with his tormenting and it didn't look like it was going to stop anytime soon.

Maureen looked down at her beloved son and stroked his flaming cheek. His seizure had ceased and he lay still in his bed. His breathing was laboured and his skin flushed. The Consultant had said the energy consumed during a fit was similar to running a marathon. Luckily, he wouldn't remember this episode in the morning. For Maureen though, it was a life sentence of worry and despair.

"I will avenge you, my darling. Trust me." But her whisper fell on deaf ears as Matt had lapsed into a deep sleep.

Chapter 2 – In the beginning…

Matt grimaced. He knew he'd had yet another seizure as his whole body ached all over. He rolled over onto the duvet, grateful for the softness against his battered body.

He knew Danny Ward was to blame but really had no idea how to stop the relentless bullying. It was easy for everyone to say 'stand up for yourself' or 'hit him so hard he'll never go near you again' but it simply wasn't in his nature. He was a gentle boy who preferred to walk away from confrontation rather than address it.

A Mother's Revenge

He thought back to the first day he'd ever set eyes on Danny Ward. That was when all the trouble, and seizures, began...

Matt had just settled into his seat in his form room, 9F, and felt quite smug and confident. He was now in Year 9 and the last two years of insecurities seemed a lifetime away. He was no longer the new boy. He'd grown quite considerably during the holidays and was just short of five foot eight. At fourteen, he was aware of the hormones raging through his body but embraced the feeling of power that came with them. He knew the next three years were important in terms of studying and was eager to continue his learning.

A sudden, loud crash, caused him to look up as a tall, dark-haired boy sauntered into the classroom and threw his bag down onto the first empty desk he saw. He had a cocky gait and, as he scanned the row of faces looking up at him, he grinned in a mocking manner. From his stance, there was little doubt that this boy knew no fear and he seemed determined to set himself aside as the Alpha Male. He stared down anyone who met his gaze and warned them off with a look that said, 'you're right to be afraid'.

At first, Matt was curious about this newcomer. His form tutor, Miss Arundel, a small, timid looking woman, stood up. "Welcome. You must be Danny? Your timing is perfect. I was just about to hand out your new timetables. Please take a seat".

Danny proceeded to retrieve his bag and swaggered towards Matt.

"Move!" It was an order.

"Excuse me?" Matt was flabbergasted. Who did this boy think he was?

Danny was unmoving. "I said, Move!" he snarled. "She told me to take a seat and I am going to take yours! Do you have a problem with that?" he challenged nastily.

Looking back, Matt supposed he should have stood up to Danny Ward. It would have probably stopped him enduring three years of absolute Hell from the boy but, in that moment, not wishing to cause a scene and hating his weakness, Matt stood up, "Take it! I can find another chair." It was a decision he would regret for many years to come.

Chapter 3 – Danny

Danny Ward groaned. He hated weekday mornings. At his mother's insistence he had taken on a newspaper round, 'to keep him out of trouble' she said, but to him, getting up at six am was torture.

He rose at five-thirty, showered, dressed then jumped on his bike, collected his round from the local Newsagents, made his deliveries and was back home at seven thirty which just gave him time to get ready for college.

College was another of life's hassles for Danny but it was made easier and much more bearable when he could play pranks on some of the kids in his classes. He'd been accused of bullying his peers but Danny didn't see it like that. To him it was harmless, adolescent fun. He didn't see the pain and insecurities his actions caused. He didn't know how many nights of tears and days of anxiety about going to College he'd contributed to and he really didn't care. Gender didn't matter to Danny either. The girls suffered just as much as the boys and he was not well-liked, as a result. That didn't bother him at all.

Ignoring the stares of hatred he attracted most days, he made his way to the science block. If there was one lesson Danny could endure it was science. There were so many distractions in the lab and, most of the time, the teachers didn't pay too much attention to what was happening in the classroom so he got away with quite a lot of mischief.

He thought back to the previous week and smiled. The episode with Matt Bellman had been particularly satisfying.

It had started, as usual, with a pinch on Matt's ruddy cheeks just to let him know who was 'in charge'. Danny loved to see Matt's frozen look of fear whenever he approached him. Like a predator circling its prey, Danny could sense the boy's anxiety and it gave him immense satisfaction. "Matty boy!" he called, grabbing a chunk of the boy's flesh, to Matt's obvious distress. "Loving your chubby cheeks this morning!"

Matt had pulled away from Danny's grasp. He was grateful that Danny couldn't hear his wildly beating heart. "Leave it out Danny!" he stammered, but his try at defence had fuelled Danny more.

"Awww what's up Matty? That's not very friendly." Danny's tone was mocking.

Matt hated the way Danny always called him Matty. It was really patronising. He could see the other kids looking at him, all aware of his discomfort, but none of them spoke a word or offered to help. They never did. They were all petrified of Danny. And Danny knew it.

Danny glanced round the Science lab to make sure there were no adults around. There weren't. The teacher, Mr Green, was late, as usual and Danny intended to take full advantage of it. He moved his hand in front of Matt and flicked the gas switch on and grinned at Matt's outraged expression, his eyes daring him to react.

Instinct took over and Matt stepped forward and turned the tap off but Danny, seeing the teacher approaching, moved away from the desk at the precise moment leaving Matt fully exposed.

Even though he knew Matthew hadn't done it, Frank Green wasn't about to confront Danny Ward. That boy was bad news. "Matthew Bellman!" The teacher bellowed. "What are you doing?"

Matt's face reddened. Before he could respond, he heard, "Detention! After school!" and watched as the teacher returned to the front of the class. Danny smirked. "Tutt tutt Matty!"

If Matt thought that was the end of Danny's daily humiliation of him, he was very much mistaken.

Ten minutes later, Mr Green ordered the students to prepare themselves for the daily experiment which was to test the reaction of potassium in water. They each had a Petri dish filled with some water. Next to each dish was a small clump of potassium.

"On my instruction," Mr Green's voice boomed into the classroom, "you will all put on your protective goggles. Then," he stressed, "*and only then*, you can drop your potassium into the water. It is imperative that you stand well back for this experiment as the results can be extremely dangerous. Do you all understa..." but he didn't get to finish his sentence because, from the back of the classroom, a massive BOOM shattered the silence.

Chapter 4 - Maureen

"Could you do the early shift tomorrow Maureen?" Tim, Maureen's boss asked. "I wouldn't usually put on you like this but Nancy has called in sick and you're the only supervisor available".

Maureen sighed. She loved her job at the Call Centre but the early shift started at six thirty am and she was still feeling the effects from Matt's seizure that morning. However, Tim had allowed her plenty of time off when Matt's anxieties were particularly bad and she felt she owed him so, reluctantly, she agreed.

She slumped back into her chair and her thoughts drifted back to the cause of Matt's seizure and how she could keep the promise she had made to her son that morning and get her own back on Danny Ward. She found it ironic, and, bizarrely, quite satisfying, that she knew so much about the boy, who terrorised her son, through checking him out on the social network sites. She knew what he looked like due to the numerous 'selfies' he'd taken of himself, the vain idiot. She had even given him a nickname, 'Turf head' due to his short brown hair being styled in the current trend of shaved at the sides with a small square of hair standing out at the top like a piece of turf. She knew that he had a paper-round. She knew he cycled everywhere. She knew that he was a loner who didn't have many friends. No big surprise there! She knew what he thought about College, the teachers and the kids. She also knew about the science incident even before she had been called to the school to collect Matt, after it had happened, because Danny had boasted about it online! That hadn't helped. Seeing him write that he had 'just blown up the science lab and taken that stupid arsehole Matt Bellman down in the process! Shame it didn't take him out completely! What a blast!' felt like a huge kick in the teeth to Maureen.

"Mme," Maureen mused. "The social networks were a great way of keeping in touch but there were definite downsides of checking up on bullies!"

The shrill ringing of the telephone brought Maureen back to reality. "I will get you Danny Ward, I swear I will!" she thought then duly answered the persistent caller.

Chapter 5 - Hit 'n' run

Paper-rounds were much better in the summer months, Danny surmised. He'd only been out ten minutes and already his hands were frozen to the handles of his bike and he couldn't feel his lips. He was beginning to wish he'd listened when his mum told him to put a hat and gloves on. The arrogance of youth!

There were never any cars out at six o'clock in the morning and, as he knew the route well, it didn't occur to Danny to look to his left before turning into Roffey Street. As he spun into the street he was aware of the screeching sound of brakes and the blasting of a horn. Although he was shocked, he recovered his balance well and even managed a two finger salute at the driver whose car he had nearly collided into. As he sped past he gave the cursing woman a cheeky grin.

Chapter 6 – Hit 'n' run (2)

Maureen, too, wasn't expecting much traffic on the roads as she made her way to work for the early shift. She quite liked driving to work in the early hours as she could use the quietness to think. She was just approaching the junction at Roffey Street when, without warning, a kid on a bike pulled out in front of her. Instinct took over and she managed to swerve to avoid him. Her hand blasted the horn and she let out a torrent of expletives. The youth just made a hand gesture at her and smiled.

Maureen frowned. She was too shocked to register the boy's face at first but his turf-like hair did look familiar. It was a style she would never forget. Danny bloody Ward!

Without thinking, Maureen accelerated up behind the boy, a steely determination in her eyes. As she approached, he turned towards her and her headlights picked out the surprised expression on his face. She didn't care. At that moment in time, all that was going on in her head was that, in front of her, was the cause of all her family's troubles over the last three years. "You're the reason my son has uncontrollable seizures," she thought. "The reason he has so little self-respect and talks of ending it all. The reason my family has been torn apart. And for that, Danny Ward, it's your turn to suffer!" With those thoughts crowding her head, Maureen turned her front wheels sharply into Danny's bike sending it crashing in to the left kerb and Danny skidding over to the right kerb.

Her heart was pumping wildly. She had felt the impact as her car had hit him. She saw him crash into the opposite kerb and heard the crunch as he landed. Without stopping, she drove on. Her hands shook so violently that it took a moment to regain control of the steering wheel. She drove off. Her eyes focussed solely on the road ahead. Had she looked back she would have seen the grotesque, broken body of Danny Ward sprawled out across the road surrounded by a slowly growing pool of blood.

Chapter 7 - Relief

By the time Maureen had arrived at her workplace she was amazed at how calm she felt. "That'll teach you Danny Ward," she thought. "Now you'll have to have a few weeks off College. That will give Matt a break from you and give you a chance to think over what it feels like to be in pain."

She felt elated. It was a 'spur of the moment' decision and she hadn't had time to think about her actions. She was sure no-one saw the incident as there were no other cars or people around. Danny himself would probably be in shock and wouldn't know what had happened. Or, if he did, at least he wouldn't know who had crashed into him. She would need to invent a story about the dent in the front of her car but that would be easy.

"Everything okay Maureen?" Leila, one of the trainees asked, seeing the pre-occupied glaze in her eyes.

Maureen glanced up at the fresh face standing at her desk. "Fine. Thanks Leila. Million miles away. It's quiet today?"

"Yeah. Day is sure gonna drag!" Leila returned to her seat and stared at the phone, willing it to ring and end the boredom.

Chapter 8 – Hunted

Pete studied the rather large dent on the front bumper of their car then returned to the kitchen. "A fox jumped out on you and you hit it, you say?"

Maureen looked up from her much needed cuppa. She had been expecting the question and was ready to face her husband. "Yes dear. That's exactly what happened. Want some more tea?"

Pete wasn't going to let it rest that easily. "Did you kill it?" he asked.

"Kill what?" Maureen's thoughts had already moved on.

"The fox!" Pete was exasperated.

"No. It ran off. Anyway, why all the questions? What about me? Don't you want to know if I'm okay?" Maureen's patience was waning.

Pete ignored her. Something about her story wasn't connecting. The dent was much larger than a fox would make but why would his wife lie? His forehead furrowed into a frown. What wasn't she telling him? He watched his wife of twenty years move towards the television. Her demeanour was calm. Perhaps it had been a fox? Pete shook his head in disbelief. He didn't know what to make of it.

All thoughts of foxes were wiped away as Danny Ward's face suddenly came into focus across the screen. "Danny Ward, a seventeen year old student from Baconsfield was mown down by a vehicle in the early hours of this morning in Roffey Street. The driver drove off. Danny was taken to St. John's Hospital where, we are told, is in a critical condition with severe head injuries. Police are asking anyone with information to come forward." Maureen pressed the off switch on the remote. Pete's eyes never left his wife's pale face.

"It wasn't a fox was it Maureen?" Pete's voice was low. "You hit Danny Ward didn't you?"

Maureen was silent for a few seconds. "I..I thought he'd be cut a little. I never thought he'd be critical," Maureen stammered. The revelation had shocked her to the core.

"Jesus, Maur. What were you thinking? What if he dies?" Pete persisted. "What will you do then?"

"I don't want to think about that. He won't. The lad's as strong as an ox." She didn't sound convinced.

"You had better hope so." Pete's voice was harsh. "I'll phone St John's Hospital. We have to know one way or another." Maureen was glad that, for once, Pete was taking charge. She passed him the phone then prayed silently for the boy to be okay.

Chapter 9 – Critical

As she walked into the intensive care unit at St John's Hospital, Trisha Ward was not been prepared for the sight that met her eyes. Her son, Danny's, face was un-recognisable. It was swathed entirely in bandages and his eyes, that were just visible through the bandages, were black and swollen. His mouth was purple and caked in congealed blood. Tubes of all colours ran from his arms into various machines surrounding him, all of which made their own strange noise. A nurse stood at his side checking his heart rate and blood pressure. Hearing Trisha's gasp of horror she turned.

"I got here as quickly as I could. That is my son. How is he doing?" Trisha's voice shook with emotion.

"I'll get Dr Briggs, er, Mrs Ward." The young nurse turned on her heel and exited the ward.

Trisha pulled up a chair and slumped into it as her legs gave way. She couldn't believe that Danny was lying in such a state. For the thousandth time that morning, she wondered who on earth could knock her beloved son down and just drive away.

"Mrs Ward?" An elderly, grey-haired Doctor appeared at her side.

"What are his chances Doctor?" Trisha dreaded his reply.

"I'll be honest, Mrs Ward, not good. Not good at all. He took quite a hit," Doctor Nigel Briggs continued. This was the hardest part of his job, telling the patient's family the facts. "Danny's skull cracked on impact and he has suffered horrific brain damage. He also has a broken cheekbone and jaw. The next twenty-four hours are critical, I'm afraid." His voice trailed off, allowing her to fully digest them. "We will call you if there is any change."

"Can I stay with him please?" Nigel noted the tremor in the small woman's voice.

"Yes, of course. I will get a nurse to sort something out for you." He paused, "I am so sorry." Then he looked over at the boy, shook his head and left the room.

Chapter 10 – Waiting...

Pete put down the phone. "They won't speak to me. Next of Kin only. We'll just have to wait. Better turn the TV back on, maybe they'll know more? Crikey Maureen! What were you thinking?" He asked for the second time.

Maureen could only stare blankly at the television. She truly didn't know.

Chapter 11 - And waiting...

Trisha had lost sense of all time as she sat motionless by Danny's bedside. Her head felt heavy and her eyes had no tears left. All she could hear was his shallow breathing and the slow beat of the monitor which confirmed that he was still alive. Barely. He hadn't moved since she'd been there. She wished there was someone she could call on for support but there was no-one. She'd divorced Danny's dad when he was two and both her parents were no longer alive. Danny was the only family she had. She took his hand into her own and caressed his soft skin. Then, as the tears streamed silently down her face, she did something she hadn't done for a long time. She prayed. It was only the continuous bleep on the monitor which caused her to stop. At that moment she knew that her only son was dead and that, somewhere out there, was a cold-blooded murderer. "Even if it takes the rest of my life, I will find you and bring you to justice!" She vowed. When she made her promise, Trisha was unaware that, at that precise moment, Maureen was handing herself in to Baconsfield Police Station.

Chapter 12 – The Aftermath

The graveyard was eerily quiet. It was seven p.m. Trisha liked to visit Danny at this time. She was able to update him with all the news without being interrupted by anyone else. No-one, it seemed, made their visits after six o'clock in the evening.

She rested her head on the black marble headstone. It cooled her sallow skin. The six-month trial against Maureen Bellman had taken its toll on Trisha and the skin over her gaunt face was taught. Her once bright, blue eyes were sunken in their dark, bruised sockets. Her clothes bagged around her skeletal frame. Anyone looking at her could have been forgiven for thinking that one of the corpses had reluctantly come to life. She did not look at all well.

She didn't feel well either. She missed Danny terribly. Kneeling beside his grave was the only solace she felt.

"It was the final day of the trial today Dan. You'd have been proud of your old mum. I held my own and even managed a cheer when the Bellman bitch was found guilty of your manslaughter. It was worth everything to see her guilt-ridden face so shocked by the verdict. Although, why she was shocked I don't know? Do you know, she never once apologised for her actions against you my love. Never uttered a word. Mind you. It should have been murder but no-one ever came forward so the prosecution had no witnesses." Trisha sighed. "Still, five years inside should keep her off the streets for a while shouldn't it and when she's free, I'll be waiting for her. I made a promise to you and I intend to keep it. I will see that justice is done." Trisha's voice suddenly became strong and harsh. She turned her head towards Danny's stone and kissed it. "Be brave my love. I miss you so much. I will be back at the same time tomorrow."

Chapter 13 – A Mother's Revenge

Maureen Bellman was indeed sentenced to five years in Belmarsh prison but, with good behaviour, her time had been reduced to just eighteen months. During her time in capacity, she had turned to writing to help off-load the terrible guilt she had felt at taking Danny Ward's young life. Along with her husband's help, the Bellman's had secured a lucrative, if not controversial, book deal and Maureen now found herself sitting in a rather crowded local bookstore, surrounded by copies of her book, 'A Mother's Revenge'.

Pete had come up with the idea of the launch to coincide with her release and it had proved a popular move. The people of Baconsfield had bought the story of the local mum who had got her revenge on the bully who had dominated the life of her family and several hundred had turned up, all eager to meet her.

Maureen glanced over at Pete and Matt who smiled back. They had been her rocks and she knew she wouldn't have been able to get through the last year and a half without their support. She was so proud of Matt. His seizures had stopped and he had been offered a place at Durham University to study for a degree in scientific research.

"Hi," Maureen was brought back to reality by the presence of a frail woman in her fifties who had approached the desk where she had been signing copies of her book. The woman's face was partially obscured by a black baseball cap which covered short, dyed- blonde hair and sunglasses which covered her eyes.

"Hi. Who would you like me to dedicate it to?" Maureen reached forward and took her book from the woman's outstretched hand.

"Could you just put 'for Dan' please?" the woman asked.

"Sure," Maureen countered and signed the inscription. As she handed the book back to the woman she felt a shiver run through her veins as her eyes focussed on the revolver nestled in the woman's palm.

"A Mother's Revenge is so apt, don't you think Maureen?" Trisha met Maureen's gaze as she slowly pulled the trigger

Black Birds

By Colin Butler

The ominous ravens and crows
Lurking by the motorway edge,
Like foraging vultures pecking at
Carcases of the car-casualty carrion.

With a minimal flap of its wings
The jet-black bird flutters down,
To perch on the black fence post,
Joining its many funereal-clad fellows.

In minutes, the fence is transformed
Into an ominous living black sea,
Exuding an air of malevolence,
Harbingers of the devil, evil and death.

The black brigade fidget and squawk
Flapping their wings impatiently,
The legion of carrion crows prepare to attack,
Their menace growing minute by minute.

Everywhere I go, omnipresent black crows
Are there, staring at me with their gimlet-like eyes,
Watching me, casting a dark shadow over me
Garbed in their bible-belt black.

United in Despair

By David Shaer

Chapter 1

Despite a smooth, dreamy, red-eye flight across the Atlantic, James Goode did not feel relaxed as the Boeing 767 commenced its gradual descent towards Stansted Airport. Of course, as the flight Captain James Goode, he wasn't supposed to be too relaxed when coming in to land – more alert and fresh.

This was the inaugural service from Sanford, Florida into Stansted and the first time that James had had the 767 and 230 fare paying passengers strapped to his backside, despite many trial flights in the same aircraft.

At 35,000 feet, he had been directed to "Turn right onto 120 and descend to 270. Line up number two to a Ryanair 737 about 5 miles ahead on the same settings." Although the instruction was simple and straight forward James felt uncomfortable and asked his cockpit crew to check and double check all of the aircraft systems.

"All clear and correct," he heard for the fourth time and he could tell by the upwards rolling eyes and subtle huffs, that he was beginning to appear paranoid.

By the time they had been directed to descend to 15,000 feet, they were running into wispy cloud and slight turbulence. Surprisingly, the cabin crew had already advised passengers to "return to your seats, put your seat backs and trays into the upright position and fasten your seat belts. All electronic devices must be switched off," and those passengers who had flown before were also looking around to see if something unusual was happening.

Captain Goode could see the Ryanair Boeing 5 miles ahead of him, although the wispy clouds were becoming thicker. But still he felt that something was odd – a gut feel of pending trouble.

As the 767 flew into a much thicker cloud, James Goode and the rest of the cockpit crew felt a strange "thwump" and cockpit warning lights and bells started up. Birdstrike at 15,000 feet was not unheard of, but this felt different. The port engine had been hit and Goode started the standard check routines. He could see that the engine was actually now on fire and checked immediately that the automatic fire extinguishers had kicked in. But then came a secondary explosion. First Officer Jason Ravinski was already in ground contact and, with a nod from Goode, had issued a May-Day call. Although the port engine had already been shut down, there seemed to be a strange vibration from the port side of the aircraft. The fire had not fully extinguished and a trail of smoke was visible from where the cockpit crew were stretching to see. Goode ordered them all back to their places. The instructions from ground control at Stansted were re-directing the flight to RAF Coningsby, which was the nearest suitable emergency location. Since this was a prime Eurofighter and Tornado base, ground control seemed to view this 'May-Day' as a far more serious problem than the rest of the cockpit crew had imagined.

Descent to 9,000 feet was rapid and controlled but James Goode was having trouble re-setting the aircraft trim to fly on one engine. It was as though he was fighting against something else.

They were now flying in much thicker cloud and the ground contact had been switched to RAF Coningsby, who seemed very calm and well-practiced.

"We need to know your expected landing weight and distribution. We already know how much fuel you have on board and calculate you will have enough to divert to a choice of two other fields if this runway is too short. But we think we can handle it easily, unless you are heavy on extra hold luggage. We couldn't get your loaded take-off weight from Sanford because their systems are down. Can you help, please?"

Goode was impressed but now concerned because he knew take off had used up far more runway at Sanford than he had expected. Perhaps their systems had already been inaccurate or failing when he was loading. Now was too late to find out.

And then the crew encountered something really scary. The thick cloud seemed to change to almost yellow in colour and suddenly the cockpit windows were covered in something slimy and sticky. Whatever they were flying into wasn't normal rain. De-icing fluid was helping to clear the screens but not totally. Flying blind was alright up here but not when you are trying to nurse a sick aircraft with one engine out onto the ground in a strange military base.

Chapter 2

Peter, sometimes known as Stetson Pete, Ivan, James and Albert had watched, for as long as they could remember, the second day of the Oval Cricket Test Match series. They even went so far back that they remembered the times when spectators were allowed to bring alcohol into the ground, so obviously many, many years.

As they had grown older, all of these days out had begun to merge in their memories, and the conversation during the day, year after year, was almost predictable. As time advanced, the merger of anecdotes became more solid and inseparable, and only the odd, really exceptional event remained distinguishable.

Like the year when they had an unwelcomed guest who stood in for one or other of them, and this Alexander person was a pompous, arrogant individual, neither liked nor respected by any of them, but, for some forgotten reason, he was thought to be an appropriate deputy.

It took mere moments for the others to realise this was a bad mistake and poor Alexander was led badly astray. By lunchtime, his speech was impaired through excessive and expensive on site alcohol, and by the afternoon he was asleep. The sun burned overhead and sticky bits of paper spelling out something vulgar were attached to his forehead. Nobody could remember what it said but it had the desired effect, so that at 'stumps,' about 6.30 pm, when he was eventually shaken back into life, the sunburn on his face was slightly less than total and left a vulgar, white, four-letter word behind.

Alexander was helped to his feet, several times, and, after the main crowd had left, was dragged to the pub outside the ground whose name none of them could remember, for a series of drinks he really didn't need. (Ed.note – Hanover Arms?)

Just before he was put on a bus, an experience that was totally alien to him, he had, however, served a purpose. It seemed that he knew of another pompous arrogant but much wealthier guy who lived so close to the ground that one could watch the game from this chap's roof-top garden, and, lo and behold, this new chap had walked past on his way home from work. Alexander greeted him, in his own unintelligible way in mono-syllabic sentences, and the guy, shook hands with whichever of the regulars were still there. His name might have been Philip or Huw, but nobody really cared as long as he extended an invitation for a drink in his roof-top garden, which he duly did. But after putting Alexander onto that bus that apparently took him to Blackheath nearly a day later, it was essential that they befriended the new guy. He had something to offer.

Struggling to portray intelligence and humour, the guys clambered up the stairs of his exquisite Edwardian house where they were greeted by a breathtaking view of South London and a couple of bottles of appalling Australian Merlot. One can always tell the true background of a pompous, arrogant City dealer by the wine he keeps at home. Then study the wine he offers to determine his view of you.

So either this chap was totally false or he was a perceptive interpreter of the state of the remaining guys. None of them was in a position to criticise. So they carefully clung to the roof garden's low walls and studied the view around, paying most attention to whether they could see the Oval ground and the score boards. To their relief, it was possible to see the game without needing binoculars and so they began the pleasant task of becoming the City dealer's best friends, so that they might get invited to join him for a future day's entertainment.

All seemed to be progressing well, especially when the host started to ridicule Alexander and to describe him as a complete waste of space. Everybody, bar Albert, thought it funny to agree and laughed out loud. Albert was more astute, working out that Alexander might still be needed to regain contact after everybody had dispersed remembering nothing of the details of their new 'best friend.' Albert was somewhat older and more experienced than the others.

As the sun began to set, some weird clouds appeared from the north, generating strange comments like "Dark over Will's mother's" and "We're doomed." The clouds grew thicker and more angry, bringing with them an unpleasant chilly wind, that carried a strange smell, almost sulphur dioxide in content. The alcohol had taken over and everybody was now seated on deckchairs, almost oblivious to the potential rainstorm. Conversation had drifted onto holidays, International Monetary Fund investment policies, Nigella Lawson's eyes, and other bits, when suddenly a sheet of rain could be seen driving its way across the rooftops from Vauxhall. Nobody thought it urgent enough to react quickly, so started to discuss where they might go to eat soon.

As the rain hit them, the transformation was immediate and startling, particularly as the rain was cold, driving hard and almost slimy in texture. Suddenly it was apparent that this was no ordinary rain as it started to sting eyes, lips, mouths and skin. In fact, it battered each person so hard that even their clothes started to disintegrate as the rain tore through shirts, jackets, trousers and hair.

It seemed like a harsh acid or bleach, cleaning everything in its path. All of the guys suddenly leapt up as best they could, and started to dash towards the door back into the building. But as they raced towards it, a gust of wind caught the door and slammed it shut. It stuck solid instantly, not giving an iota as each of them tried to yank the door open. As the wind and rain beat down on their backs, they could feel it burning through their clothes, even ripping out tufts of hair from their sticky heads.

Hammering on the shut door was to no avail, as they were all outside and nobody was indoors. One of the party, thinking laterally, pulled his mobile phone from his pocket and, despite his freezing cold, wet and sticky hands, tried to dial emergency services. But as he finished dialling, he could see the phone disintegrating in smoke in front of his eyes. He turned with pleading eyes to his colleagues, only to see them already dropping around him, lifeless. Whatever was happening to them was much more than just a 'Rain stops play' moment – it seemed to be stopping life.

Chapter 3

Charles was an engineer by training and qualification but was teaching ignorant students how to use computers. He didn't want to do it, neither did they. But both of them were being paid, he as a technical tutor in an East Anglian college, they as apprentices in a government training program for youngsters with attitude problems.

As the course progressed, both parties hated each other more, they because they wanted to be anywhere else and he......for exactly the same reason.

But, in the end, they both had to pass an end of term exam, about which the students had to be more concerned than he, because failure could mean being cast aside and receiving no benefits. Charles, however, had to pass because he had a much more ambitious target. All his life he had wanted to fly. He had been an Air Cadet from the age of sixteen but had ever so slight colour recognition issues. As a consequence, he was deemed colour blind, which hacked him off twice over. His first was because it was so minor that it should not have affected anything. The second reason was that his mother was adamant that the examining board were corrupt, ever since they had de-frocked both of the men in her life. Charles's father had been an experienced flyer who had been grounded following an incident in 1958 when a Lufthansa DC4 had been "buzzed" over Northolt. Sadly Charles's father's alibi had been the clandestine affair he was having with the wife of his Commanding Officer, which he obviously couldn't use, whereas the actual pilot of the offending RAF Trainer was really the son of the same Commanding Officer – so Charles's father was on an all-round loser every which-way. Needless to say, he lost and was dismissed summarily, bringing to a rapid close, two near-perfect careers.

Charles brushed himself down and started again, whereas his father took it very badly, never worked again and died soon after, a sad inebriate.

In the meantime, Charles had become an armchair and simulator trainer, not flying personally but teaching hundreds of youngsters good flying etiquette and disaster recovery. Although he was good, in fact quite brilliant, a major downfall in the number of new recruits dealt him another cruel blow and the RAF decided to 'let him go.'

Teaching, in the meantime, had become his new skill and he had also taken up micro-light flying and teaching others how to do it. His enthusiasm extended rapidly to his students and soon they had acquired six Taylor micro-lights and developed skills sufficient to be able to perform formation flying displays.

Inevitably, some of the students were better than others, and one of them, in particular, was more adventurous than all of the others. In fact, Biggles, which was obviously not his name but that by which he was known by the others, became the expert in the art of stunt flying, something not recommended by anybody in the know. Taylorcraft were held together with string and sticky tape and were prone to disintegration when pushed. Biggles had escaped two such incidents with only minor injuries, much to the chagrin of his colleagues, who thought the pompous git deserved to be maimed.

Charles could no longer control him in classes and formation flying was becoming too dangerous when Biggles was doing his own thing.

So, early one Saturday morning, Charles had prepared the six for what would probably be their last formation display and Biggles had been ordered to toe the line and behave, or suffer the consequences. He shrugged insubordination and carried on regardless, although all of the team had to admit that, on this particular day, Biggles flew brilliantly as Red Leader. He led the whole formation in wide, sweeping, wing-overs, brought them through on a low-level pass in diamond formation and finally broke away to perform a victory roll, at which point everybody expected the craft to fall apart.

But Biggles had stretched the aircraft to perfection and turned the victory roll into a steep climb, which would normally finish in a stall spin at about two thousand feet. Today, however, was different and Biggles took his craft up a notch or two and was swooping with a triumphant shriek, first from 5,000 feet, then from 6,000 feet and finally pushing up to just short of 8,000 feet. At that height he was dangerously close to running into cloud, which is always reckless, because you can't see anybody else hiding in the cloud. Similarly, neither can they see you and Charles was getting exasperated. He called and shouted, fired red warning flares and finally turned and walked away – just as a blood-curdling scream came from high in the heavens.

Charles turned and looked upwards, only to see the Taylorcraft floating downwards, empty and without Biggles. Urgently he scanned around but nowhere could he see the missing flyer falling from above. The scream had echoed around and seemed to continue above the clouds. As the micro-light fell slowly, Charles could see that it appeared to be flying itself and even lined itself up for a gentle touch down, without suffering any damage, apart from the missing Biggles.

Charles quickly rounded up the other flyers and divided the ground area into six separate grids, assigning one to each flyer and one to himself, giving them instructions to cover each grid systematically until they found any trace or evidence of Biggles.

After twenty minutes, he called them all back but nobody had found anything. "Get back out there until you do," he instructed and even those who despised Biggles began to feel guilty. The night began to roll in and the clouds grew thicker. Still there was no sign of Biggles. Nobody had any idea what to do next but calling the police seemed to be the most logical solution.

The police were somewhat less than enthusiastic, mainly because they already knew Biggles, as a part-time special constable, who was a severe pain in the butt, but also because he had been missing for only a couple of hours. They assumed he had gone home and not told anybody, but, since nobody seemed to have his personal address details, this was fairly academic.

Charles, however, was worried. He had heard the scream and thought it bizarre. He expected to find a gory mess somewhere but it was already too dark to see everything. The group carried on searching into the night but were getting nowhere. Eventually fatigue took over and the search was abandoned until daylight. Each member of the search team just hoped that Biggles would miraculously appear and it was all a joke or a mistake.

Chapter 4

Fishing had always been one of Jonathan's solutions to stress and pressure. The very nature of his job involved constant, unexpected, long working hours and usually he worked alone, on messy, difficult problems created mainly by other people's stupidity and lack of common sense. He ran the hardware support team for a multinational manufacturing and distribution conglomerate and people were constantly losing things, from netbooks, laptops and hand-held devices to articulated trucks, trailers and combined harvesters.

Today had been one of his worst days for months, since a whole Italian accounts department had been burgled overnight and every single computer item stolen, on the evening before quarter end. Results were paramount but having no hardware on which to produce them had failed to be covered properly during the previous year's disaster recovery tests.

Jonathan had been up for nearly forty two hours without a break and was beginning to talk rubbish. His command of any language was letting him down badly, and obscenities were beginning to be heard by all the wrong sort of people in senior management.

Suddenly Chris, Jonathan's boss from the States, rang through demanding to know where the results and reports from the previous disaster recovery tests could be found.

Jonathan felt that this was not very constructive but may have thought that too loudly as he was being escorted from the business premises by some strong men in white coats. One of them may have smote Jonathan, who may have re-acted rather recklessly as he brought a chair down on the head of one of the white coats. Before they were forcibly separated, Jonathan had thrown down his security swipe card and left the building. The white coat was sitting on his butt feeling rather inept, particularly when a group of onlookers cheered and clapped.

Jonathan was not a man many people liked but on this occasion most were prepared to make an exception, as cheering, whistling and hand-clapping reverberated throughout the premises.

But Jonathan was nowhere to be seen. He had gone immediately and was already half way en route to an overnight fishing lake he knew a couple of miles away in secluded brick-fields. By the time security had notified the local police, it was amazing how many people had forgotten where Jonathan lived, what his name was and nobody seemed to have his mobile telephone number. In fact, the local police were so short-handed due to some existing missing person enquiry occupying their restricted resources, they asked if somebody could ring back in the morning when they might be able to help.

Jonathan's boss in the States was still hanging on to his phone, believing that Jonathan was just dealing with his request for the papers for the previous disaster recovery tests. After twenty minutes, he worked out that he had been cut-off and was now after Jonathan's head. Sadly he was far too late and then he was cut-off deliberately by a steaming local manager.

In the meantime, Jonathan had collected his fishing kit from the boot of his car and was now settled down in his collapsible fishing chair with his line already cast and a bottle of Bordeaux Superior nearly half consumed. Nobody was going to disturb him, especially since it was already 10.37p.m. and he was firing up his Kindle with a new Joe Pickett story by C.J.Box, Breaking Point. How appropriate!

Just as he reached the bit where Singewald and Baker meet Kim Love for the first time in Cheyenne, an enormous splash deafened him and soaked him, but not in water. Even by FBI standards, this was out of order.

Jonathan leapt up and tried to rub the liquid off his clothes, but it was slimy and sticky. In fact, as he rubbed his jacket, the sleeve came off in his hand. His hand felt raw and started to bleed. Fighting the urge to run, Jonathan knew that he had heard a substantial splash. Struggling to find a torch in his fishing bag, Jonathan began to realise that there was an eerie silence all around him and something was not normal. Finally finding his torch, he knew that it felt wrong. Sticky was an understatement, but it was light – very light – almost as though there were no batteries within. As he tried to turn the switch on, he could feel it was futile. The torch was disintegrating as he tried to look at it. Ever the I.T. man, Jonathan reached for his mobile phone, even if only to take a photograph or two. It was already smouldering as he fired off a couple of quick shots, then tried to e-mail the products to as many people as possible. Ironically the first picture went to his boss in the States, who deleted it instantly. However, by the time he received the second picture which showed an image that looked like an oily man trying to crawl out of a lake, the boss in the States realised this was something important and immediately tried to call Jonathan. The effect was not dissimilar to a lightning strike. The explosion reverberated around the spooky silence and

Jonathan's blood-curdling scream could be heard for miles. Which was fortunate, since one of Jonathan's old colleagues and an ex-flame, Janice, had tried to follow him as he left the building. She knew about the brick-fields and the lake but had not yet found it. The scream was all she needed. She was only about two hundred metres away and was crashing through the undergrowth now searching for the scream. As she approached, she could hear groaning and moaning, which she recognised as a standard I.T. greeting.

"Feck, feck and bloody feck!"

Jonathan was a man of few words but each one counted.

"Greebo," she called in response, which obviously meant something in I.T. speak, because Jonathan stopped screaming and strained to listen.

"Jan – over here, but mind the bloody water – it's lethal. How the hell did you get here? But thank Christ you did."

Janice had now tracked Jonathan down and was about to remonstrate with him for not remembering that this was where they had made love for the first time. But when she saw him, she changed her mind. His face was blackened and all his hair had been singed off. His clothes were burnt and elbows and knees were poking out of all sorts of strange places.

"Don't touch me!" Jonathan screamed. As Janice drew close, she could see a weird glow all around him and realised that he was fully charged. She just managed to stop herself when a sudden violent crack of static electricity shot out of Jonathan's head and he collapsed clutching his temples with flat, burnt hands. The scream he emitted this time sounded far worse than anything she had ever heard before and, after one violent twitch, Jonathan lay motionless on the floor with his eyes shut.

Regardless of safety, Janice threw herself on top of Jonathan, urgently seeking a pulse. First aid was not one of her attributes and she began to panic. This was different — she had some unfinished business with Jonathan and he wasn't going to get away this time. She rolled him over and started push-ups on his chest. After about a dozen, she stopped and tried the kiss of life she'd seen given once. Three attempts at that and then she went back to push-ups again but this time she started to sing "Nelly the Elephant packed her trunk and said goodbye to the circus; off she went with a trumpety trump — trump trump trump" then went back to the kissing bit again.

After three identical verses of Nelly the Elephant, and three mouths full of heavy breathing, Janice finally opened her eyes and saw that Jonathan was watching her intently and smiling.

"You bastard," she said and nearly slapped him, stopping herself only just in time to throw her arms around him and burst into tears.

"God, that felt good," smiled Jonathan, but he failed to move quickly enough as Janice completed her full slap. This time she meant it.

But whatever thoughts they were having were interrupted by a gurgling, slimy sound as the lake behind them opened up to reveal the man whose image Jonathan had sent on one of his shots. The man was strange, yet he seemed to have presence. His movement was more of a staggering limp, as though he were trying to escape from the lake but was being held back by invisible forces. Each step upwards from the mud showed a hidden strength. The most notable feature was the sound. Despite his obvious strength, he groaned with each step he attempted and the squelch of mud, oil and effort echoed around, bringing an 'eerie, sickening wincing pain with each movement, as though he was suffering from broken limbs. Every step sounded as though it would be his last. But still he kept coming. There was a driving force that portrayed the desire to succeed.

Chapter 5

"Can anybody see where we're going?" came the somewhat panic-stricken voice of the First Officer. Nobody replied. Jason Ravinski asked again. "For Christ's sake, help me here. I've got about as much vision as with a blind-fold and bringing this bird down on one engine needs a bit more from each of us." Captain Goode appeared not to be focusing, his eyes looking glazed.

"No," he suddenly responded, "this isn't going to work. I can't get the bloody bird stable. We're dragging to port and I can't set the trim to overcome it. I'm going round again."

Ravinski heaved a sigh of either mild relief or irritation – not even he knew which. At least he was no longer alone in thinking that they were in trouble.

"RAF Coningsby, Ground Control. This is Sanbird 72 and we're encountering some strange sensations. We need to go round again. Over."

"Sanbird 72. We're tracking you but go round again? You're not cleared to land yet and you're linked into Control Tower – not Approach. Nobody here's lined you up. What's happening? Over."

"RAF Coningsby, we got an instruction to descend to five zero and line up on runway 05 and switch to 123.30 which we will do at 5,000 feet. Over."

"Not from us, you didn't Sanbird 72. That sounds like Wattisham. Have you been talking to RAF Wattisham?"

"No, Sir. Is that far from here?"

"Too far for you and it's for Army helicopters now. Our runway is 9,000 feet long and we can handle you. Theirs is about two thirds of that. Stick with us, Sunbeam, and we'll get you down safely. Don't switch controllers at all. Stay on this wavelength, 122.10 and we'll talk you in from Control Tower. We won't switch you to Approach. Over."

Captain Goode suddenly assumed a new power. He knew something had been wrong and this proved it. He turned to Ravinski and said, "Trust me, I knew something was wrong. Let's stick close together on this and we'll get the old bird down. I'll re-take controls now – I want you checking everything around us. Make sure the transponder is working and we're tracking everybody up here. Something weird's going on. I'll fly – you protect."

First Officer Ravinski smiled and nodded. This was what had been lacking since he had flown all those missions for years in the USAF – a proper leader when the rest of the world is in attack mode.

New found strength appeared and the aircraft turned discreetly right and climbed slowly back up to 8,000 feet and settled. It was as though something had been jamming the controls.

Despite still being unable to see forward through the screen, Captain Goode now turned the aircraft and followed clear instructions to change direction, descend to 5,000 feet and line up for approach to runway 07. The drag from the port engine seemed to disappear, although it was still trailing smoke. The talk down continued but this time it was smooth and as the aircraft approach the runway, everything appeared to be under control.

As the aircraft descended smoothly, the Control Tower kept talking altitude and direction, which was amazingly formal but, on this occasion, Captain James Goode and his crew had never welcomed British formality as much. The landing could hardly have been smoother and even First Officer Ravinski applauded gently as the aircraft failed to bounce on landing. He was also of the opinion that all American pilots have to land twice, mainly because he was of Russian descent.

Ironically, once the aircraft was on the ground, the problem was being able to park. Although fire-tenders and medical teams had attended the landing, expecting things to go wrong at that point, the front of the aircraft was now covered in something disgustingly slimy and impenetrable, so thick that even the crews' side windows were incapable of being prised open.

"Sanbird 72. Well done, good flying and thank you." RAF Conningsby Control Tower was being as British as only the British can be.

"No, thank you, Conningsby Tower. We'd like to thank all of your guys personally but we've still got one helluva problem left. We cain't see. Our screens are totally blocked with some kind of slimy, writhing, smelly shite. Any ideas?"

"Sanbird 72. We'll take you off the runway and park you out of the way. We still have to do Customs clearance on you and that's going to take about twenty minutes before we can get anybody here. Sorry, guys but rules is rules."

"Conningsby Tower. We don't have a problem with that but we do have a vision problem."

"Sanbird 72. Follow the white pick-up with flashing amber lights and he'll lead you."

"We got a bigger problem now. First we can't see anything through our screens with this layer of gunk but, and I think this may be much worse, we just lost our starb'd engine too. It sort of died with a squelch. Something sucks big here and we think we were very lucky to get down in one piece. I think whatever took out engine one has just taken out engine two. We are being shut down. We need help in a hurry. Got any ideas?"

"Negative, Sanbird 72 – in fact we're just receiving some disturbing news from all around us. East Midlands, Lakenheath and Mildenhall airfields are all closing down. Sounds like something similar. Wriggly, slimy, maggot-like stuff stickin' to everything. We'll try and get a fire-tender to you – see if we can hose it down."

"Negative, Conningsby. Don't let anybody out in this shit. We'll just sit here and hold. You won't get anything else down in this crap, so the runway can wait."

With both engines out of action, the 767 wasn't going to move. Coningsby Control Tower tried to warn anybody around to avoid the area and nothing was allowed to descend below 20,000 feet. But the "slimy gunk" appeared to be forming a blanket across the Home Counties and was creeping across the land, initially at ground level but rising rapidly, firstly up trees but rapidly floating through the air. And then, with a tremendous roar, the 767 exploded into flames from end to end. Nobody was going anywhere ever again.

Chapter 6

The sound of smashing glass echoed around Kennington as the police broke down the patio doors leading onto the roof-top garden of Huw Schoenberg's house. There the police were confronted by the distressing sight of a mound of decomposing bodies, possibly three or four in number – it was difficult to determine. A neighbour had heard the screams of agony earlier and, after all went quiet and nothing more happened, had decided to knock on the front door. All he could hear was a ringing, an unanswered telephone and nothing else. That seemed unusual, so, for first time ever, he decided to call the police. No, he didn't know the neighbour's name, how many people were living there, what the neighbour's telephone number was or even when the neighbour would be back from work. In fact the position was so typical of London all over, where nobody knew anybody, unless there was the possibility of a party or an office affair.

But this was gory and even one of the police officers was seen to throw up. The neighbour declined to say if he knew any of the corpses, although he did think that he may have recognised a pair of cuff-links, which was about all that was distinguishable of the heap that had at some stage consisted of grown men. The stench was sufficient to deter anybody but the police officers, with one exception, expressed gratitude for the neighbour's assistance. The exception was preparing to throw up again but he had spotted alone that the bodies outside seemed to be moving – almost as though they were wriggling. He kept trying to attract the attention of his colleagues but nobody seemed interested, until finally one of turned and screamed.

"Jesus, this lot is on the move! Come out here guys. It's alive with wriggling bloody maggots." And then he also joined his vomiting friend. His colleagues ran outside again and realised that this was now serious. Although the bodies were seemingly all very dead, they were shimmering across the roof-top garden, albeit slowly but definitely on the move. The wriggling maggot effect was all embracing. One of the officers had the presence of mind to get everybody alive back indoors and then shut and barricaded the doors. Serious help was needed but of what sort?

Chapter 7

Biggles' colleagues were due to go out searching again. Day was about to break and Charles had already rung each member of the group. All, however, were up, awake and ready to go. So by first light they had already broken the land into grids and were splitting up into well organised search parties. If anybody was going to find Biggles, it would be they.

First light or not, the conditions were miserable. The dawn drizzle soaked through everything and penetrated, like a depression that just won't clear or go away. There was a constant damp wind that carried moisture like a woollen jumper holds a cold sweat, unfashionably clinging, smelly, unwanted and unpleasant.

Nobody could even raise a greeting smile, regardless of an underlying group need to be optimistic. Within fifteen minutes, Charles could sense that this was going nowhere and called the group back together.

"Look," he said, "nobody expects this to be fun, but we've got to stay positive and ever keen. We'll find him and when we do, we're going to celebrate wildly. Whatever may have happened in the past is all behind us — we've just got to get out there and motivate each other. I've never lost anybody before and we're not starting today. All we know is that Biggles' machine came back in one piece, so we're going to find him out there somewhere. I want us to keep in touch – and I don't mean by radio, phone or any other device. Let's keep calling to each other, telling everybody where we are, what we see, what we hear but, most importantly what clues we're finding. Shout them out so we can all hear – I want to be able to track and record it all so we don't miss anything. The slightest clue will get us excited and we are going to get very excited. I've got a feeling we're on the verge, so let's be alert, careful but, most of all, let's scour every single inch out there. We're gonna find him and when we do, he is gonna owe us one helluva drink. So let's get out there and start shouting as you move."

The group all looked at each other for a moment and then realised that Charles was right. Any other attitude would mean that they just weren't looking properly. So they all turned and set off, with almost a skip. And sure enough, within five minutes, a call reverberated throughout the gloom. But it wasn't a call of excitement – more an aghast call of horror.

"Christ, quick – all get over here, I need your help – big! Now!" The voice was steeped in panic and suddenly people started running blindly.

"Here – near the lake – I've got something – Oh, my God!"

As the group descended on Christopher, who had made the discovery, they could see what appeared to be an article of clothing half buried in the mud by the lake. As they got closer they could see that it was the shirt that Biggles had been wearing the previous night, but it wasn't complete. It was mostly half of one sleeve but it had been severed by a scorch mark, so it extended from elbow to wrist only. Charles leapt in first, grabbed it and sniffed.

His colour drained instantly and he examined the section of sleeve over and over again. Finally he stopped and turned to the other guys.

"I think this might be my fault – I might have shot him with one of the red flares!"

"No, quick over here – I've found him!" came a strange voice. They all turned and were mortified to see a tall, huge man, whom nobody knew. He was seriously large and seemed to be lumbering towards them carrying a body. Both of them were covered in oil and looked like ghosts striding out of a lake.

Charles stood still, frozen with fear but was not even thinking of retreating.

"Stop there," he called to the enormous guy, who seemed to be about seven feet tall.

"No – there's a pulse – he's not dead – but he obviously needs help immediately. Can anybody call for help, we need it now?"

Another one of the team, Jack, was already on his mobile phone and had reached someone.

"Ambulance – we need an ambulance urgently. There's a man who is barely alive and may have fallen from an aircraft into a lake. Where? I don't know – where the hell are we?" he called to his fellow fliers.

"North 52.18, East 0.27", replied the big man, "very close to Cambridge Airport." Everybody looked at each other but Jack was already repeating the co-ordinates.

"Any chance of the Air Ambulance, please?" he asked. "We think this is life threatening." He stood there listening, then announced "Apparently all aircraft movements have been grounded in the UK," and shrugged.

The big guy expressed total lack of surprise and began to talk. He said that he had been fishing when it started to rain. But the rain had been strange. It had been very, very heavy but seemed contain an oily, slimy substance which caused all of his fishing colleagues to pack up and go. He was about to when he heard his colleagues screaming and saw them collapsing, apparently lifeless. He slipped and fell into the lake, which he thought was already polluted, so he scrambled to get out. But, as luck would have it, he realised that the lake seemed to counter whatever was in the air and he didn't feel anything other than wet. Close to the shore was moored a small dinghy and he swam to it. But as he got closer he realised he was in deep water and climbing into the dinghy would not be easy. After a couple of attempts, he pulled himself up into one side of the dinghy but it suddenly turned turtle on him, possibly knocking him unconscious at the same time. Now the upside down dinghy was on top of him, protecting him from the rain. Then he began to realise that he could breathe again, yet he was pinned underneath the upturned dinghy and trapped. He decided that was probably the best place to be and climbed up into the structure of the boat and fell asleep. There he had stayed asleep and uncomfortable until shouting voices had woken him the next morning – the Biggles' search party. His fishing colleagues had perished but both he and now possibly Biggles had survived, because, perhaps, they had both escaped from whatever was in the air.

Admittedly, Biggles had fallen several thousand feet into the lake and landing on a lake from that height was about as soft as landing on concrete. So he'd had the right to pass out and possibly suffer a couple of broken legs too. Hence his unconscious silence. His shallow breathing had probably also saved his life.

Chapter 8

Jonathan was slowly recovering from what appeared to be a lightning strike but he wasn't concentrating. Janice was now trying to hold him in her arms but he was struggling.

"What happened to oily man?" he asked.

"Don't know what you're talking about," said Janice, obviously not interested.

Jonathan searched for his mobile phone but with no success, when suddenly they both heard wailing sirens. Instantly their concentration was destroyed and they turned their attention to the new sounds, which seemed to coming in their direction. As the wailing grew louder and louder, they could also hear other voices. Totally out of the blue, a red flare illuminated the whole area around them.

"Over here," screeched a voice and then other people started to shout, trying to attract attention. They could hear various people giving all sorts of different instructions, when suddenly Janice screamed "No, over here!" But her call went unanswered as a couple of people tore into the foliage around them calling, "Who the hell are you? This is our ambulance, our crisis, our disaster. Sod off."

Before she could answer, Janice trod on someone and shrieked. Immediately she was surrounded with all sorts of people, all shouting conflicting instructions. One of them seemed to be older than the others, so she grabbed him and asked him what the hell was going on?

"No time, but we've just found a friend who fell from a plane and he's badly hurt. Who are you?"

"I'm with a friend who looks like he just got struck by lightning, so can we share your ambulance?"

A moment of silence followed before both Janice and the older guy started to bombard each other with questions. Jonathan sat up and held his hand up.

"Stop – let's just get on with it. I don't need medical treatment. Let's just get the other guy sorted out."

Suddenly the large and strange guy appeared and said, "Something really weird's happening here – why aren't we all dead?"

Everybody turned on him but nobody could answer.

Charles took the lead and explained his issues from the day before, which killed conversation stone dead. Finally he said, "We found Biggles just a short time ago but he doesn't look very good at all."

"He's not alone," said Janice and looked at Jonathan, who dutifully winced with pain.

The huge and strange guy intervened and stood addressing everybody present.

"I don't know any more than anybody else but what I do know is that this part of the country seems to be grounded by poisoned rain. Not far from here a commercial airliner has come down and it sounds as though Biggles here may have suffered the same fate. There's bound to be more out there, so let's just pool our resources." The large guy seemed to know much more than anybody else and this concerned Charles, who had begun to study him closely. He exceeded 6ft 6inches, which was big by most standards. He was broad and looked strong but he had an air of senior management about him. He was obviously a man of some intelligence and strength but nobody in the group seemed to know him.

"Who are you?" asked Charles, deciding that any other approach would take time, and they didn't appear to have any time.

"It doesn't actually matter," responded the big guy, "but I work for a specialist government department and we have been expecting this day for several years now. Your friend Biggles is one of my colleagues and he got too close — we actually call him Icarus in our office."

Nobody smiled.

"So can we just get him to hospital — like now?" asked Janice. "Jonathan seems to think he doesn't need any attention but in my eyes you look like shit." Jonathan winced again.

The large chap raised his right hand, almost in treaty, and said, "If I thought there was any chance of getting anybody out here, I'd get straight onto it but I understand there is a general lockdown until it appears to be safe."

Even as he spoke, another sound of sirens approaching shattered the peace and everybody stood in dumbstruck silence. But not for long. Suddenly the siren-led transport passed and kept going, obviously not interested in this incident but something far more powerful. Janice set off in chase but to no avail. After a few minutes, she returned, cursing and muttering, only to confirm that there were several fire tenders and numerous other emergency vehicles but no ambulances.

"Sounds like the aircraft problem," said the large guy, "but that's about thirty miles away. As I said, I don't think we've got any chance, other than to take them ourselves. Anybody got any transport?"

Jonathan turned rapidly and said, "I ask again, who the hell are you?"

In the silence that followed, the only sound was the fading wail of disappearing emergency vehicles.

"OK," came the reluctant response. "My name is Mike Menton and I head up the CAA Accident Investigations team. Several hours ago a Boeing 767 fell out of the sky and nobody survived. We need to find out why and how, and what happened to Icarus/Biggles."

"I may have shot Biggles," said Charles, "albeit with a red flare. However, I don't think I shot down a Boeing airliner. But if he was up there in the clouds, maybe I did."

The silence boomed even louder. On a very late cue, Mike finally stepped up and put his enormous hand on Charles's shoulder.

"There's very little chance of that. It's more likely the plane had a massive bird strike, although at fifteen thousand feet it's not very common."

Charles noticeably sighed with relief but asked, "So if it wasn't bird strike, what was it?"

Chapter 9

"Maggots," came the one word response. The speaker was a new individual who had apparently appeared from nowhere. Everybody spun round to see who had spoken and were all surprised to see a short, young guy dressed in very scruffy denims and filthy trainers.

"Shabby!" replied Mike, "How did you get here? I thought you were going to stay in the office."

"If you'd answered any of your bloody text messages in the last hour, I would have done. Don't you keep your bloody phone turned on?"

Mike started rummaging through his pockets and finally appeared with nothing.

"Damn. Looks like I've lost it. Sorry. What's been happening?"

"Oh, not much," replied Shabby. "People dropping dead in London, East Anglia, Home Counties, Liverpool and Manchester, just to name a few. You're needed at a bad site in Kennington. Like about two hours ago. Look at the state of you. Did you fall in something?"

"Kennington? South London? Has there been an accident there? That could be disastrous." Mike Menton suddenly became very agitated.

"No, no," replied Shabby. "This is strange. Something fell out of the sky but it wasn't a plane. The local police have asked for technical assistance and you drew the short straw. However, I think you ought to know that it may have something in common with that 767." And without any warning, Shabby turned his back on the others and mouthed something to Menton that looked like a very exaggerated "Magg Otz"

"Pardon," said both Charles and Janice.

Mike Menton put his hands on Shabby's shoulders and turned him around slowly to face them. "Go on, tell them. They've got much of the story so far and we need to keep them informed, because they can all help us."

Shabby's face showed it all – embarrassment, hatred and anger. But he knew how to handle himself professionally and drew all of the people together.

"Ladies and Gentlemen. This is not totally evidenced yet but it would appear that we are being forced to ground all aircraft, or divert them away from the UK, due to some strange atmospheric conditions. During the last twenty four hours, we have been subject to some very heavy and weird rain storms that seem to have included some strange substances, which have given rise to physical damage to equipment that would normally be considered to be safe and sound. All I can tell you is that these are not normal conditions and we would not normally issue any specific instructions. But I can advise you that we are working urgently to ensure that there is no risk to human health and normal service will be resumed very shortly."

"Bullshit," muttered about half of the group. The other half just shook their heads in disbelief, but were too polite to comment. The first half of the group, however, was not happy and various questions about findings to date crushed both Mike and Shabby on the spot.

"Look," said Mike Menton, "you're going to find out eventually but there is something in the rain that we don't understand. We're just trying to make sure that nothing slips through if we can stop it. Our main aim is to keep everybody safe — hence grounding all flights. Your friend Biggles is very lucky, although he probably doesn't feel that currently. All I'm going to say is I am not going to guess what this is about. We're going to be ultra-careful." And with that, Menton and Shabby turned and left.

Charles, Jonathan and Janice all looked at each other and shrugged.

"So what the hell are we supposed to do with Biggles?" asked Charles. "Much though I'd like to get him an ambulance, it doesn't look likely. Has anybody got access to a car?"

Janice nodded, "But it's a hair-dresser's MX5" she added sheepishly.

Jonathan's reaction was beautiful: "You weren't expecting me to ride in that, were you?" a thought he suddenly wished he had kept to himself.

"Bloody right," she said, "why on earth would I offer you a lift? Charles, let's see if we can get Biggles safely to the hospital. You sit next to me and we'll get Biggles across us somehow. Jonathan – you can help carry Biggles with us."

Chapter 10

Transferring Biggles to hospital was relatively easy. Getting him admitted was a totally different issue. Nobody really knew his proper name, let alone his National Insurance number. The nature of his injuries – possible broken ankles, fell out of the sky, burn injury on a wrist and unconscious – made it difficult to fill out a single form for any hospital department. Other questions, such as religion, ethnic minority, address, next-of-kin and date of birth had to be left blank as well. His occupation was also elusive to everyone, other hobbies – a secret policeman, being a stunt pilot – seemed somewhat eccentric. But since this was the UK, nobody seemed too anxious to ascertain his insurance company, so eventually he was admitted, albeit without anybody really knowing what to do with him.

So, as is often the way, the most junior doctor on call had Biggles added to his list. The doctor, known to his colleagues as Shavreem, because nobody could recall or pronounce his real name, decided that he was going to make his name on this mysterious patient and set to with all sorts of x-rays and tests. After a couple of hours, still unconscious, Biggles had been diagnosed with two broken ankles, a forearm burn or gun-shot wound that was mostly superficial, but would need plastic surgery, and then the most amazing lung injury. It appeared to Dr Shavreem that Biggles had been attacked from within his throat by something live and bacterial. The worrying aspect was that the doctor thought that Biggles had swallowed something, choked on it and tried to cough it up, merely moving it partially from his stomach, back into his mouth and into his lungs. Upon closer examination, the doctor decided it was still alive and trying to eat its way out of Biggles' body, by any route, whether available or not. Inevitably Biggles was going to die but the question was when and how.

Dr Shavreem was about to concede that he was out of his depth and call for help when he suddenly saw a small reflection from one of Biggles' ears. Upon closer examination, Dr Shavreem almost passed out and was grabbed by one of the hospital orderlies before he fell. The assistant turned to see what had caused the problem and threw up immediately. Biggles' ear was writhing with maggots. Dr Shavreem reciprocated the kindness of the orderly and helped him away to the discretion of a staff room out of the sight of any patients or relatives.

By the time he returned to Biggles, all sorts of nursing staff were charging around trying to look efficient but, in reality having no idea whatsoever on what to do. Dr Shavreem stood about six inches taller than his normal height and said, "Ladies and gentlemen, please stand back and let me carry on with my patient." Everybody recoiled like they had touched an electric fence and moved away relieved. Shavreem asked one of the less attractive nurses to give him a hand and her response was immediate.

"Why me?" she asked, not knowing whether to be proud or hurt.

"I've been watching you for several weeks now, Nurse Abram, and I think you have excellent patient bedside manner, and this patient is going to need much of that when we get him on the mend. If you don't mind, I would like you to work with me on this."

The young nurse, naturally shy and almost trembling with fear, turned instantly scarlet and put her small, elegant hand into her own mouth, thereby simultaneously concealing her chewed fingernails. Dr Shavreem patted her on the shoulder without appearing to be patronising and smiled at her, making her scarlet face turn almost white.

"Don't worry, I won't bite your head off," he continued and she almost returned a smile. The rest of the staff had already glided away with relief and Shavreem was able to carry on as though this was a normal working partnership.

"Actually, I wanted someone to talk to about this and I think you could be the right person. I really don't have a clue what to do with this guy but between the two of us we could work on him until we get a great success or a complete failure. Would you mind sticking your neck out with me on this? I understand if you say no but it could do us both a big favour if we get it right. What say you?"

Nurse Leila Abram nodded gently and both of them looked at each other with a small wink. "Blind leading the blind?" she asked.

"Bloody right, but what the hell?" came Dr Shavreem's smiling response.

"Actually, I've been studying the notes and although we know very little about this guy, there is one thing that's really intrigued me," she started, and immediately stopped in case she was out of order.

"No – carry on – I've got a theory too, so let's swap notes," replied Dr Shavreem. "You first."

"That's not fair," replied the nurse, with a smile, suddenly realising that maybe nursing wasn't so bad after all. Somebody had actually noticed her and this guy seemed alright. Working with him might help her boost her confidence, which was at rock bottom currently and if they did really crack this case maybe it was a best foot forward moment.

"I get the impression that this guy fell out of the sky into the lake but his injuries had already happened before then, apart from his ankles. I think his lung, throat, stomach stuff is what we need to look at and whatever happened there could be critical."

Dr Shavreem smiled and said, "Brilliant. We're on the same track here. Except I think this is not the only case. I have also learned about a couple of other weird incidents that might be related. Did you hear about a plane coming down with engine troubles? It strikes me that something strange is going on upstairs because this plane's engines sucked in something that caused one to catch fire and the other one just seized up, just before it blew up. If this guy's swallowed something up in the sky, it might just be related.

"Let's see what we've got, unless, of course, you have anything else," he added as a late after-thought.

"Well, actually, I do," added the nurse, feeling boosted and more confident each moment. "The people who discovered this character weren't alone. I understand that there were some outsiders who appeared around the discovery of our man. Rumour has it they may have been government people, perhaps trying to cover up what was going on. But one of them apparently mentioned the plane incident, which was big, before he got called off to something in London. My source tells me he knew the exact location of this incident, including grid references. No normal person would even understand those, let alone use them. I know this makes me sound like a bit of a sad anorak but I know somebody in air traffic control, NATS, and he told me they'd had an emergency yesterday when a Boeing 767 made an emergency landing at a British military base with engine intake issues and slimy cockpit windows. Both engines appear to have been damaged in flight by some form of air strike and the rumours have mentioned slimy maggots. Maybe Biggles here has been up to something messy?"

Dr Shavreem stood open-mouthed. His assessment of Nurse Abram had been way off course. She was bright, intelligent and very observant. Not only that but she was becoming more attractive with every word she said. And she hadn't finished.

"My brother and I............damn. I didn't mean to say that. NATS staff are all sworn to secrecy, especially over "incidents," and this, until now, is just another "incident." But he thought we might have had loads of admissions because of this 767. It looks as though there was a massive cover up because over 200 people have gone missing and nothing has been said yet. The flight was due to land yesterday but is reported "missing" as though in wartime action. But still it is low key. This news embargo is total nonsense. How can you 'lose' a 767? And this 'government' man? Who the hell is Mike Menton? Or his side-kick, Shabby?" Dr Shavreem was impressed with his new assistant, and hoped she was going to pursue this further. He need not have worried.

"Neither of these characters is known in the circles of any CAA department. I have good insight through my brother into these types of department and something is being covered up. Why would the CAA be investigating a non-crash? Why would they be involved with a Taylorcraft incident when nobody was killed? Particularly if the pilot was shot? Even if it was with a red flare?

"This doesn't hang together. These two strange guys are trying to cover something up. The two guys don't add up themselves. And what would they be needed in London for? They should be where the plane caught fire. Something sucks here, big."

"Aah! I may be able to contribute here," interrupted Shavreem. "I used to know something about fishing and pond life. Sometimes peculiar things happen with the pond water because it is usually stagnant. Algae and bugs survive with strange properties to the extent where new breeds develop unexpectedly. Our Biggles man fell out of the sky, which isn't surprising from what I read in the notes. If he was shot by a flare, he probably fell out of his flying machine by letting go instinctively. So normally he would have died hitting the ground. However, he fell into the pond – broken legs – but I reckon some of the crap he swallowed might have saved him. So if the pond contains some form of remedy to whatever the problem is, I reckon we need to move quickly before other evidence can disappear."

Nurse Abram stood with a beaming smile on her face, almost rubbing her hands with glee.

"I've always been interested in forensics and I wondered how I might bring them into my life. I think you have just done it, thanks," she said exuding happiness. "I'm on my way."

"Make sure you get the right pond," said Dr Shavreem.

"I think the one with the police blue tape all around it might be a clue," said the nurse, combining a smile with a wink. And then she was gone.

Shavreem returned to his patient and once again examined his ears. The maggots were white, writhing and active. They seemed to surge upwards from within the patient's ears and were fighting to breathe. But they seemed to be lacking the will to take over the world. Perhaps they were beginning to tire.

Chapter 11

Mike Menton and Shabby had reached Kennington without being challenged but knew that they were treading on thin ice. The CAA cover might have been accepted in Cambridge but the trouble was that there was no back up and whatever they said could be ripped apart effortlessly.

Their other fear was that the problem could get out of control without their being able to intervene. It was already way beyond their remit and only their anonymity could help them proceed where others were failing in large numbers. In reality, if they didn't find the cause of the problem quickly, any solution could be worthless. Not that they actually had a solution.

Following a quick call to announce their potential arrival, they flashed their ID with cautious optimism. To their surprise, Menton and Shabby received only a nod and walked straight upstairs to the scene. The bodies were still slumped on top of each other but deterioration had already commenced. Menton was angry and demanded to see the officer in charge.

"That'll be you, mate," came the abrupt retort. "The two of us have only just come on shift, and we know sod-all."

Menton snarled and demanded to know who had despatched these officers. The shrugged response was not what he wanted or expected, so still he sought names. One of the officers offered to ring the police station manager and hand his phone over to Menton, who snapped and said he had no intention of speaking to such an imbecile but merely intended to screw the career of his commanding officer. In reality, he was powerless to do anything, but he wanted the evidence protected. So he cleverly negotiated with the two policemen that revealing their senior's name would protect their own careers. Naïvely they believed him and gave him the identity of somebody about whom he knew nothing, for just the moment. But his main concern was to protect the bodies. Then he would throw his weight around.

Menton noticed the sudden arrival of a young lady, who was armed and angry. When he saw that she was armed, his attitude changed until he realised that it was with a large glass jar. Menton froze, because now his attitude would have to change yet again. He turned towards the girl and tried to beckon her away from the two policemen. As soon as she saw him, she spun on her heels and strode purposefully away from the police, who were getting rattled by her insistence on access.

She reached Menton in about eight paces and leapt into conversation before he could get a word in edgeways.

"You're the guy who was at Cambridge earlier. God you're hard to find."

Menton was shocked that he had been followed and found, particularly by a girl with a jam-jar. "I might ask who the hell you are and why you're following me? You'll get nothing from me until you explain yourself," he snapped.

"Do you think I'll get anything afterwards?" she asked astutely.

They stood facing each other in impasse mode.

Menton cracked first. "But you're only........"

"A girl? How dare you? I'm involved in the forensics on this case and you're covering up stuff which could be of major help to us. I don't even care who you are but if you carry on obstructing our investigations, I'll make sure you get nothing back – and, believe me, I can." Nurse Abram felt vomit rise in her throat as she knew she had gone way too far and, any second now, would get put down enormously.

But to her total amazement, the other guy with Menton put his hand on Menton's shoulder and said, quietly, "She's right, you know. Come on, we're getting nowhere on this case and maybe she can help us."

Menton turned on Shabby and, for a brief second, looked as though he would deck his colleague. But suddenly a discrete smile appeared on his face and he bowed his head forward, almost in shame.

With a wink to his colleague, he turned and faced Nurse Abram and started an apology. But before he could open his mouth, the nurse waved an index finger at his face and said, "Don't even think about making any form of apology unless you mean it. I can see through people like you all the time." She poked him in his shoulder to emphasise the point and Shabby had to stifle a shriek of laughter.

"Good on you, girl," he thought, "it's about time someone did that to him," and failed to control a smile.

"OK, OK," said Menton, "you go first then."

Leila Abram had been waiting for this moment in her life and now that it had arisen, she wasn't going to miss such an opportunity.

"Right," she began. Shabby crossed his arms across his chest to savour the moment. "You waltzed into Cambridge as though you owned the place but, from what I hear, all you did was contaminate the evidence on site. For all I know, you've probably done the same here, so until I get my forensic samples, you're barred from touching anything. And if you even think of going over my head, you're as good as dead. I've got very senior level sanction to be here, probably even more senior than you could dream about. So let's start off on the right foot. You obviously know some secrets that you're withholding but I've already got a partial solution which might be of help to you. So, without beating about the bush, you show me yours and then I'll show you mine." She crossed her arms but not until she had wagged her finger again at Menton. Shabby was beside himself trying not to burst out laughing.

Menton stood still and silent for a second, then offered his hand in shaking mode. Leila Abram tensed her body and then grasped Menton's hand as though she was going to break it. He knew a good handshake when he met one and this was one of those. He smiled slightly and held on just a second too long. Leila didn't just withdraw her hand, she almost shoved

Menton's hand an inch back into his arm. She was fully in control.

After a deep breath and what seemed like an eternity, Menton relaxed and looked Leila straight in the eye. She glared back, which surprised even her. He finally opened his mouth and said, "This is very hard to start to explain because none of us really knows where the beginning is. I also work in forensics but from a very different angle compared with you. My role is that of chemical warfare investigator and, as I am sure you can imagine, it's not an easy or respected task. Most of the people I talk to are murderers, terrorists and mad. I therefore have to assume that my life is at risk, which it usually is. Shabby here is the perfect partner, because nobody thinks he's a nasty bastard. He should win an Oscar for some of his performances but this time we're in trouble. We think we know what the weapon is but we really don't have a clue who is the perpetrator. Any help you can give would be superb but I am really going to have to get moving very quickly because the weapon, as you already know, is lethal."

Menton paused for breath and Leila Abrams could feel herself ready to fall apart. Her aggression had subsided and suddenly she was about to become the very minor player she really was. But she still had one last item in reserve; one more card to play. And as though the Gods were on her side, a blood-curling scream came from one of the police officers. They both turned and ran towards him, to be confronted by something that brought them to an instant standstill. One of the bodies had moved. In fact, it was dragging itself free of the others heaped on top of itself. Stetson Pete had gleaned some protection from his large tasteless hat because his mouth had probably not collected as much rain in it as had the others and he was now throwing up. Leila surged forward with her jar extended and captured whatever vile coloured bile was now trailing from Stetson Pete's mouth.

"Great," she said, "all I need now is a sample of the maggots themselves, although some of this stuff might have some regurgitated samples." A small plastic bag was thrust into her hand and she found new, writhing maggots instantly.

Menton and Shabby both grasped their mouths but slightly too late. Leila was surrounded by vomiting men, which made her smile ever so briefly but restored her confidence and upper hand status.

"Whilst you're all puking your hearts up, I've got business to do. Get this guy," she aimed her pointy finger in the direction of Stetson Pete, "to St Mary's in Cambridge to Dr Shavreem as quickly as possible. I'll tell him he'll be there within the hour." She aimed her instruction at the two duty policeman, who shrugged and looked away. "No, you. I'm talking to you. Do it now." Menton nodded his approval, which appeared to smooth the ruffled feathers, before Leila turned back to him.

"I'm taking samples back with me but I need to go via my potential solution location. D'you want to come with me?"

Menton and Shabby both nodded, still unable to talk.

"Good," she said, "we'll take your car – it'll be bigger than mine, and probably has flashing lights on it."

The guys nodded again and she swept out clutching her jam jar and plastic bag, closely pursued by two fairly dishevelled and slightly confused people. As they reached street level, Menton managed to raise an arm, albeit very briefly for fear of being sick again, and a black BMW, with discreet blue lights flashing from within its radiator, came gliding in, allowing the two men in the back, so Leila slid into the front seat.

"Where to?" asked the driver.

"Back to where you came from," replied Leila, "near Cambridge."

The driver looked at her, the two guys in the back seat and shrugged his shoulders in question. "Like the lady says," muttered Menton and the car took off with wailing sirens and flashing lights.

Leila was impressed as they wound through all sorts of vehicles that moved out of their way. By the time they had reached the pond where Biggles had been found, the police presence around the blue tapes had been reduced to one very young and nervous special constable, who reluctantly gave up his empty tea flask to enable a sample of pond water to be taken. Leila promised him she would replace it personally, although absolutely nobody believed her. Particularly since she didn't even take his name.

"Back to St. Mary's," she commanded and Menton nodded confirming approval again.

Dr Shavreem nodded as she marched in with the two men trailing behind her and patted Leila on the shoulder. "I got the sample you asked for," he said, "and it seems I have a new patient coming in. Is there anything else you would like me to do, Boss?" he added, and winked. Shabby and Menton looked with horror at each other, at which points Leila swung round to face them.

"We should get an answer on this quickly," she said and strode off clutching her jam jar half full of vomit and her wriggling plastic bag.

"One amazing lady," said Menton, to his feet. Shabby had stopped feeling sick and was smiling again.

"Should I go with her?" asked Shabby.

"I wouldn't if I were you," replied Shavreem and everybody agreed instantly.

Dr Shavreem slipped off to find his new Stetson covered patient and Menton and Shabby mentioned, half-heartedly, that perhaps they would like to see him if he recovered. Secretly they both hoped Shavreem would deny them access but he smiled and said that it would be a pleasure. Both shook their heads. This wasn't turning out to be one of their better days.

Within minutes, Leila Abram came bouncing back, covered in smiles. Trailing behind her, Dr Shavreem looked pensive but not negative. Menton and Shabby both hoped that an explanation for both attitudes would come verbally but Shavreem insisted that the two men followed them back into the hospital. The visitors assumed a hint of grey in their faces but Leila was enjoying this. Almost skipping, she led them into a small office which appeared to be chaotic. It seemed part laboratory, part children's play room with miniature toys scattered everywhere. She grabbed something that looked like a small bicycle, about three inches long, and almost dragged the two men by their ears to peer into the basket-like contraption attached to the handle bars. In the basket, which resembled a beaker with liquid in it, there was nothing other than clear water. The two men shrugged and looked at each other.

"That was a couple of those maggots and I dropped some of the murky pond water on them. And now it is just clear water. The maggots have gone – disintegrated – vanished. It looks as though we may have the cure. All we need now is the source, the cause." Leila smiled so much that she even showed dimples no-one had seen before.

Chapter 12

Stetson Pete was not good and Dr Shavreem was struggling to keep him alive. By throwing up, he had cleared his stomach to an extent but his lungs had been contaminated and his ears were now alive with maggots. Menton, looking now almost green in the gills, was close to being sick again but he had already wretched himself empty. As his own stomach began to turn again, he grabbed a glass of water sitting by his hand and was about to drink from it when Leila shrieked and snatched it from his hand, spilling much of the contents onto Stetson Pete's face, including his ear.

With a hiss and a sizzle, steam poured upwards from Stetson Pete's ear and he winced. Leila grasped Shavreem's arm.

"Wait," she snapped, "This could be interesting. The water in that glass was a by-product from the pond water that had been poured onto the maggots. Whilst it seems to have destroyed the maggots, it looks as though it can now self-generate. Look what it's doing to his skin and the other maggots."

Everybody, except Menton, stood in awe and watched the process kicking in. Menton was looking for anything into which he could throw up. But even he could see that something good was happening and forced himself to watch. He could almost hear a whirlpool sucking sound as Stetson Pete's ears started to slurp in the liquid and the maggots seemed to disappear in a squeak and almost a wisp of smoke. Within seconds, Stetson

Pete began to groan, and people could hear his stomach rumble. The guy was almost dead but hungry.

Shabby stepped in front of everybody and took a deep breath. Menton, suddenly recovered, leant over towards him and said, "Not now, Ray. We need to discuss this elsewhere first." Shabby nodded and the two men muttered some feeble excuse and left before Leila or Shavreem could stop them. Leila was about to shriek again, when Shavreem gently grabbed her arm and walked her towards the door. Shavreem leant over and, sliding one of his hands under the nearest desk, and set off a string of very loud alarm bells. They could hear all of the hospital security doors slamming.

Chapter 13

Menton and Shabby didn't even make the first door before it slammed in their faces. They turned round looking for an alternative escape route and realised that they were going nowhere.

"Shit," was Menton's all-embracing response. He turned and was facing Shavreem and Leila, both of whom appeared incandescent with rage.

"How dare you," started Leila. Shavreem thought about restraining her, but changed his mind. She had already raised her right arm and he thought that a sharp slap in the face was almost justified. What Shavreem hadn't anticipated was her fully clenched fist spanking Menton's nose so hard that blood spurted everywhere. At that point, she was supposed to dissolve into tears, but she raised her fist for a second blow. Shavreem intervened but not without deflecting the second blow.

"Right, we've made the point," said Shavreem, jumping to Leila's defence but it was not needed. Menton put his hands up, partly in self-defence but partly conceding the battle.

"I'm sorry," he said, clutching his bleeding nose, "but we have a real issue here. Let me explain."

"Would've been better earlier," said Leila, trying hard to calm down. "We've done an amazing amount to help and you were just walking away? I don't normally break noses but, in your case, I was prepared to make an exception. I would say I'm sorry but I doubt you'd believe me – so just start talking before I change my mind."

All three men looked at each other with eyes portraying fear.

"Go on, talk."

Shabby stepped forward holding his hands up and said, "This is very serious. We've been chasing a new form of security breach which seems to have got out of control. Obviously we're both sworn to secrecy but, provided this stays within these four walls, we'll tell you. Can we count on that?"

Shavreem and Leila attempted to nod but Menton and Shabby both insisted on words and handshakes, although the Menton/Leila relationship hadn't really reached that stage of recovery yet. Nevertheless they shook hands, albeit tentatively.

Shabby drew another long breath and started.

"In this age of evil warfare, the use of deadly gases creates too much attention. There are many other types of damaging evil and we think we've encountered something uncontrollable. You may have come up with, albeit unwittingly, the solution to the problem we haven't fully discovered. Provided we keep it to ourselves, we would like to work on this together but it is far too high profile for us to make that decision. How am I doing so far?"

"Bullshit!" said Leila, obviously still preparing to let rip another punch. "You've actually said nothing yet that can't be read in a tabloid newspaper. Come on, give, or you'll be joining your friend here in A&E."

"OK, OK," said Shabby. "We think we've uncovered the controlled breeding of an innocent type of moth that creates something almost harmless on the ground. But modified to work in the air, specifically in artificially inseminated rain clouds, the end product could be used to threaten civilisation as we know it. Hence the downing of a Boeing 767, a single light aircraft, pollution of a town, city or country. We had no idea how it would work but it seems to have been started and you may have come up with a cure."

Shavreem stepped forward and asked, "So what happens now?"

"We don't know," replied Menton, "but I can tell what we think might happen. These moths are called the spindle ermine moths and their caterpillars strip trees bare as the larvae eat the leaves of trees. We've found a row of trees in a forest that look like an avenue of ghosts. The silk from the larvae make the trees look as though they are wrapped in an enormous cobweb. But we think someone has been breeding them specifically to use for far more lethal purposes and that's where the maggots come into it. If your theories are right, we shall have to go back to your pond and examine the contents of that in much more detail. But I would hazard a guess that you've got it right. But, in the meantime, I can't stop you from dealing with your patients until I report this all back. I know I should but I genuinely think you can help these guys. Waiting for the strategy from on high could involve people you might be able to save from simply dying.

"So this conversation hasn't taken place and you carry on doing what you're doing. I'm going to escalate our findings but I'm afraid you'll have to work fast because suddenly this place will be swarming with undesirable nerds.

"And now, if you wouldn't mind, we need to leave."

"Sorry – no can do," said Leila, causing Shavreem's right eyebrow to rise. "Security here requires that approval to release the doors comes from the both the Secretary of the hospital and the Security Manager, both of whom are key-holders."

"And?" questioned Menton.

"They will only grant that after they're happy that the "whistle-blower" has been traced and the risk encountered has been overcome. Nobody else is authorised to do that," said Leila, almost controlling a smile. "Oh, and by the way, the Hospital Secretary is on holiday."

"So who the hell is deputising for him?" retorted Menton.

"For her," replied Leila, "and you'll have to ask the Security Manager. You're confusing me with someone who gives a damn. As far as I'm concerned, it stays locked."

Shavreem recoiled. But both Menton and Shabby reacted by turning slightly red and also by instinctively raising their right clenched hands.

"Oh that's right – go on, hit me. That'll help you a lot. Any second now about ten armed security guards will burst through the door behind us, and they are trained to attack first and ask questions afterwards. So I suggest you simply lie face down on the floor and put your hands on the backs of your heads – both of you. Seriously. Now."

With a violent crash, the door behind Leila burst open and two fully armed police officers threw themselves onto the ground but with rifles pointing at Menton and Shabby. Behind were a team of a further six fully armed support, with two familiar faces.

Chapter 14

Janice and Jonathan looked remarkably different in full armed police uniform, although his face seemed to have staged a miraculous recovery and his hair had re-grown. Leila, despite her relief, looked at both of them as though she had seen ghosts.

"How come you're............you know......different?"

Janice waited until her colleagues had grasped, searched and hand-cuffed Menton and Shabby and marched them away. She then turned to explain.

"Although I've worked with Jonathan before, my IT days were fairly low key, because I have been training to be an armed officer for over three years. This is only my third call because, believe it or not, we rarely get full alert calls. I was already designated to this case about three weeks ago and when we first got the call about Biggles, who's also one of us, we were on full alert from then. The trouble was that Biggles is a complete pratt and never knew when to cool off."

"But that doesn't explain Jonathan, though," said Leila. "He looked like total shit when I saw him last."

"Correct," said Janice, "he was feeling like it too. However, let me introduce you to Detective Superintendant James Wilkinson, Jonathan's twenty minute older twin brother. My taste in men has always been shit, and I chose the wrong brother. But this one is married, totally reliable, and a decent chap – and also one of my bosses. Otherwise I'd tell you the truth about him too," she added, nodding at D.S. Wilkinson, who extended his hand in greeting.

Leila shook it, without trying to crush it, but the policeman still winced.

"I'm sorry," he said, "it's just a bit of a sports injury."

"What, fishing?" asked Leila, in mock disbelief.

"Actually, yes," he replied, with red face. "I slipped over carrying a load of fish and jarred my shoulder."

"Tell me it wasn't the pond where we found Biggles," Leila giggled.

"I can't. It was and all the fish fell back in and escaped," blushed the policeman. "We were following those two pricks and trying to set up a discreet surveillance. It so nearly all fell apart but the Terrorist Squad have also had their eyes on them for months now and I nearly blew it. If that guy hadn't shot Biggles with a flare and if Biggles hadn't fallen into that pond with all my fish, none of this would have happened and we would have been in the wrong place. But the reality is these guys are dangerous. They've been trying to perfect this dreadful product to sell it overseas to known terrorists. Your antidote has only just happened in time because our sources tell us release was imminent."

By the time he had finished, the Detective Superintendant was pleased to have run it past a stranger because he knew that a Press Release was on the horizon and the Press would be far less accommodating. In fact, he was hoping that it could be deferred for some time in order to ensure that there were no further members working with the two detainees. There was still an issue of a plane load of passengers and crew who were dead and the problem of the general grounding of aircraft in Eastern England.

"I wonder if you two might have any spare time to work with us for a few weeks to devise a plan on where we go from here," Wilkinson asked Leila and Dr Shavreem, who both snorted with laughter.

"Er, we work in A&E and the chances of our getting any time off for you to take us out for even a burger dinner is non-existent," they replied, almost in union.

"We're both due at least three weeks' holiday leave we can't take, so if you can swing something for us to help you, you will be an even bigger miracle performer than any living person on this earth," said Leila. "By the way, how is your brother?"

"Sorry, I don't know," shrugged the Detective Superintendant, "I've been a bit busy the last few days. Janice?"

"I despair," replied Janice, "I was about to ask you."

"He's upstairs on Lakeside Ward," smiled Dr. Shavreem, "I don't suppose you even knew that. What is it with all this work stuff? I despair too."

Turning around and beckoning Leila Abrams to follow him, Shavreem strode off into the fading daylight, business concluded but far from resolved. One day this would all be put to bed but the only thing that everybody agreed to at this moment was that nobody knew exactly what had happened then nor what was going to happen next. Their frustration and despair was not going away yet.

Dawn of a New Day

By Colin Butler

Just another day dawns,
People desperately searching for food,
Innocent children playing in the park,
Little Mitsuko riding his new birthday bike.
Whilst office workers punch their time clocks,
And soldiers exercise on the parade ground.
The clock ticks slowly round to eight-fifteen,
Some thirty-two thousand feet above Hiroshima
A lone aircraft silhouetted against the clear blue sky
Slowly, the bomb-bay doors open.............

In the land of the rising sun
A man-made fireball consumes all before it,
As a living hell rages all around me.
I see a man blasted out of existence
Leaving just a shadow burnt into the stone.
The dense choking, dust cloud
Is followed by black toxic rain.
I see death and destruction as far as my eyes can see.
Somehow I've miraculously survived- but later
My skin erupts as a mysterious sickness overtakes me.

The Wretched Man

By Elliot Thorpe

Chapter 1

The Underground station of City Road had been closed to the public years ago. Charles Tavistock was confident that no one could or would find it either on any map or by footfall. It had been adapted for Tavistock's needs, the many rooms once used by train staff and engineers alive again with movement. He stood at the long, bleach- and chemical-scarred work bench, surrounded by test tubes, beakers and phials. Dominating the far end of the lab, as close to the wall as the curved ceiling would allow, was a tall glass tank. It was filled with a gently moving thick liquid and connected to the mains. Suspended in the jelly-like water was a woman, naked and attached at the temples and hips by glistening tubes.

This wasn't where Tavistock lived, of course, but he spent more time here than anywhere, even the elite Langelaan Club on Pall Mall. His home, in rooms overlooking Hanover Square, was tall and airy - in great contrast to this damp and deep-level laboratory. During moments of contemplation that sometimes lasted for hours, he often he found himself at the tall sash window smoking on an opium pipe and watching the bustle go by and young couples in love sharing lunch and more with each other on the grass.

But down here, beneath the world, he need not think about those above him and it didn't matter if it was day or night, summer or winter.

His war pension was more than adequate to keep him in the lifestyle he wished, able to pay for City Road and his research. And his research was all that drove him.

Nevertheless, he found it useful to keep abreast of matters and he continued his read of the day's papers.

Tavistock glossed over the side-bar of woman falling under the wheels of a taxi cab in the night, instead focusing on the British Empire's claims on its nation states weakening after the Great War. There was a strong possibility that England's key position in the First World could easily be threatened. The death of the King earlier in the year and his eldest son's unpredictable reign so far brought many to the same conclusion.

"We could all be Communists by the end of the decade," he commented to his assistant, who went by the name Spike, simply to air his thoughts as oppose to really wanting to engage in any proper form of conversation. Spike was a mute, anyway, so no exchange could be had even if Tavistock had the proclivity. "I doubt even our indispensable Government will be short-sighted enough to agree with Europe. Berlin has an agenda and is certainly heading down a path it shouldn't. The Olympic Games there were a precursor for something. No, I take that back. We won't be Communists. We'll all be damned Nazis."

Spike was a tool, as inanimate and disposable as the lab equipment and, when he became surplus to requirements, he would give his body parts to Tavistock's studies, without consent of course. For now, Spike allowed Tavistock to retain his air of elegance when stalking the streets for his latest subject.

The Wretched Man

The night just gone had been very successful. It had started off in the usual pattern, with Tavistock himself strolling proudly through the streets of London as though he was simply enjoying the sights, with Spike trailing behind by a few yards, ever watchful of his master's movements. Tavistock was a big man and knew that his presence in a crowd was noticeable. Spike on the other hand was small and wiry, like a weasel, and could easily snake through the busy streets.

Tavistock would spot a potential target and trail the person, more mindful of keeping his distance if they were with someone. A few swirls of his cane, pre-planned signals like some cryptic semaphore display, meant that Spike knew Tavistock's intentions.

Tavistock never knew names, never wanted to know names. Anonymity was the order of things, but the person he had chosen this night was with a lady friend. They weren't married (he looked for a ring), Tavistock always sure of that. The lady friend had called her companion Arnold and Arnold was highly responsive to the woman's attentions, so much so that neither of them realised that Tavistock had been stalking them for the last forty minutes.

The cane flashed in the air, triggering Spike into action as the coupled crossed Henrietta Street, a taxi honking as it tried to avoid them. But Spike was quick and with a great shove with his shoulder ensured Arnold's companion fell under the solid tyres of the cab, crushing her chest, killing her after a few moments of agonised breaths.

In the calamity and panic that ensured, the despairing Arnold had been dragged into a side alley by Spike and subjected to the contents of the mute's entomologist's killing jar.

Dead as his lady friend, he was put atop a rag and bone cart (belonging to another on Tavistock's payroll) and covered by a heavy canvas sheet. The horse and cart moved back out into Henrietta Street, passing by the commotion of the woman mangled by the taxi.

Spike disappeared into the crowd. Tavistock, once he'd marked the target, had long since vacated the area. He'd spend the next couple of hours in a West End flea-pit watching the latest Karloff talkie.

They had met back at the lab with the cadaver, which lay under a sheet on top of a forensics table bought as part of a job lot from the Old Surgeons' Hall in Edinburgh.

Arnold lay there as Tavistock finished a meal of cold meats and cheese at his work bench, a bottle of Ernest Gallo given to Tavistock by the wine tycoon himself open and breathing, which was more than could be said about Arnold.

Chapter 2

Harry Pogue didn't like the countryside. The warm air was thick with maddening bugs, clumping and hovering together at the first sign of dusk. The pollen made his nose itch. He much preferred the gloom of London Town, the chugging of the traffic and the life that a busy city brought.

The spate of murders that had broken out across the capital, sparking panic amongst the population, had spread to the area surrounding Croydon Aerodrome. Each adult victim, gender seemingly irrelevant, had been found with severe rigor mortis, the condition apparently occurring immediately after death according to the sensationalist headlines. Their faces expressed shock (and fear, Pogue was convinced), with eyes bulging, tongues lolling and swollen. Each victim's skin was pale and yellow. Other than that, there were no visible cuts or bruises. It was as if they had been poisoned.

Pogue was looking now at a body in a hedgerow in the exact same condition.

The inspector scratched the top of his head, where his hairline was receding. A brown bowler was clamped between a couple of fingers. He leant against the bonnet of his prized car, a royal blue Triumph Ten-Twenty.

"This woman," PC Abbotts said as he checked his little note book, "is a Mrs Hurndall. She was last seen this morning after taking her children to school. On her way back home, she stopped by the local farm to pick up two dozen eggs."

Pogue shielded his eyes from the sun as he looked around him. "I wonder where the eggs are. Is this farm nearby?"

"Twenty minutes."

"By car?"

"On foot."

"Car it is, then."

Soon huddled behind the wheel of the Triumph, Pogue drove them down endlessly twisting country lanes towards the farm. They'd left PC Stranks behind to guard the crime scene, such as it was.

Abbotts in the passenger seat, as he cradled his custodian helmet, had to admit to himself that he was enjoying this brief foray into the country, even though the murder that brought them here meant that their search for the culprit had spread far wider than central London - further than Pogue's actual jurisdiction.

An Imperial Airways 'plane roared overhead and Abbotts watched its path up into the sky.

Pogue saw the almost wistful expression on the constable's bewhiskered face. "Not on your wages, Abbotts. You just might be able to afford a trip if you become commissioner."

"At least thoughts of such things don't cost nothing, sir."

"Just keep your head out of the clouds. There's enough going on down here to occupy you."

The rest of the journey was made in silence until Winterbourne Farm came into view.

It was a small set-up, mainly chickens and a trip of goats or two. A herd of cows could be seen in a top field. Two outhouses sat at odd angles within the perimeter fence as one tractor rested forlornly nearby. A boggy weir made up the landscape behind the farmhouse, clearly an area too dangerous to be navigated.

Pogue pulled the car up alongside the house. The engine shuddered into silence.

Chapter 3

"Who does he damn well think he is? He has no scientific training - at least none of note. No basis for any of his judgements."

Dr Fabyan put down his pen, the ink from its nib blotting his fingertips. Sighing, he wiped them clean with a kerchief from a pocket and looked across the table. His golden pince-nez was giving him a headache and so he removed them, rubbing gently the red indents either side of his chubby nose. "But he is a recognised patron of the Alliance."

"And that gives him the right to comment on how we carry out our profession, does it?" Rasurel took a long drag on his cigar. He was of French birth, medically trained as was Fabyan, but of the opinion that Charles Tavistock had no legal standing either as a scientist or as a doctor. "He won't even take the title of practitioner. Surely that tells us he should not be allowed to...well, to practice!"

"The Socialist Medical Alliance welcomes his support," Fabyan replied, the formality of his position as chair of the Alliance taking over. Yet he was still hesitant to minute this conversation. "Dr Rasurel, you know how important funding is for us. The Civil War in Spain is showing us the need of some sort of national service for the treatment of health. We have to look to the wealthy to help the poor. At least initially."

"But have you read his papers, Robert? He seems to think he's writing for some pulp fiction pamphlet." Rasurel paced, his wingtip shoes making no sound upon the thick carpet.

Fabyan didn't know how to answer his agitated colleague. It was true that Tavistock's researches were unorthodox but his donations to the SMA meant he was given unalloyed access to the most modern equipment of the day. The fact that Tavistock had taken most of it to some undetermined location was something the SMA tried hard to ignore. The deal had been that Tavistock was to carry out his experiments on site but Fabyan and the SMA's chairman Dr Block had realised after a time that what Tavistock was researching could not be condoned. They reluctantly agreed that the hardware could be kept elsewhere. It was either that or losing Tavistock's very generous endowments.

Rasurel had not been party to that agreement and rightly so felt the need to question Tavistock's ethics. It had left Block and his fellows with a bitter taste in their mouths.

Fabyan stood and circled around the table. The long bookcases against the wall were dark in their teak veneer. He hadn't read Tavistock's thesis but he knew through conversations with Block as to what it contained. "There are many things we can learn from the insect world. They have many advantages over size and stamina."

"If you are telling me that you agree with his methods then I have grave doubts about our moral standing." Rasurel tapped cigar ash into a large tray in the middle of Fabyan's desk.

"It's not that, George, but..."

"What did the Police want?" Rasurel asked.

In the distance, the great bell in St Stephen's tower began to chime five o'clock.

"The Police?" Fabyan feigned surprise.

Rasurel saw through the expression. "Yes, Robert, the Police. They were here yesterday. You know they were."

Rasurel was direct, forceful and Fabyan found him intimidating. Becoming flustered, he stumbled over his words but managed to explain to Rasurel that Block had had a private audience with them that no one else was party to.

"Then Dr Block will tell me," Rasurel said.

Chapter 4

Constable Abbotts stood quietly in the farmhouse kitchen, his notebook in his right hand.

The sink was loaded with dirty crockery and utensils. The smell from the cold stale water was sickly, a mixture of Rinso and turned meat. Abbotts had to guess that it had been there for a good few days. Mrs Abbotts was the only one in his own household who did the dishes but all the same, Mr Hurndall could have at least made some effort.

Pans dangled from crude hooks above the central kitchen table, clanging slightly in the draught as Pogue entered and closed the door behind him.

"Now then, Mr Hurndall..." the inspector began.

Mr Hurndall stared at the table and the butter dish atop it. It seemed a markedly better thing to focus on than Pogue's pouting expression opposite him.

"I need to know the time you last saw Mrs Hurndall." Pogue felt finishing with the word 'alive' to be inappropriate given Mr Hurndall's current state of mind.

Mr Hurndall didn't answer, didn't respond. But he'd heard Pogue all the same.

"Were you working in the stables?" prompted Abbotts, pencil in his left hand poised to take notes.

Silence. Abbotts rephrased the question. Hurndall's eyes flickered up for a moment then back down to the butter dish. The tiny painted cows along its edge pranced in the very way that cows don't.

"I haven't got any stables."

It was an answer at least.

"Where do you keep your herd?"

"Cowshed."

"And the goats?"

"Cowshed."

Pogue was a city man. Where this farmer kept his animals really was of no consequence to him but his trained mind meant he was interested to keep Abbotts questioning Hurndall.

"So you were in the cowshed?"

A nod.

Pogue looked keenly at Hurndall. The man's face was dark and ruddy, a sign of his outdoor existence. His hands were like slabs of ham, scarred and soiled.

"Taking the cows in or letting them out?"

"Cleaning up their shit."

Abbotts paused in his note taking, altering the expletive for a more conservative description. "And Mrs Hurndall, had she left for town by then?"

"About then."

"What time?"

"Seven o'clock."

"Are you sure?"

"I can tell the bloody time, you know."

Abbotts saw a glint of a watch chain in Hurndall's waistcoat and nodded. "Of course, sir. Didn't mean nothing by it. And she'd gone to get eggs?"

"That's right."

"But you have chickens."

Hurndall frowned slightly, as though it hadn't previously occurred to him. "The birds ain't laying."

Pogue leant back in his chair. "I'm not hands-on with the countryside and all that, Mr Hurndall, but why would that be so?"

"Are my chickens suspects?"

Abbotts found this odd. Hurndall's wife had been found dead in a ditch some miles away from home but he saw the need to reply with sarcasm. In Abbotts' book, that was a sign of guilt.

Pogue also picked up on this and glanced over at the Constable. "Will you be around for the next few days, Mr Hurndall?"

Hurndall snorted. "Can't leave the farm. I'm short of labour, now."

Strange again. Abbotts concluded it was the farmer hiding his feelings. He closed his note book as Pogue stood. An odd rattling sound seemed to come from the far distance outside. Abbotts was not sure Pogue had heard it so paid it no mind.

"Well, if you do decide to go on a trip, telegraph me at the Skylark before you go. Constable Abbotts and I will be there for a couple more days. Just to finish our investigations, you understand."

"Please yourselves. That hotel's full of toffs and rich bastards. Strangers, too. You'd be better off questioning them. Find the thing that killed my wife."

And there it was: the only audible sign of grief the two Police officers were likely to get from the farmer.

"We'll do our best, sir," said Pogue. "Do you mind if we take a look around before we go?"

Hurndall became rather agitated at this but quickly calmed down and shook his head. "Of course not. Just don't disturb my girls. No eggs is one thing. No milk...that's another."

"They won't even know we're there," Abbotts said quietly as he and Pogue made their farewells, leaving Hurndall at the kitchen table.

Outside, the sky rumbled as a summer storm, not the first this year, made its presence known.

"We'll have a quick look around, Abbotts, and then head back to the hotel."

"What are we looking for, sir?"

Pogue positioned his brown bowler firmly on his head and navigated the muddy track towards the two outhouses. "Anything to pinpoint Hurndall to his wife's last location."

"So you think he did it?" asked Abbotts as he followed, his Police-issue boots soiled with every stride.

"Not for me to judge, Constable. We can only gather the facts."

The cowshed, the larger of the two buildings, met them with a gloomy, dusty stare. The big doors were already half open as Pogue pushed them wider. He caught something under his fingertips, a pearly dust spread along the edges of both the doors, as though something had brushed against them. Some of the powder was sprinkled in the mud at their feet.

"What is it, sir?"

"Some sort of residue. Got a handkerchief? Clean, preferably"

Abbotts obliged and Pogue wiped the doors, collecting the specimen. The handkerchief disappeared into his coat pocket, folded and secure.

"Do you hear that?" Abbotts asked, a hand on Pogue's upper arm. "That buzzing. Sort of a rattling. I heard it earlier in the kitchen. Listen…"

Pogue tilted his head, frowned then shook it. "I can't hear a thing. We're not that far from the airport though so it's probably a 'plane taxiing."

Abbotts saw the logic and followed Pogue into the dark cowshed, flicking on his torch-lamp he'd grabbed from the car on the way by as the shadows swallowed up what was left of the daylight.

The straw crunched under their feet.

The lamp swinging around from its handle, the light undulating across the beams and stacks of hay, produced the oddest shapes. Something caught Pogue's eye and he asked Abbotts to hold the lamp still.

Nothing moved but Pogue had been convinced something had been positioned against the far wall. A tall, black thing, not unlike a large man in an Inverness cape.

"Must be my bloody eyes playing tricks on me," Pogue murmured but still reached inside his coat for his 38 Special. The revolver sat tidily in his grip, cocked and ready. "Shine it over there to the left."

Abbotts took his truncheon from his belt as he moved the light, displaying the far corner of the cowshed. There was nothing there but Pogue seemed to be convinced otherwise.

A ladder revealed itself and Pogue followed with the tip of his gun to where it stopped. A shelf, wide enough to walk on ran around the edge of the building high above their heads. It disappeared to the right, where it was darkest.

"I'll take a look, sir," suggested Abbotts but Pogue shook his head.

"Something's not right, Abbotts. I'll go."

Abbotts tried to light Pogue's way as much as possible but it was difficult. "Are you sure about this? Perhaps we should go and get Constable Stranks."

Pogue looked back over his shoulder and raised his eyebrows, turning back to the ladder just as a heavy shape came crashing down it, knocking Pogue clean off his feet. As his head hit the semi-hard surface of the barn's floor, his revolver went flying.

As the shape tumbled past, the buzzing noise filled the cowshed. Quickly, Abbotts dropped his truncheon and dived for the pistol. He grabbed it swiftly and shot at the retreating form. A screech. Something heavy lashed out, something bigger than an arm. It knocked the lamp clear from Abbotts' tight grip.

The black figure scuttled towards the doors and vanished into the evening twilight.

"What the hell was that!" Pogue gasped, pulling himself to his feet.

"Don't know, sir," replied Abbotts as he grabbed the torch. "But whatever it was, I think I got it. Look."

Abbotts indicated the floor with the lamp, in particular the peculiar trail of pale yellow pus that snaked towards the doors.

Chapter 5

The business card was plain, white and had delicate gold lettering embossed on just one side that read:

> *17b Bottle Street*
> *Piccadilly*
> *W1*

Alice Delambre looked at the house number on the black front door and back down at the card again. Definitely the right place. Even though it appeared to be adjacent to a Police station.

In her late twenties and looking every inch the English Rose, she had been made a widow by the same conflict in Afghanistan that Tavistock had survived. Her husband, Captain Eric Delambre, had promised she would be looked after if anything was to happen to him. Eric's war pension and shaky business links in the Africas kept Alice on the edge of comfort. Thick blonde hair tied back and under her hat, Alice reached forward a gloved hand and yanked at the metal pulley to the side of the door.

Somewhere inside, a bell rang and moments later the door opened. Two eyes peered out under bushy eyebrows. A beaky nose flared and a thin lipped mouth split as the man asked for her name. When Alice replied, it was as if he didn't believe her. He sighed with the weight of the world upon his round, narrow shoulders and beckoned her in.

It was only as she crossed the threshold that Alice realised the door had no lock or handle on the outside.

Behind her, as she stood in the hall and removed her hat, the door thudded shut, cutting off completely the noise of the street.

It appeared to be a normal house as she looked around. Black and white tiled floor, red-papered walls and a grandfather clock ticking ominously to itself. A fern sprouted from a huge Chinese vase at the foot of the stairs. It was almost as tall as she was. There was a smell of boot polish in the air.

The man, presumably the butler, waved her through to the drawing room.

There were five standing men in impeccable military uniform. Another, in a black pin-stripe suit, was sitting behind a wide mahogany desk. On the wall behind them above the fireplace hung a scarlet red flag, in its centre, in a plain white disc, the striking angular symbol of their beliefs.

Alice swallowed hard and raised her right arm straight. "Heil Hitler."

Gregor Samsa, gauleiter of the secret London division of the Nazi Party, acknowledged her salute to the swastika. Peering at her over his round glasses, he waved at her to step forward.

"Did you bring it, Frau Delambre?" he asked coldly, subtle German accent lacing his words.

Reaching into her coat, Alice produced a thick wad of papers, folded but torn in places. "It's all here." She dropped them to the table, disturbing the slight layer of dust on the desk.

"All of it?" Samsa pulled the papers towards him and Alice could have sworn he almost licked his lips.

"All of it, Herr Samsa, and it wasn't easy."

The Nazi did not break his gaze on the documents. "I do not care. You did as you were instructed. That is enough." He waved her away. Alice stood firm. Finally those steel grey eyes looked up from the papers. "I said: that is enough."

"No."

Samsa stood and removed his glasses, eyes flicking to the five SS officers then to Alice. "You have not worked for me before. I am perhaps willing to overlook your impudence."

"I want my money. I was told I'd get good pay for this. I've got kids to feed."

Alice felt the officers moving in closer to her. She leant forward to snatch the papers back. Samsa grabbed her wrist, squeezing slowly and hard.

Alice bit her bottom lip, not willing to show how much his increasing grip hurt. "Captain Delambre's annuity is not enough for you? That I find hard to believe. Do not deceive me, Frau Delambre. It would be wise to leave now before your children wonder why their mother has not returned home."

"I'm not scared of you," she replied, defiant in her poise.

"Perhaps not," Samsa replied, his tight hold on her unrelenting. "But my officers can be a little...heavy-handed when giving bad news. I'm sure little Ben and little Polly will be most upset."

Alice tensed. How did he know their names? She had the feeling that her children wouldn't be safe with their nanny for much longer. "Please, let me go."

"Of course. That was my suggestion to begin with." Samsa clenched harder before releasing Alice's wrist. "You will be paid in good time."

Alice rubbed her sore skin, her hat squashed under one arm.

Samsa and his men watched her leave, waited for the front door to open then shut again before focussing on the sheaf of papers.

"Gentlemen, we have here the means by which our beloved Führer will exercise his control and dominance over the whole world."

Almost theatrically, Samsa unfolded the papers, flattening the creases and ironing out the edges with a lead crystal paper-weight from the desk drawer.

"Was ist das?" one of the officers asked, peering at the anatomical drawing the now unfurled document displayed.

"I do not understand," another said. "How can this help our movement?"

Chapter 6

The little bell above the door jangled as it closed.

"Where are you, Weller?" A shuffling from the back of the shop, in the room behind the counter, told Tavistock where the mole-like shopkeeper was. "Come on out. You have something I want."

It was a bric-a-brac sort of store, no focus on one particular style of product. Any customer diligent enough to see past the grot could find all manner of trinkets and delights, all at reasonable prices.

Up high on shelves around the walls, a number of bell jars each displayed a taxidermist's dream. To Tavistock's left were more treasures: foot long statuettes, ornamental weaponry, a perfect crystal replica of a human skull, the light from the single bare bulb hanging from the ceiling dancing across its curved surface. Lengths of carved wood were stacked in the corners, ornately decorated wooden chests and equally bland crates became surrogate tabletops for an incredible array of beautiful gold and silver chalices and plates, trinket boxes, medicines and many other curios too numerous to take in. It was like a museum's storeroom.

As Weller appeared behind the counter, his nose wrinkled between fat cheeks, Tavistock put down the gold-capped glass phial he was juggling between his hands. Weller huffed as he grabbed the phial, its powdery red contents settling, and put it out of reach behind him.

"I've got nothing you want," he said.

"You know that's not true," Tavistock hissed, motioning to the contents of the shop around them. "Out of all of this, you have something I need. I know you have something I need."

"It's not for sale," Weller replied, moving out from the counter and to the door, where he was about to spin the tatty 'open' sign to 'closed'. "And anyway, we're closed. You need to leave."

"Lock the door, then," said Tavistock nonchalantly. "I would prefer that we are not disturbed." The cosh slid from within his coat pocket.

Weller saw the weapon in Tavistock's gloved hands and began to sweat. He sweated easily. His nerves were shredded at the best of times and his esteemed visitor wasn't helping them. "I don't want any trouble, Sir Charles."

"There'll be no trouble. Not as long as you complete the sale. Now lock the door."

Weller closed his eyes briefly as he slid the stiff, heavy bolt up, the door now fixed from within. He turned back to Tavistock. "I'm not sure where it is."

"I don't need any excuses, Weller. You have it here. You will sell it to me." With his free hand, Tavistock pulled from another pocket a large handful of ten shilling notes. He dropped them to the wooden floor and watched, not without disgust and pity, Weller scrabble around to collect them all up. Before Weller could finish, Tavistock stepped on the back of the shopkeeper's right hand. "Bring it to me or I will break your fingers."

Weller nodded, whimpering as Tavistock stepped back. The cash had already disappeared under his waistcoat. Rising to his feet on short legs, he grabbed a stepladder, leant it against a free-standing tallboy and ascended to dig around in its top drawer.

Tavistock's dark eyes flashed with excitement as Weller withdrew a round shape swathed in heavy sackcloth, needing both hands to lift it clear. It was about the size of a large melon. While he did not help Weller come back down the steps, little interested if the man fell, Charles was anxious that the wrapped Istalifi pot itself would not break. The trepidation made him forget briefly an ache in his left leg. He held his breath until the pot was safely resting on the counter and he hurried over to it, almost pushing Weller out of the way.

"Now take it and go," Weller breathed, unlocking the door and motioning for Tavistock to leave. The door was flung open and Spike dashed in from the street, taking the sackcloth parcel from the counter at Tavistock's instruction.

Weller watched it and the two men go, shoulders sagging as he realised that others would most likely come for the pot, too, and that he would have to fend them off. Tavistock hadn't been the first (it was difficult to try to forget that religious man from Sardinia), but Weller knew Tavistock would be the only one to utilise its contents as they were meant to be. Tavistock also was the only one willing to pay a princely sum for it.

Patting the money inside his waistcoat, Weller decided today's trading was over so shifted the bolt back up once more, pulled down the blind and retreated into his office behind the counter.

Chapter 7

A gloved set of knuckles was rapping on the back of Pogue's skull. It made his temples sore and his brow ache. It was lucky he had his eyes closed because he could just imagine the sunshine making the whole headache thing worse.

But wait. It was the middle of the night. He was asleep. Wasn't he?

The tapping ceased, started again and woke Pogue up.

His head was still painful from striking it against the barn floor but the knocking was coming from his hotel room door.

Dragging himself out of bed, dizziness doing its utmost to try to keep him horizontal, he staggered to the door and prised it open, seeing in the hallway Abbotts looking agitated in his pyjamas.

"What time is it?" Pogue mumbled, feeling for his wristwatch but remembering the doctor who had attended to his head wound taking it off.

"Very sorry to disturb you, sir. It's 6am."

"What do you want?"

"Telegram from the Yard. We're expected back there now."

Pogue took a moment to adjust to being awake. "We've got some loose ends here to tie up first. Hurndall's body-"

"...already on it, sir. She's on her way to London now, to be kept with the others."

"Did the Yard say what was urgent?"

Abbotts handed Pogue the telegram, its reddish pink paper thick under the touch.

INSPTR H POGUE =

REQUIRED TO RETURN WITH ALL OFCRS TO YARD =

CASE CLOSED =

WILSON +

Pogue read it again, not quite believing what it said. Case closed? Unless someone else had solved the murders, surely the case had much more life in it yet! And there was the matter of that person who attacked them in the barn.

Wilson, albeit Pogue's superior, had better have a good reason for this, Pogue cursed to himself. He told Abbotts to meet him and Stranks in the Skylark's reception and proceeded to get dressed.

London was an hour or so's drive and the route Pogue took brought them in at Blackfriars, in time to see a steamer, with a cacophony of blowing sirens and thundering paddle-wheels, chug east down the Thames towards Wapping and eventually out to sea past the estuary.

Nosing the car through the busy streets along the north bank, Pogue finally pulled into Scotland Yard, his temper seething as he prepared to confront his superior officer. Stranks and Abbotts knew to keep quiet and were grateful for the opportunity to carry on their duties elsewhere in the Yard.

Wilson's office was on the third floor and Pogue wasted no time in getting there, a ring of sweat around his hairline as he rapped firmly upon Wilson's door.

"I know what you're going to say, Pogue," Wilson began as Pogue stopped before the chief inspector's desk. "But let me speak first."

"Sir..."

"Inspector Pogue," Wilson growled with resonance, "I am your superior officer and you will listen to me. Now sit down."

Pogue waved his arms like a nervous band leader and sank into one of the two chairs on front of the desk, his hat turning between his hands.

"A letter. It is addressed to me personally. Apparently you are named in it." Wilson gave Pogue the sealed envelope, who glanced at it thoughtfully.

"I don't recognise the handwriting."

"There's no reason why you should, but I do. It is from a Dr Block."

Pogue frowned. He wasn't familiar with the name.

"Dr Block and I are on the board of the Socialist Medical Alliance and we have been friends for many years." Wilson nodded to Pogue to open it.

"You know the contents of this letter, sir?" asked Pogue, as he slit open the envelope.

"Dr Block informed me of what it reads. I was at first reluctant to accept what he was saying but I have to concur it is the only way forward. Please..."

Pogue turned the single piece of paper over then back again. Both sides had the same immaculate handwriting as the envelope. He began to read.

My dear Chief Inspector

I am not prone to flights of fancy nor have I ever been or consider myself to be delusional. Yet it is with complete clarity and of sound mind that I write this account to you. You are a man of esteemed standing and respect within the SMA as well as the Metropolitan Federation and it is this that gives me comfort to know that you will take all steps to ensure our respective professions' credibility remains intact.

Your men have been investigating these peculiar incidents across the capital for nearly two months now. Inspector Pogue is no closer to making an arrest. You are unable to determine the cause of the incidents themselves.

Is it my belief that without help you will never find the person responsible and for the incidents to cease.

No trail or clue has led you to the SMA but I am able to tell you that this is where you may ultimately end your search.

If you do, you will bring disrepute to the Alliance. Remember too that many of its members have close links with the Metropolitan force.

I ask you, Chief Inspector Wilson, to cease all investigations and give no further bulletins to the *press. The incidents will stop, of that I can assure you.*

The SMA are involved but I will not divulge how. By default, the Met are involved, too. There are other, wider European matters afoot that will soon push this affair into insignificance, so there will be no visible repercussions.

I say again, this case is closed and you will treat it as such.

With sincerity and my faith in your own

Dr Nathaniel Block

Pogue sat back in the chair, the letter hanging between his fingers. "Is this..?"

"...a confession?" Wilson stood and stared out the window. The distant noise of a Wolseley's bell rang through the streets. A lock of grey hair, avoiding the imported Pomade, fell across his high forehead. "It would be hard not to reach that conclusion."

"He is clearly protecting his own, sir." Pogue placed the letter and the envelope back on Wilson's desk and stood.

Wilson turned back to face him. "This case isn't closed, Harry."

"I thought as much."

"I still want you to work on it. But this has to be hush-hush. Dr Block must be of the assumption we are not carrying on with this."

"I'm happy you've said that. I completed my report as much as I could before you called us back."

Wilson nodded, looking perturbed. "The body...Hartnell?"

"Hurndall," Pogue corrected.

"Hurndall – in the same state?"

"In every detail. Constable Abbotts said it was being brought back with the others."

"Yes, that's something else that we need to keep to ourselves."

"Sir?"

"I was lunching at La Contessa yesterday," began Wilson, his large frame dominating the window, "when I happened to overhear a conversation being had behind me. I did not turn around to have a look and I did not recognise the voices, but they were quite convincing with their knowledge that the bodies had all been moved from the mortuary."

"Where to?"

"They didn't know but my luncheon companion who joined me shortly after also knew that they had gone."

"Dr Block?"

"The same. He told me," and this was where Wilson moved close to Pogue and grabbed him by the elbow, "that they had disappeared. No one knows where to but I believe Dr Block does. Of course, his persuasive argument qualified by that letter means I have agreed to drop the case and therefore I could not pursue that line of questioning. But you, Harry, you will be my eyes and ears out there, my bulldog never letting go of a scent."

A knock came at the door and Pogue recognised the silhouette through the frosted glass.

"It's Abbotts."

"Do you trust him?" asked Wilson, to which Pogue nodded. "Enough to work with you on this?"

"Indeed, sir."

"How many bodies did we have on the slab?"

"Fourteen, sir," Pogue confirmed, "fifteen if we include Hurndall."

"You need to find them. Come," called the chief inspector to Abbotts, who entered, embarrassed to be in the presence of such senior staff.

"Sorry to disturb you, sirs," he began, helmet clamped under his arm, "but I thought you needed to know what we found in the barn."

"Barn?" queried Wilson, Pogue swiftly telling the story of the attack by the big shadow-like figure.

"We had the yellow mucus examined by the forensic pathologist," continued Abbotts.

"And?" Pogue prompted, recognising the Constable's hesitancy.

"He referred it on. This is the entomologist's findings."

Abbotts handed Pogue a file.

"Entomologist?" frowned Pogue as he opened the brown folder.

"Someone who studies insects, sir."

"I know what it is, Abbotts," snapped Pogue. "What on earth made Lockhart refer it to a damn bug doctor?"

"Because the results show it was hemolymph, sir. Insect blood."

Pogue's jaw dropped and he didn't even bother to read the report.

"An insect? Abbotts, are you saying we were attacked by an insect?"

Wilson then pointed out the obvious, something that Pogue and Abbotts had both realised at the same time. "Pogue," the chief inspector said slowly, lighting a Craven 'A', "didn't you just say that the figure that attacked you was over six feet tall?"

Chapter 8

The curved ceiling and walls of the tunnel were cold to the touch as Tavistock moved, surefooted, over the live tracks. Trains came along this route, servicing the Northern Line, far more frequently that he would have liked, but it was deep beneath the streets of London and therefore secure enough for him to carry out his research. It also meant that the tunnels gave him easy access to the south whenever his experiments demanded it.

Feeling the breeze increase towards him from the gloom, Tavistock sidestepped into a nearby workman's alcove, neck tilted to fit his wide and six-foot tall frame within its confines, and waited for High Barnet service to growl by. His lab coat, already stained with chemicals and all manner of spills, scuffed against the black walls.

No one on the Metropolitan-Vickers locomotive saw him but he saw them, as clear as day, sitting, standing, sleeping, talking: all oblivious to the world outside their carriage, outside even their own limited imaginations.

The smell of carbon filled his nostrils as the train trundled off down the tunnel and Tavistock knew he had minutes to reach his lab before the next service came by.

He almost flew down the tracks to the heavy door that kept the world at bay and opened it, using a lock combination not unlike a bank safe.

The thud as the metal entrance slammed shut being him echoed through the tunnels, a few passengers a couple of miles away on the platforms at Angel casually glancing up then back down to their newspapers.

Tavistock leant against the door, shoulders relaxing, feeling safer here than he did anywhere else these last few days.

Even with the dull pain in his leg, he strode with purpose into the main room of his laboratory. Arnold was still on the table, naked as the day he was born, but with his innards distributed around him, turning a peculiar yellow. The smell of his flesh was beginning to turn sickly-sweet. At Arnold's head was a beaker, a rubber tube snaking out into his gaping mouth. In the beaker was a thick slime.

Tavistock had been monitoring the effects of the slime on the human interior and finding no difference to tell of was preparing to test it on a live subject. Spike would need to go alone tonight and find a suitable guinea pig, for Tavistock had a prior dinner engagement at the SMA.

Then, like a blow across the eyes, Tavistock's vision suddenly blurred, fracturing like a kaleidoscope before settling. The pain that followed was unbearable and he scrabbled about the lab, knocking the beaker clean to the floor, looking for something to cover his sight from the burning glare of the light bulbs hanging above him. He crunched the glass, almost slipping on the spilled contents. Reaching out, he went elbow deep into Arnold's open chest, turning his nose up with disgust.

Sleeves sodden now with blood and putrid entrails, he ripped off his lab coat and threw it to the floor.

"Spike!" he yelled, quite unkindly.

His diminutive assistant was by his side within seconds, already on his way to his superior when he'd heard the glass smashing, seeing that Tavistock's eyes were streaming with tears, red and inflamed.

"Get me the saline!"

Washing his own eyes out with the salty liquid, having snatched the bottle from Spike's gnarled hands, they stung about as much as the light he could not cope with. Pushing past Spike he stumbled to the large cupboard adjacent to the glass tank, knocking into it as he felt for his overcoat.

The tank was so heavy and the glass so thick that the woman within didn't even stir in the suspending liquid.

But nevertheless Tavistock stopped and touched the glass with such tenderness then, as if apologising to the woman for his clumsiness, that it took even Spike aback, who had seen over the years his employer go through a whole gamut of emotions.

Then Tavistock seemed to collect himself together once more and flung the overcoat around his trembling shoulders.

Spike could only watch, not understanding what Tavistock was thinking or indeed where he was going, but Tavistock was certainly determined in his actions – until he paused and frowned, obvious consternation crossing his face. He turned back to his assistant, the overcoat slipping from his shoulders to the dusty floor.

"No, Spike," Tavistock stammered, hands to his forehead, "I have to succeed. I have to…before this takes me over completely." Lowering his arms, he looked at the backs of his trembling hands, the epidermis dull and grey. "This cannot happen to her too, not to my beloved Isabella."

Spike nodded and picked up the overcoat as Tavistock moved back into the centre of the lab and to a workbench adorned with phials and papers.

The motionless woman in the tank stared, sightless, back out at them but Spike was convinced just slightly, so very slightly, that her eyes flicked momentarily in Tavistock's direction.

Chapter 9

Delambre knew she was being followed and at first didn't quite know what to do about it. Mid-afternoon meant it would be getting dark soon.

The man in the black raincoat and trilby had been some yards behind her since Cambridge Circus. She'd not got the money to jump into a cab so had to make her own way back to City Road, a good forty-five minutes on foot. It had started raining too and her hat was getting heavier on her head the wetter it got.

Picking up speed for a quick left up Southampton Row and then a first right lost him for a moment but, pausing to catch her breath in a doorway, she saw him appear at the end of the passage and she was convinced he was one of Samsa's men. She knew then that she could not lead the Nazi back to where she had been headed. He gestured to someone else unseen then hared towards her.

Skirts hitched, Alice broke into a run, hearing the man's jackboots on the cobbles gaining behind her.

As she ran into the road, a charabanc braked and swerved to avoid her and a horse reared up, throwing the milkman from his cart. It whinnied as the milkman cried out. The ground was cold and hard beneath him.

The Nazi was suddenly upon her has she stumbled to avoid the prone milkman, his leering face and bad breath close.

Lashing out with her right palm, Alice struck the Nazi full at the base of his sternum. He staggered and fell, winded and in pain.

He feebly waved to his colleague to resume the chase as their quarry headed for Chancery Lane, Alice hoping that their knowledge of London was vague.

Even though these men were Nazis, they had been in England since 1932. Their understanding of the capital and its wiles was as familiar to them as any Londoner born and bred, moreso after the intense studying their Führer had insisted upon.

Guessing she was ultimately heading for the river and the Police station at Waterloo Bridge, Erich von Wer back-tracked, intending to cut her off at Aldwych.

Picking up speed again, Alice raced through the busy streets, ignoring the bemused faces of those she passed by. She dashed past a Police public call box but never thought to use the telephone it contained within the little cupboard set in one of its thin blue doors. She dared look over her shoulder and to her surprise could no longer see her pursuer. But she didn't slow and kept running, using what she thought was an advantage to widen the gap. Her blood pounded in her ears as heavy as her feet did against the pavement.

As she turned a corner, the Embankment just yards ahead, a great black limousine crawled to a stop in front of her. She skidded to a halt, using a lamppost as anchorage as a darkened window in the big car slowly wound down.

She didn't want to wait to see who it was. Spinning around to flee, she collided with von Wer who pinned her back against the lamppost briefly before dragging her kicking and screaming into the back of the vehicle.

Samsa gave an evil smile as he pushed her down into the plush seats next to him while Erich cuffed her wrists and motioned for the driver to pull away into the heavy traffic.

Chapter 10

PANIC ON NORTHERN CITY LINE
AS ANOTHER VICTIM FOUND DEAD

Pogue sipped at his tea, sighing between each swallow. The headline that screamed out at him from the evening press meant that Wilson's attempts for a subtle investigation would now be impossible. It also meant that his working day was far from over.

The Chief Inspector had shown him the paper amidst a flurry of words and growls and pacing. "How the hell did the press get hold of this before we did? We can't make them know it's linked to the other deaths. I'll release a statement in the morning."

"It says a woman was found dismembered between Hampstead and Golders Green," said Pogue, reading the front page. "The workman who found the body is currently being treated for shock."

"Treated with ale and pound notes, probably. He's got Fleet Street eating out of his hands. I've sent a car to collect him. You and Abbotts get yourselves down the tunnels and see what else you can find. The Transport Board have been told not to touch the body. You can interview the workman when you get back."

"What about the timetable?"

"Edgeware services are being stopped at Camden Town. You've got two hours, Harry, until they need to start up again."

Pogue downed the rest of his tea, tepid by now, and pulled on his raincoat, bowler already in place.

It was a quick journey to Camden and he and Abbotts were met by the station master, a proud old veteran of the Great War. As the Police officers were led down to the tracks, via a spiral staircase, the emergency access route, the man expressed how appalled he was that such a thing could happen on 'his' line. Abbotts smiled wryly at the man's ingrained military pomp.

"The current is off but please still be careful," he finished as they walked along the platform to the tunnel mouth. A train was standing silent and still, its doors open and devoid of passengers. "Your lot are already down here tramping all over everything."

"Sir," said a smart young Constable who stepped into the light from out of the tunnel to meet them, "it's this way."

"Thank you, McTighe." Pogue removed his hat and gingerly stepped down between the running rails, noticing how deceptively high the platform was.

Lights hanging every few yards made the tunnels even more eerie than Abbotts already thought they were as he followed the inspector and the young officer. Pogue queried the press interest and McTighe settled his mind by explaining than no journalist had been down here and that all the initial reports had come from the workman himself. But the fear the workman had caused as he had fled the tunnels had reverberated through the passengers as though they'd seen the body themselves. There was even talk of a giant insect living down in the darkness.

Pogue and Abbotts looked at each other.

"I'm sure that's just peoples' imaginations running rife, McTighe," Pogue said quickly, seeing the look of worry across the youngster's face. "Pay it no mind. All rumours remain as such until proven otherwise."

"Of course, sir," McTighe responded, feeling a little foolish, as they came upon a curve in the tunnel and lamps brighter here than elsewhere.

Admittedly, Abbotts had not seen much in his career to date but prided himself on his stoic approach in the face of adversity. Nevertheless, what was left of the woman lying across the tracks before them made his stomach churn and brought tears to his eyes.

There was a man a short way away with his back to them and on his knees. He appeared to be examining the base of the curved wall.

"That's Mr Tavistock," McTighe said to his colleagues, calling the man over.

Tavistock turned and stood up, grey tie skewed and waistcoat smudged with oil. His jacket was hanging over a lamp stand.

"Mr Tavistock," began Harry, offering his hand. "I'm Inspector Pogue. This is Constable Abbotts. I'm leading this investigation."

"A pleasure to meet you, Inspector," replied Tavistock, manners perfect and poise even more so, especially for a man his size.

His handshake wasn't as strong as Pogue had expected and felt the slight tremor in the grip. "Everything alright, Mr Tavistock?"

"Yes," Tavistock responded, immediately thrusting the offending hand into a trouser pocket. "Just a shock – all these murders."

"Murders, sir? You believe she was murdered?" asked Pogue, gesturing to the victim with his hat.

"I meant deaths, Inspector. All these deaths. Does something to a man, you know. Even if one has seen action."

"Indeed," came the inspector's reply. "I take it you've seen a lot of action, then? Where were you stationed?"

"Kabul."

"Kabul," Harry Pogue nodded, wanting for that moment a cigarette. He circled the crime scene, as much as the tracks would allow, and rubbed his chin. "Nasty business, this."

"It is. Very nasty."

Abbotts frowned, looking between the two men. Tavistock was an upright man, head and shoulders over Pogue, and with a slight limp to his gait. He was stony faced whereas Pogue could go through all manner of expressions. Clearly the inspector was sizing Tavistock up.

"What's your position here?" Pogue asked suddenly. "You're not with Police forensics."

"I was asked to attend the scene."

"Who by?" asked Abbotts.

Tavistock looked back at the Constable. "Dr Block of the SMA."

"Is that so?" Pogue knelt by the body. The woman's head was some feet away while her torso was tidily folded up between the rails. An arm was missing from the root. Pogue was no expert but even he knew that it had been torn out and not shorn off by a passing train. "We can get that verified, Mr Tavistock."

"Do so. You will find my credentials to be sound."

Pogue nodded to McTighe who disappeared up the track towards the tube station, his task given.

For the moment, Pogue would assume that Tavistock was here under Block's instruction, which would make sense if this murder was to be kept out of the papers any further. Leaning near to one of the rails, he slipped something glinting into a pocket out of Tavistock's line of sight then stood.

"Can she be identified?"

Tavistock moved over to the woman. "Her removed arm, such as it is, cannot be used for fingerprinting. Her remaining one, possibly so."

"She looks like she's some sort of maid, sir," pointed out Abbotts, looking at the blood-stained pinafore she wore. "Not very old."

"Take a small unit, Abbotts, and go door-to-door. We'll assume she's local for the moment. A household will be missing her before long. No mention of a death, though. Just a missing person at this stage. Understood?" Pogue scratched his head as Abbotts complied and headed off in the same direction as McTighe. "Mr Tavistock, will you begin to gather together the, ah..." he gestured around him, "the evidence, please. I have ordered a van to take her to St Peter's. You can carry out your post-mortem there."

"I have my own facilities," said Tavistock. "I work best with my own equipment."

"That may be so, but this is a Police matter and therefore you will do as I ask or Mr Block will be informed of your uncooperative nature."

Tavistock's jaw vibrated as he ground his teeth.

That's got you, Pogue said to himself. *If Dr Block is so insistent on keeping this quiet, this Tavistock chap has to comply.*

Tavistock's stern expression broke into what could be construed as a smile. "Of course, Inspector. I have no wish to stand in the way of our esteemed Police force."

Pogue knew the man was being sarcastic but let it go, standing around until Tavistock, with the help of a strange little man he called Spike, had collected the body and its associated parts ready for the mortuary attendants to take to safety and out of public knowledge.

Chapter 11

Dr Rasurel stubbed his cigar in the middle of the newspaper's headline, the heat burning a neat circular hole.

"Tavistock is behind this. I know he is."

Fabyan looked flustered, always uneasy whenever Rasurel started questioning Block and Tavistock's actions. "That may not be the case. I know you are unsure as to what Tavistock is doing but that doesn't mean his conduct is unethical to the point that people are getting hurt."

"See sense, man!" roared the doctor, throwing the paper to Fabyan's desk. "Benefactor or no, Tavistock has to be accountable for what he is doing!"

"But we don't know what he is doing," offered Fabyan, gently patting the newspaper for fear of the rest of it catching fire.

"Exactly my point!" A great cloud of smoke lingered around Rasurel's head as he exhaled a lung-full of his cigar. "I spoke with Dr Block and do you know what he told me?" Fabyan dared not answer so simply shook his head, his pince-nez sliding off his nose. "The Police are using Tavistock," finished Rasurel.

"But surely that is not unusual? After all we and the Police Federation have close links."

Rasurel leant on the back of Fabyan's chair, ash from his cigar dropping to the carpeted floor. Fabyan tried to ignore both it and the uncomfortable proximity of the oppressive man.

"The Met already has Rowan Lockhart for that: the country's foremost expert in forensics. I should know! I trained him myself!"

"Yes, that's correct," responded Fabyan, as though Rasurel's statement needed to be qualified. Which it didn't.

"And Lockhart's since been taken off the case completely." Rasurel perched on Fabyan's desk and looked out the window. The view across Regent's Park was all but obscured by the night. "Now why would that be, eh?"

"Perhaps because Dr Lockhart isn't a member of the SMA?" offered Fabyan.

Rasurel agreed. "I need to know who is in charge of the investigation."

Fabyan thought for a moment then walked to a bureau, pulled down the top section and handed Rasurel a newspaper a couple of weeks old. "I meant to throw this away but never got around to it. It's the first major feature the press ran on the murders."

Rasurel opened it up and stopped at the fourth page. "Inspector Harry Pogue," he noted, scanning the fine print of the broadsheet. Then, looking across to Fabyan, he said, as if Fabyan was an underling: "Call Scotland Yard. I want to meet with him."

Chapter 12

Something like 125 miles of track snakes this way and that under the highways and buildings of London, criss-crossing beneath the capital in an apparently frenetic yet ordered system of tunnels and stations. As much as the streets above, the tunnels are the veins that keep the city alive.

Two members of the extensive team of maintenance crew that kept those veins open were standing on the tracks, watching the Police clear away the evidence of the latest victim.

"All yours now, gents," the last of the Constables said, giving them a relaxed salute, and headed off to the station platform.

Chick, leaning on his broom, nodded in reply then turned to his companion. "We ain't got long, Wilbur. The Edgware service needs to start up in a while."

Chick's colleague whistled to himself as he moved into action. Wilbur was a short overweight man, invalided out of Amiens towards the end of the Great War and finding comfort in the dark tunnels that he spent so much of his time in.

Chick on the other hand was never quite clear on the subject of his own past and Wilbur, as much as he had tried, could never draw Chick into any form of conversation about it. Wilbur ultimately respected the man's privacy and the two often worked in silence.

Lamplights undulating, they moved steadily down the tunnel, checking each section of the track, the couplings and the electrics, cleaning away any debris left naturally or by recent events.

This they did every night, once the Underground system had been shut down after the last service of the day — but this evening was a special case and Chick had insisted on double pay for starting his shift earlier than usual. Wilbur was just grateful for the money.

Slowly and methodically, the tracks moved under them and Wilbur wondered how Gerald was feeling, the one who had found the body. Chick didn't want to talk about it so Wilbur got on with the job, resuming his whistling, the two of them alone in the half-light.

Chalk Farm station was up ahead, just around the gentle curve in the tunnel, and Wilbur could just make out the light from the platform reflecting on the dull, black walls with their endless pipes and wires.

Something crunched under his foot so he stopped whistling, stopped walking and looked down, swinging his torch close to his boots. There was some form of black powder over his steel-caps and he knocked it off with a shake. As he lifted his foot, he noticed something move and he gasped.

Chick wandered over to take a look, assumed it had been a large rat, shrugged and kept walking. Wilbur had to assume the same so followed Chick. But Chick stopped suddenly, having trodden in another pile of the same odd powder.

A gentle chirruping rose up around them, the tunnel amplifying the sound.

"Is that a bird?" asked Wilbur, lifting the lamp above his head. "Sounds like a bird."

"It's nothing. Just a train in the east tunnel," mumbled Chick in his broad Scots accent. "We've got to get going if we're going to get this finished."

Wilbur knew Chick was right and tried to ignore the peculiar noise. Perhaps it was a train. After all, similar noises did echo out from the tunnels moments before one arrived at a station. "Get your broom and let's clear away this stuff."

Chick put his broom into action, pushing the powder into the crevasses to the sides of the tracks. Wilbur noticed how it shone at a certain angle with a strange pearly iridescence. He felt something else under foot and jumped back. This was bigger. And he could see it scrabble past his boot.

"There...there!" he yelled, pointing, and Chick swung the lamp to see.

"My God...what is that?" Chick said, peering closer.

The thing was some sort of beetle or insect or something. It was bigger than one of their boots, its back oily wet with long yellow-green antenna swaying in the air, as if sniffing them out.

Chick and Wilbur watched motionless as the creature rested its front legs on one of the tracks.

"Not seen one as big as that before," whispered Wilbur, a chill across his shoulders.

"Who knows what lives down here, mate," responded Chick, tensing further as the insect scuttled a few feet away and stopped, rising on its hind quarters. "I wonder if there's any more of them..."

The query was somewhat redundant as suddenly a whole swarm of the things appeared from nowhere and headed towards them in one seething, glistening, chittering mass. There were probably hundreds. The two men didn't wait to count.

Wilbur and Chick spun where they stood and hurtled back towards Camden Town but they were not as fast as the insects that crawled over their feet and around their legs.

Wilbur realised that the creatures weren't actually interested in them – they also seemed to be running. And from what became apparent as Wilbur turned to look.

He screamed and stumbled, falling into Chick who in turn fell upon the rails, skull cracking like an egg on the metal.

The insects stopped as one, suddenly sensing the fresh blood seeping from Chick's prone form and turned to smother the Scot.

Wilbur didn't even try to help his friend up because the huge monster launched itself at him from the darkness, a great vile beast of an insect, as tall as a man if not taller still. Six spindly, angular legs collected Wilbur up in a horrific embrace, its thick, disgusting, swollen abdomen pulsing as it pressed on Wilbur's own chubby stomach. Great mandibles open and closed with slavering, jerky motions, drooling over Wilbur's mouth and chin.

Wilbur hollered, the insect slobber falling into the back of his throat and clogging his windpipe.

Panicking as one is want to do in these situations or when suffocation is unavoidable, Wilbur twisted and wriggled but the size of the insect was too great and the more he struggled, the tighter the grip became.

Even though his airways screamed to be opened, no further sound came from Wilbur, apart from the crack of his rib cage as the insect bore down on him with its full weight.

Within seconds, the creature had sucked the very nutrients from Wilbur, leaving him dead, yellow and stiff, a look of sheer terror upon his once-kindly face.

Chapter 13

After a journey that seemed to last forever, Alice had been kept in a stark, white empty room save for a wide, hot spotlight protruding from one wall. Even with her eyes clamped tight shut she could still not dim the incessant glare and her head had begun to pound.

They had asked her very few questions, instead tempting her with then withdrawing the offer of refreshment time and time again.

They had not threatened her or hurt her, apart from the torturous light of course, but from what she could understand from their hushed whispers, they were eager to find for themselves the source of the anatomical drawings she had sold them.

But it was when she had been presented with her twin children that she realised they were not going to give up until she told them. Ben and Polly, so very young and looking painfully vulnerable in the white room, broke her to tears and it was easy for her to tell her captors exactly where Tavistock's private laboratory was.

Her initial feelings of relief were shattered when Samsa swept the twins away, out of the room, his power over her strong while he kept them from her.

She continued to weep as they gave her back her clothes, dressing quickly and trying to ignore the burly SS guard staring intently at her.

And now she was back in the limousine, parked on the corner of Graham Street, the boarded-up main entrance of City Road station clearly within view.

Von Wer turned around from his position in the front passenger seat to address his gauleiter.

"The man will have no way in," he said, beaky nose twitching. "The woman is lying to us."

"I do not believe so. I do not hope so." Samsa caressed Alice's blonde hair and she grimaced. "Her children are very dear to her."

"This is where I meet him," Alice said. "He insists on secrecy. I can't get into the lab when he's not there. It has to be pre-arranged."

"And when are you intending to 'meet' him next?"

"Whenever he needs me or needs me to get something that his assistant can't manage." Alice looked down at her lap, hands wringing. "He telegrams me. There is no set time."

Von Wer repositioned himself, sitting forward again. "We are wasting time."

"Frau Delambre," began Samsa, "you will do something for us."

"I can't do anymore," she whispered. "You know where he works. Please...can that be the end of it?"

"Just a little more. You will go home. Erich will stay with you. When the telegram is received, you will bring it straight to me here."

"But that could be days away!" she exclaimed. "I want my children back!"

"In good time, Frau Delambre. You bring me Tavistock. I bring you your children."

"But all you wanted were the drawings! You never wanted Tavistock himself!"

Samsa placed a gloved hand on Alice's knee. She looked down and pushed it away.

"You were quite willing to sell us Tavistock's medical notes. Now you have a conscience? It is perhaps a little late for that."

Chapter 14

Harry was finishing his fifth cup of tea of the morning when Abbotts told him that Gerald Moorcroft, the Underground workman who had discovered the woman's beheaded corpse, had been found dead amongst some rubbish bins outside Waterloo Station.

He'd not been killed in the same way as the other victims, but his throat cut in a single clean stroke, almost with surgical precision.

"That's a shame," Pogue said. "He was a nice chap. Not a threat to anybody."

"Somebody had a motive."

Pogue nodded. The murderer may have had an interest in what Moorcroft knew but to resort to killing him did seem somewhat excessive — unless Moorcroft was no longer of use.

As it was, Pogue and Abbotts had already been able to interview Moorcroft on returning from the tunnels and now Pogue picked up the dead man's statement, focusing on an intriguing piece of information that had been revealed.

According to Moorcroft, Tavistock was at the scene of the woman's murder immediately after Moorcroft had found her but Tavistock had told Pogue that he'd been called there by Block to view the scene from a forensic standpoint, implying that he would have arrived there some time after.

Either Moorcroft was mistaken or Tavistock was lying, and Pogue had no reason to think Moorcroft could get an important detail wrong. Further, there was no benefit if Moorcroft had set out to deceive. Pogue lit a cigarette. Now that Moorcroft was dead, he couldn't be cross-examined against Tavistock's story. But Tavistock could still be cross-examined against Moorcroft's.

"Let's bring Tavistock in."

"Under what grounds?" Abbotts asked, foreseeing a difficult conversation being had with Tavistock

"To clear up an issue, nothing more. No deceptions on our part." Pogue put the statement down then fished in his jacket pocket. "That reminds me, I found this in the tunnel."

He placed on the desk a semi-transparent, curved piece of pearl-coloured material, interwoven with black vein-like strands. It was about as big as a large hand and ragged on three edges, as if had been torn. Abbotts poked it with a pencil. It was hard, like impossibly translucent Bakelite. The two Policemen didn't need Lockhart or an entomologist to tell them what it was.

"An insect wing," Abbotts breathed.

"A bloody big one, too."

"Sir, I…"

Pogue saw Abbotts looking tense. "I understand your worries, Constable. The whole idea of giant insects is nothing short of ludicrous but we have to remain focussed."

"Yes, sir," stammered Abbotts. Pogue was right: they were heading into territory that was alien to them, to their way of thinking and logical Police procedure. But people were being killed, murdered, and if talk of giant bugs was a link or simply a horror story then they would find the truth.

"Smoke?" offered Pogue.

Abbotts shook his head. "No thank you, sir. Not on duty."

"Come on. Let's have a nice little chat with Mr Tavistock."

As they left Scotland Yard and took a Wolseley to Tavistock's last known address on Hanover Square, Pogue did his best to continue to reassure Abbotts to simply treat all of it as a murder enquiry, just as they had been doing before the notion of insects was mooted.

Tavistock's flat was on the third floor of an elegant Victorian house. Pogue rang the bell a few times but no one answered. There was no sign that the bell even worked. Abbotts craned his neck to see if there was any movement from the windows.

As Pogue kept trying with the bell, a short man in a white flannel suit came up to them, walking with a cane topped with a bird's head moulded in silver. Bespectacled, he had a mass of white hair combed away from his face and a thick goatee beard around his small mouth. "Can I help you officers?" he asked politely, smiling as Pogue doffed his bowler.

"Do you live on the Square?" asked Pogue.

"Well, yes, right here..." the man replied, pointing at the front door with his cane. "First floor. Is everything alright?"

"Yes, just routine...Mr..?"

"Ferguson."

"Mr Ferguson," acknowledged Abbotts. "We're trying to reach Mr Tavistock."

"Sir Charles, you mean?"

Pogue raised his eyebrows. Abbotts got out his notebook.

"Yes, Sir Charles," Pogue responded. "Your neighbour. I take it?"

"Odd fellow, if you don't mind me saying."

"Not at all. Please go on."

"Well," continued the man, leaning on his cane, "he keeps himself to himself most of the time. But I did have cause once to knock on his door."

"For what reason, Mr Ferguson?" Abbotts was poised with his pencil.

"There was an awful stench coming from his rooms. I had to tell him, wondered if some sort of animal had got caught somewhere."

"And it was definitely from his flat?"

"Sure as mustard," nodded Ferguson. "Damn fellow wouldn't open the door but I knew he was in there."

"We won't take it personally, then," retorted Pogue, trying the bell again.

"All the crashing and banging. But he did open the door eventually. Just a crack mind. Wouldn't let me in. But the stink was dreadful."

"What did he say?" Abbotts asked.

"He said it was the drains. I knew it wasn't. Lying he was."

"How did you know it wasn't the drains?"

"Three floors up? The pong would have been at ground level and definitely in my flat, too."

"The stench was isolated?" asked Pogue.

Ferguson nodded. "Either of you fish?"

"Erm, occasionally," said Abbotts, thinking then of warm Sunday afternoons by the river with his son.

"It's the same smell you get with the maggot jar."

Abbotts knew exactly what Ferguson meant, and Pogue had a fair idea, too.

"Did you ever find the cause of the smell?"

"No, Constable. It came and went. All a bit odd."

"You've been very helpful, Mr Ferguson." Harry Pogue put a hand on Abbotts arm, indicating that the conversation was suddenly over. A little bemused, Abbotts slid the notebook back into his breast pocket, pencil neatly against it. "We'll let you enjoy the rest of your day."

"I can let you in, if you want?" Ferguson said suddenly.

"Sir Charles clearly isn't there. We have no appointment and we're unable to wait," said Abbotts.

"I mean into his flat."

"You have a key?" Pogue frowned. For someone so private as Tavistock apparently was, why would this neighbour have one?

"Of course I do. I'm his landlord. I own the building."

Chapter 15

"I don't care if this bloody toff is linked with the SMA. If you feel you're on the right track, then that's good enough for me." Chief Inspector Wilson poured a generous measure of Jameson's into a glass, no ice, and handed it to Pogue.

"Thank you, sir." Pogue downed the drink in one, hot on his larynx. Sipping only made it last longer. "Tavistock's place didn't smell like his landlord described but he had quite large collection of books about bugs and things: finding them, collecting them, breeding them. Insect lover's heaven. Then there were the plans of City Road."

"That's been shut for years, hasn't it?"

"That's right. Closed in '22 when they were widening the tunnels and it never reopened."

"And the Transport Board have just left it all as was down there?"

"Yes. Trains don't stop there anymore naturally, but if one's quick you can still spot the platform whizz by."

"So what would a rich bloke want with Underground station plans? Is he going to buy it?"

"If he is then it sets a precedent for others. But really - what would he want with it?"

"The plans themselves looked well used. Dirty and covered in grease and what have you."

"He's down there, isn't he?" concluded Wilson.

"I think so. And he did say to me that he had his own facilities to carry out a post-mortem. There was no sign of that in his flat. I wouldn't have expected to see any anyway, if I'm honest, but something does lean towards City Road as being the place where he was going to take the woman's body back to."

Abbotts' silhouette appeared at the frosted glass door again. He knocked and entered. Following him was a pristinely dressed individual, the crease on his trousers sharp enough to cut paper.

"Sorry to disturb you, sirs," began Abbotts. "But this gentleman insisted on speaking with Inspector Pogue. He-"

"Thank you, Constable," the man said, cutting off Abbotts somewhat rudely, Pogue thought. He had a slight accent. "Officers, who is leading this investigation?"

"Investigation into what? And we are addressing whom?" Wilson put his own whisky glass back on his desk.

"I am Dr Rasurel. The investigation into these murders." Rasurel peeled off his gloves and folded them over his left hand. "I want to know who appointed Sir Charles Tavistock as your forensic 'expert'."

"Dr Rasurel." Wilson held out a hand. Rasurel took no notice of it. Wilson recognised the name from the SMA but had never met the man before. He dropped his hand to his side. "It is a pleasure to meet you. I am Chief Inspector Wilson, and Inspector Pogue here is running the case."

Pogue stepped back as Rasurel moved towards Wilson.

"I assure you, Chief Inspector," Rasurel said, completely ignoring Pogue, "the SMA will not stand for the Police side lining an esteemed member for an untrained obsessive."

"Untrained?" Wilson pulled himself to his full height. "Are you saying that Tavistock is not qualified to carry out post-mortems?"

"You didn't check?" Dr Rasurel snapped.

"We didn't appoint him," said Pogue. "A Dr Block did."

"Hmm. And the woman's body. You have it at St Peter's?"

Pogue nodded. "Yes."

"It is not."

"I beg your pardon?" Wilson faced Pogue. "Where the hell is it?"

"Before you start laying blame at your own door," Rasurel interjected. "Be assured that there was every intention of it going there. It's just that it didn't arrive."

"How the hell do you know this?" Pogue demanded.

"*I checked.*" Rasurel moved to one of the chairs. "May I?"

"Please," Wilson said, gesturing for Rasurel to sit.

"I am not a young man and standing is difficult for me." He pulled a fat cigar from an inside pocket, clipped the end with a gold-plated cutter and lit it. "I do not like Tavistock. I do not like his approach, his manner or his methods. Dr Block seems to feel that the man's money is worth ignoring his...his ways."

"Money?" Abbotts asked.

"He is a benefactor for the SMA. And a rich one at that. Block is a doctor but he also wishes to be an accountant. He sees the francs – no, forgive me - the pounds. Tavistock has a fascination, quite unnatural I feel, with the insect world. He is convinced that we can learn from them. I wouldn't be at all surprised if he is damn well mating with the things." Like bullets from a gun, Pogue and Wilson, with Abbotts in tow, shot from Wilson's office, the door banging as they went. Rasurel puffed calmly on his cigar, looking down at its length between his fingers. "Was it something I said?"

Chapter 16

The lights flickered, went out, flickered some more then steadied, their yellow glow washing over Tavistock's lab.

The power needed to recharge the tank was phenomenal and tapping into the Underground's electrics had been easy. It was also the main reason why Tavistock had chosen to set up operations in such an inaccessible place.

He hovered around the perimeter of the tank, careful that the connections feeding into Isabella were secure and the current was sound. The air around him crackled and hummed, alive with energy.

Isabella was subdued again, floating gently in the thick liquid, after a lengthy and disturbing thrashing. She'd struck her head against the tank wall and had knocked herself unconscious but a slight burst of current had brought her back to a motionless but conscious state.

The buzzer, the harsh, grating sound, made him jump. He'd been expecting Alice (his telegram to her was marked urgent) but he was annoyed that she had arrived at such a delicate moment.

"Spike," he called, "keep the current steady. Too much and she'll arrest, too little and she'll comatose."

Spike nodded, sitting at the bank of controls, all dials and valves and spark plugs. A gauge, its grey arrow hovering near the centre, the safety zone, sat at the top of the desk and Spike glanced quickly between it and Isabella as Tavistock wiped his hands on a cloth. He had to keep it steady. Tavistock's wrath would be unalloyed. The buzzer rasped again. He could see Sir Charles becoming agitated, saw him clench his hands, the darkening skin across his knuckles glistening.

A third sounding of the buzzer and Sir Charles gave a momentary look at the tank before hurrying through a maze of tiny, shoulder-width corridors, originally workmen's access, to a single metal door: the hidden exit to the street.

Tavistock was a strong man, years of hard labour in the Great War and then Afghanistan saw to that, but the massive bolts and interlocking mechanisms he installed were stiff - and rightly so. Not even a battering ram could penetrate.

He paused before grabbing hold of the heavy locks.

There was always the need to stop before he opened his world to the sky, to the reality above him, to be sure that the status quo would remain.

Yet the reality for him was markedly different. It was of death, pain, suffering, as if a grave was forever open and beckoning for him to fall into its maw.

Holding on to the bolts took him back, every time, to his tiny prison on the outskirts of Kabul.

He recalled the heat of the metal, warmed by the sun, blistering his fingers as with agonising strength he tried to slide them back to free himself. But he never could. The power eluded him for so many months that death seemed the only option.

He remembered with such clarity his captors defecating and urinating over him from outside his cage in the desert, laughing and cussing, in their cruelty keeping him barely alive.

The insects, the incessant, relentless drone of insects. They crawled in his hair, burrowed in his ears and in places so humiliating that he was still scarred from where the British doctors eventually cut them out.

And to this day, he still saw the child's face in his dreams, the child he slaughtered. The child that carried the gun.

His mother, the little boy's mother, and the curse she put upon him when he was imprisoned for killing her son. The guards had jeered at him at first, damning him and his kin, but as the curse took hold, they began to fear him.

The mother's act of vengeance had taken a different turn and Tavistock had just about learnt to control what was inside him.

But now, so many years later, that control was wavering and he had to find a way to save his darling Isabella before it dominated them both entirely.

The cold iron bolts under his hands now, keeping out the London that was on the other side of the thick metal door, had to contain him. He knew it to be the only way. Contain him until Isabella was free once more.

But he needed help. Spike whom he couldn't stand and Alice, his cook, cleaner, housemaid and lover. Both were loyal to him and he often dismissed that loyalty with little thought.

With a tremendous pull, he cranked open the locks and swung the door out, the fresh air caressing his cheeks and stinging the backs of his hands.

"At last!" said the man standing at Alice's shoulder, a German lilt to his voice.

Tavistock stared at him, eyes wide, looked behind him to the group of sharp-suited men and then to Alice, her face drawn and so terribly sad. What had she done!

"You bitch!" Tavistock spat and went to pull the heavy door shut, but the men pushed Alice clear and Tavistock back down the little corridor.

Tavistock stumbled and fell. The man, Samsa, stood over him.

"I have waited so long to meet you, Herr Tavistock. Please," he indicated for Sir Charles to stand, "shall we?"

Chapter 17

Pogue and Abbotts, with an unfit Wilson trailing behind, had left the squad car two streets way, the mid-morning traffic heavy and unrelenting. A team of twelve officers were still in a Bedford van and Wilson was hesitant to allow them to join them on foot in case they spread panic amongst the pedestrians.

Reaching the street level building of City Road's tube station, they waited for Wilson to get his breath back and stole gingerly over the broken fencing and to a tiny hidden entrance, its metal door half-open.

Pogue pulled out his revolver, Abbotts his truncheon, and they stepped into the gloom.

The first thing they noticed was the smell, like maggots or rotting flesh, becoming more pungent the deeper in they went. The heat, as they traversed in single file, increased too, reminding Wilson of the hothouse at Kew.

The narrow corridor twisted and turned but always headed downwards. Eventually, the light became brighter and the space wider.

Pogue stopped them and held up a hand. "Voices," he whispered. "Listen…"

Quite clearly, they could make out two distinct voices. Once sounded like Tavistock but the other was accented.

"French?" asked Abbotts.

"That's bloody German," Wilson corrected, voice low. "What the hell are the damn Bosh doing down here?"

"Your *friend* was very easy to convince," the German was saying. "Perhaps you should pay her more and she would not sell your secrets."

"I've got nothing to say to you," came Tavistock's indignant reply. "Those drawings are useless without the correct scientific knowledge."

"We have our own scientists. We will interpret them. The Führer enjoys the unusual. He even has a team digging in Cairo for trinkets that will aid our cause. And with creatures like you at the head of our army, we will be invincible."

"But you said you wanted to help him find a cure!" A woman's voice!

"Frau Delambre, how misplaced your ideals are. Why would we want to suppress such power?"

In the corridor, Wilson tapped Pogue on the shoulder. "We move in."

Pogue nodded. "Ready? Abbotts, are you okay?"

Abbotts nodded, his nerves shredded. But he was an officer of the law and so his own fears had to be set aside.

"Let's go!"

With a clattering of boots upon stone, the three men stormed Tavistock's lab.

"This is the Police!" cried Pogue. "Nobody move!"

Nobody did – for a split second.

Then Tavistock dove under a bench and the men in suits, moving too quickly for Pogue and the others to count, scattered.

Pogue fired, missed, fired again, got one of them in the shoulder and fired a third time, striking the glass tank in the corner.

A great cracking sound reverberated around the curved walls and Tavistock stood, horrified, as he and everyone else could do nothing but watch the glass split slowly and steadily, the weight of the liquid it contained pushing against the weakness.

"No! NO!" Tavistock suddenly rushed to the tank, pressing against it as if it would stop the inevitable.

It was then that Pogue realised with horror there was a woman behind the glass. What was this Tavistock capable of? He couldn't tell if she were living or dead but by Tavistock's reaction, the tank breaking was something he could not cope with so logically she had to still be alive.

The glass finally gave way and showered Tavistock and the floor in a thick, creamy ooze.

"Isabella!" Tavistock cried out in anguish, frantically scooping the liquid back over the woman's twitching form. But it was no use. The stuff was seeping away across the floor, reaching the booted feet of the dumbfounded men. The tubes coming out of her skin flailed like snakes, crackling and sparkling with energy. Alice screamed as the control desk, where Spike still sat transfixed, hissed and caught alight, power threading back down the connecting tubes to Isabella.

Spike fell backwards off his stool then hurried around to Tavistock. Tavistock struck out with the back of his fist, sending Spike flying.

"Get away from her! Don't touch her!" he screamed.

Wiring and tubes glowed hot and threw out a series of sparks, erratic, blinding. Tavistock grabbed Isabella's hands but was thrown back himself as she burst into flames. Isabella found her voice then as she awoke, smothered in fire and liquid and screaming her way into death.

The flames jumped from her writhing form to the benches, desks, and any electrical source it could find.

Tavistock shook himself and stood, looking down at his hands. They had become twisted, as though arthritis had set in all of a sudden. Sir Charles roared and spun to face Pogue and the others.

"You did this! You!" he hissed, clawed hands pointing, accusing.

"My God!" Pogue exclaimed, clutching a hand across his mouth.

Tavistock's features had changed, dropped, his face sagging to one side.

As they all watched, Tavistock's skin darkened and he fell to the ground, embryonic, shuddering. His back arched, the lab coat ripping as his body seemed to expand through his clothing. Arms twisted into new positions with a new set of limbs, dark and covered in coarse short hairs, digging their way through the flesh either side of his torso.

Then in a shower of skin and cloth and an inhuman shriek, Tavistock launched himself to his feet.

But it wasn't Tavistock. Not anymore.

Abbotts cried out, falling to his feet in terror. Samsa and von Wer on the other hand seemed elated with what they had just witnessed.

"It works! It is *beautiful!*" Samsa cried, but the other SS members thought otherwise and darted for the narrow exit.

"Stop! Stay where you are!" ordered von Wer to his men but they either did not hear him in their fright or chose to ignore him.

The winged insect that used to be Tavistock quickly cut them off, and cut them down, before they could escape. Their bodies, torn asunder, were scattered over the floor in their own blood and in the tank's liquid.

Von Wer drew his Luger but his hands were shaking too much to determine a clear shot of the creature that was flitting with such speed and grace before them. The ochre glow of the flames reflected off the creature's glistening exoskeleton.

Pogue pulled Abbotts with him and headed in the other direction, firing as he went. He hit the creature in the shoulder and it screeched, heading towards Alice. Instead of pinning her down, it grabbed her with multi-jointed legs and trampled over the inspector to scurry across the lab, taking Delambre with it. Pogue remembered the plans he had seen in Tavistock's flat and knew where the insect was headed: to the other exit that opened directly to the tunnels.

"We have to stop him! Once he's in the Tube system, we'll lose him forever!"

Wilson launched himself at Samsa, but the German sidestepped him and trailed after Pogue and Abbotts. He too wanted to capture the insect but for reasons Pogue could not condone.

"Harry!" called Wilson, pulling himself to his feet, coughing as the smoke and flames grew thicker and hotter. "I'll get help!"

Pogue for a brief moment considered Wilson's cowardice in retreating but it did make sense that one of them was able to alert others. He even smiled as he thought what Block and the SMA's reaction would be.

"Come on, we've got a bug to catch!" he said to Abbotts who grimaced and followed against his better judgement.

"You kill it, I kill you!" Samsa spat as he barged past them. Abbotts went to tackle the Nazi with all the skill of a fullback, but Samsa lashed out with a boot at the constable's chest then pulled his own Luger out from under his leather overcoat. "Stay back! The creature is mine!"

Von Wer helped his *gauleiter* to his feet and together they stumbled into the tunnels.

"With any luck Tavistock will do a good job on them," Pogue breathed.

"But, sir...that's not right," gasped Abbotts. "Even if those chaps are bloody Bosh we can't leave them at the mercy of that thing."

"I understand your sentiment, but he's got that woman. Having the Nazis for lunch might mean he'll leave her alone. Come on!"

The tunnel greeted them with a cool embrace, a shock compared to the sweltering, burning heat in the lab. They could hear the two Nazis' faint footsteps in the distance and cautiously followed the sound.

Chapter 18

The tunnels seemed to be without beginning or end, forever curving away behind and in front of Samsa and von Wer. The two Nazis may have had an exact knowledge of London but down here they were literally in the dark.

A heavy breeze came flooding out of the gloom towards them and realising what was coming, Samsa dived to the wall, pressing himself as close to it as he could, gesturing to von Wer to do the same.

The train streaked by. The noise of the clattering on the rails was deafening, with the lights from the interior bouncing on-off-on-off against the tunnel walls. As it rattled away, Samsa breathed out. The distance between him and the train had felt like less than an inch.

He looked over to von Wer but his colleague had disappeared. Straining to see, he noticed von Wer's Luger under the tracks so reached down to get it. As he did so, his hand met with a sticky mass, warm and soft.

Raising it to his face to see what it was, he gasped and nearly choked. It was blood and flesh.

Von Wer had been sucked under the train, his end ignominious and probably quite painful. Tucking the spare Luger away, Samsa wiped his hand clean on his coat. No matter. At least the spoils would all be his now, as it should be. He would capture the creature single-handed and take it before his beloved Führer in Berlin.

Treading between the tracks, the floor beneath him seemed to glimmer and undulate and he had no comprehension that it was a scurrying mass of giant beetles coming from the walls to consume the raw meat on von Wer's shattered bones.

Tap, tick, hiss.

Tick, tick, tap.

The train had long gone and Samsa assumed another wouldn't be along for a few minutes yet.

Hiss, tap, tap.

Something brushed past his shoulder. He spun but could see nothing.

A touch to his face! He batted the air away with his hand, pointing the Luger to nothing before him.

The wind whistled down the tunnel. A junction was ahead, where one line met another and a further moved deeper beneath. Samsa heard a train change tracks, wheelbases rumbling and clanging against the rails.

The touch came again, the peculiar noises disguised by the distant, unseen carriages.

Samsa turned, convinced he was being followed, but sure it wasn't by the ineffectual Metropolitan Police officers.

Then the insect came down on him without further warning, throwing him to between the rails. The thing was huge. Two compound eyes swivelled in their sockets while mandibles chomped and clicked. He spied a mouth – he assumed it was a mouth – opening behind the mandibles, a stench like rotting flesh coursing up his nose.

Samsa more in shock than anything began to laugh at the absurdity.

"Die verwandlung."

The insect's jaws snapped at him and he hit his right wrist briefly on the live track. He screamed in pain, the Luger flying out of his grasp.

The insect spewed vile, burning acid over his face and neck. He managed one last agonising scream before the regurgitated substance melted away his jaw and his tongue.

Some distance away, further up the tunnel, Pogue and Abbotts heard the death cry and broke into a canter, the tracks hindering their ability to fully run. But it was enough to see the insect pull Samsa's flaccid body up and half-fly half-scuttle with it away from them and down a corridor adjacent to the tunnels. Abbotts swiped up the fallen Luger.

Behind them, a train trundled along and the two officers hurried as much as they could and dived down the corridor before it struck them.

The corridor sloped down and they realised they were in a passageway that connected the Tube system to the sewer.

Beneath them was a wide circular room descending to a shallow pool, air holes to the street above (Abbotts hazarded a guess it was Monument) giving spots of light that allowed them to see relatively well.

Suspended from the vaulted roof were over twenty leathery cocoons. Pogue immediately realised that within them were most of the missing bodies. The insect that was Tavistock was up there now creating a hard shell around another: Samsa. He shuddered. This was the monster's larder. And it smelt like a maggot jar.

"Tavistock!" Pogue shouted, his revolver drawn. Next to him, Abbotts comfortably gripped the Luger. "Tavistock!"

The huge creature above dropped in front of them, splashing in the few feet of water.

It was hideous. There was no other way to describe it. Swollen abdomen, transparent wings that left a pearl-coloured powder on everything they brushed against, six spindly legs. Abbotts could take no more and vomited over his own boots.

The insect's massive head twitched and tilted, mandibles detecting the odorous discharge.

"Let us help you," Pogue said. He didn't know how but it seemed the right thing to say. "There has to be a cure."

The insect screeched and scuttled up the wall, acidic spittle trailing from its mouth. It seemed to be looking between the two officers. Pogue was worried that it was considering Abbotts as weak and wondered if that glistening hide was bullet-proof.

"Please…" Pogue uncocked his pistol and placed it carefully on the brickwork flooring beside him. He raised his hands.

Abbotts, composing himself, a handkerchief at his lips, said: "Sir, what are you doing?"

"I have no idea. But I hope it's right."

Abbotts swallowed hard, his throat and nostrils burning.

The insect landed back in front of them and seemed to lower itself as it crept nearer.

"I think he understands," whispered Pogue.

"He?" Abbotts stepped back and the insect jerked in his direction.

"Wait!" Pogue grabbed Abbotts forearm. "Don't move an inch."

From behind them, quite suddenly, was such a commotion of boots on brick and shouted orders, causing the insect to shriek and fly up to the cocoons it had created.

Wilson had arrived with a team of officers, one of whom was armed with a flame-thrower.

"There is it! Bring it down!" he barked.

"No! Wait!" Pogue cried but one of the new arrivals aimed a rifle and brought the creature down with a clear shot at one of its wings.

"Burn it!"

Pogue watched, with surprising pity, as the flame leapt from the barrel and caught the insect's back, the hard shell giving some protection.

"Again!"

"No, sir!" Pogue shouted.

"It's a damned monster, Harry! We can't let it live!"

The flame spoke again, this time catching the cluster of cocoons. They lit up immediately and the insect screeched, almost desperate, Pogue felt. One fell and split as it landed in the water. Alice, covered in a yellow pus, tumbled out. Abbotts gingerly padded around to her, all the while his gaze on the monstrosity before them.

Another rifle shot, this time in the creature's abdomen. Then, after a reload, a leg, the limb coming clean off.

The insect shuddered in the water then, dragging itself to the officers, something remarkable happened.

Before their very eyes, the thing became Tavistock again in a cruel and painful metamorphosis. But the change wasn't quite finished and lying there, half out of the water was a gruesome man shaped liked a katydid, or a katydid shaped like a man. But in whatever way it could be described, Tavistock's twisted, swollen face looked up at them, tears streaming from human, bloodshot eyes.

He raised an insect-like stump.

"Help me. Please help me."

It was a pathetic voice and Pogue could see the pain behind the façade. There was only one way that Tavistock needed such help but Pogue needed to have answers first. He knelt at the water's edge, parts of the remaining cocoons dropping around them and half-decomposed bodies spilling out.

"What did you do?" he asked quietly.

Tavistock looked back at him and tried to find the words, his lips engorged.

"I turned her. I made her like me," he whispered. "My Isabella…"

Tavistock wanted to die, but needed to confess. He had never been a religious man. He wasn't even an evil man. But taking the story of Isabella to his grave would be something he didn't want to do.

So, through bouts of excruciating pain, he told Pogue of his time in Afghanistan; of the curse that had been cast upon him; of the visitations of the ancient Celebrants and of the Deep Ones; of how he had come home to England and how he had not been able to control the changes at first and how he had infected Isabella through their unions. She had begun to suffer the same fate. A cure was all he had ever wanted for her and had been desperate to find one before his own body was taken over completely by the insect inside.

But he had failed. Isabella was dead and his own body ruined and burnt beyond repair. And he knew deep down, buried in the human soul that he still had, that there was no cure. If there ever had been.

Leaning on the stump, Tavistock pulled his other arm from under his body, a claw at its end instead of fingers. He motioned for Pogue's revolver.

"Pogue…" warned Wilson, as the inspector clamped the pistol in Tavistock's grip and cocked it.

"It's alright, sir," responded Pogue. He didn't quite believe in curses but something *had* happened in Afghanistan. Something unnatural. "It's alright."

Slowly and deliberately, Tavistock raised the gun to his temple and closed his eyes.

"No!" cried Alice, pushing her face into Abbotts' chest.

The shot rang out and the insect who wanted to be a man collapsed lifeless into the water.

In a tiny alcove out of sight of all sat Spike, hugging the Istalifi pot close to his chest, rocking gently back and forth. A single tear for his wretched master ran down his cheek.

Chapter 19 - 128 Years Later

The largest section of the Underground's Central and West network was closed to the public while the electro-magnetic cushioning system (which had long since replaced unwieldy iron rails) underwent a routine safety check.

It only took one engineer to service an entire stretch of line and even then it was done remotely. The engineer didn't even need to leave home to do it.

But tonight the Underground Network Control system had detected an anomaly and a visual check was needed before Unc would switch the power grid back on.

Ryan Isaiah had dragged herself halfway across London and the SoftTab in her pocket would only stop bleeping once she had physically patched it in to the domain socket at the station in question.

Reaching the brightly-lit and antiseptic west-bound platform of Tottenham Court Road, Ryan unrolled the flexible tablet and connected it to the socket in the stationbot's chest.

The stationbot, whom she had nick-named Dave, was a big, rectangular box with a single yellow lens for an eye flush against his white plastic outer shell. He looked more like one of the old automatic ticket machines back in the noughties, a consensus being that androids in the Underground system looking human was somehow more unnerving down here for the passengers who absurdly packed themselves aboard the trains for their daily commutes.

"Hello, Ryan," Dave said politely in a smooth, faux-American accent. His lens whirred and contracted as he focussed on his human counterpart.

"Hi, Dave. What's up?" Ryan tapped her password into the SoftTab's keyboard.

"There is a blockage on the line," Dave responded, acknowledging the password. "Unc is unable to confirm what it is."

"Have the cleanerbots been down there?"

"Yes."

"What did they find?"

"They found nothing."

"Patch me in to their cameras."

"I cannot do that, Ryan."

"Why not?" Ryan got frustrated with robots. They only offered bits of information and she had to act like she was conversing with a child most of the time.

"Their cameras were taken off-line."

"By you?"

"No, Ryan."

"By Unc, then?"

"No, Ryan."

"Then who did it?" A blur of fingers and the SoftTab's screen brought up a series of images of the line Ryan was standing by.

"I do not know."

"Where are the cleanerbots now?"

"I do not know."

"Then they're likely to *be* the blockage. Has Unc considered that?"

"I do not know."

Dave didn't seem to know much tonight.

"The grid is off, yes?" Ryan checked via her SoftTab but still asked.

"Yes, Ryan."

"Okay. You wait here. I'll go see."

Ryan took her SoftTab with her as she jumped down onto the smooth line and into the tunnel. She would have wi-fi to keep in touch with Dave.

And so Dave waited. His computer mind had not been told to do anything else and he stayed like that, waiting, for the next four hours. Nothing on the platform moved, the electro-magnetic line stayed quiet, not even a mouse coming to investigate.

Eventually, when Ryan hadn't reported in, Unc automatically linked in to Dave's hard drive, running in fast-forward the complete exchange between the stationbot and Ryan.

The four hour gap of nothing went by for Unc within seconds and then the data stopped.

When Unc was unable to interpret the image that appeared immediately before Dave's camera ceased functioning at 7.18am, it dialled its human superiors for guidance.

The brief, somewhat blurred image from Dave's memory that Unc sent them was played, rewound and paused over and over again until they were convinced of what it was they were seeing.

"What else can it be?" one of the team said, a woman.

"It hasn't just crawled over the lens?" said another.

"No," countered a man. "You can see it comes out of the tunnel. Up from the tracks."

(Even after all this time, the terminology had stuck.)

"Where the hell did it come from?" queried the man. "How many more are down there?"

"You want to go check?"

"Well it's definitely an insect," came a statement from the rear of the boardroom.

"But if this image is correct..." began the man.

"Why wouldn't it be?" someone interjected.

"...then the bloody thing is six feet tall."

The Old Overcoat

By Colin Butler

Purchased at Burtons in its prime,
The height of fashion and style.
Now a victim of wear and time,
Hanging forlornly in the hall.

Travelled to London on the eight fifteen train,
Rubbed shoulders with expensive suits.
Protected its owner from wind and rain,
Hung in the boardroom with top hats and canes.

Many private soirees it has seen,
With gorgeous ladies, blonde and brunette.
What stories it could tell a racy magazine,
Its fabric redolent with expensive perfumes.

Visited the opera and concerts galore,
Nestled next to expensive furs.
Sadly now relegated to the gardening chore,
Like its owner, now well past its best.

A tear in the pocket, stains on the cuff,
A button hanging dejectedly down.
Good intentions to mend, never enough,
As they both await their inevitable end.

Council Crème

By Simon Woodward

Chapter 1

Basildon and District councillor Sir Jeremiah Hoggs-Warch was sitting down to a coffee with his aide Mike Jenkins discussing the latest league tables for crematoria and cemeteries.

Sir Jeremiah held out his cup of coffee. "More cream, Jenkins," he demanded.

"Of course, Sir Jeremiah." Mike poured out the contents of the small pot of real cream.

"Halt," Sir Jeremiah said as he held up his hand. Mike stopped.

Jeremiah continued to shake his head. "I don't like this one bit, Jenkins. These are grave matters. We're going to have to visit this crematorium."

"But why do we need to visit? It's one of our best performing crematoria; the crème de la crem. So to speak." Mike smiled at his little jest. His smile didn't last long.

"You stupid boy," came his boss' retort. "Once a plebeian, always a plebeian."

"Erm. I don't think you're allowed to say that."

"WHAT?" bellowed Sir Jeremiah. "Are you titled such as I?"

"Er. No."

"Would you say you work hard?"

"Yes, of course, Sir Jeremiah. Always." Mike responded not knowing where things were going.

"Working class?" Sir Jeremiah continued to push.

"I suppose."

"Is your name Mike or Michael?"

Mike's brow furrowed. "Mike is on my birth certificate."

"Therefore you are a plebeian," Sir Jeremiah concluded. "Look it up in the dictionary. This is the last I'm going to say on the matter."

"Yes, Sir Jeremiah."

"Now, to the question at hand; why is this crematorium doing so well? Isn't this a little strange?"

"Possibly. But with the increase in mortality..."

"We don't talk about that," Sir Jeremiah interjected.

"Alright. Let me re-phrase. Foregoing the increase in mortality..."

"JENKINS! We DO NOT talk about that."

"Of course, of course. With the new throughput..." Jenkins paused for a moment ready for the expected quick and sharp interjection. But none was forthcoming, so he continued. "With the new throughput figures due to..." Mike Jenkins paused again trying to think of a phrase the councillor would like. "With the new throughput figures due to more permanent visits?" Mike raised an eyebrow as he looked at the councillor.

"Good, Jenkins. I like that; 'More permanent visits'."

"It ought to be expected," Mike concluded.

The councillor nodded. "Across the board, yes. But not just one of them. Something's going on and we need to find out what."

Mike Jenkins nodded agreement.

"Get Timms from the former Health & Safety department to visit this crematorium. He spends most of his damned time on his righteous arse denying responsibility for anything. God knows why we pay people from that department. He can go and not be responsible in situ at the crem."

★

Mike walked down the stairwell to the former offices of the local health and safety executive.

Although it had been six months since the government cuts and mergers had been announced the office changes were still underway.

"What?" the decorator asked Steven Timms. "You want me to complete a risk assessment before I open that tin of paint?"

"Of course, Mr Brushbins. You know it's for your own good."

"Mr Timms, I've already completed a form for that."

"But the colour has changed..."

"The COLOUR!!!" Mr Brushbins interrupted as a beetroot scheme replaced his normal pale pink facial colouring. Sort of like a chameleon, but without the beetroot background to be matched.

"If you'd let me finish," Timms started in an exceptionally calm manner as he was well used to people he met going ballistic for no apparent reason. "You have changed the size of the paint pot, it's not really to do with the colour, though I'd best follow up on that point – thanks for the pointer – the risk is likely to have changed."

In the straitened times Mr Brushbins had to concede. He didn't want any competitors getting his gig, though giving up had crossed his mind many, many times.

"Okay, Mr Timms. Have it your way. I will get the risk assessment done. It will mean delays to the decorating though."

"I understand, Mr Brushbins. I truly understand. But we can't have you injuring yourself can we? God forbid if you get killed, due to some mishap, and you decide to sue the council. It wouldn't be right. Especially as it would be your fault."

If it was possible for steam to suddenly be expressed from any person's ears it would be his, right this minute, but the decorator managed to keep control. "No. You're right, Mr Timms. I would hate to benefit from compensation after my death. It's just wrong."

"I knew you would see it my way."

Mike knocked on the door to the office suite. "Ahem!"

Steven Timms turned around. "Mike! What brings you here? Good news I hope."

"Well..., sort of. I think. We've got a crematorium hitting and exceeding targets."

Steven Timms paused before responding. "I see."

"You do?"

"Of course."

"But they're hitting and exceeding the targets," Mike reiterated.

Timms nodded, knowingly. "Yes."

"That's the problem?"

"Of course. Everyone knows targets aren't defined to be accomplished – I mean if they were we'd all be out of a job. A target is defined to make sure it can't be hit. Hence, allowing any government department, or council one, to exponentially grow its staff head count to compensate for the issues and thus generate more employment."

"Ah! I see," Mike said.

"So you understand that when a school, or police service, or crematorium hits its target there must be something seriously wrong, because hitting a target is made to be impossible."

Mike's conversation with his boss was becoming clearer in his mind. He now knew why the Basildon and District crematorium at Gowers Bifford had to be investigated.

"Mr Timms, I've been instructed by Sir Jeremiah Hoggs-Warch to tell you to visit this extraordinary crematorium and find out what, exactly, is going on."

Steve Timms felt like he was being made responsible for something and, that, certainly, wasn't how any health and safety officer operated.

Steven Timms shook his head. "Sorry, Mike. No can do. It's not my responsibility. How the crem. operates is solely the responsibility of the owners."

Mike nodded. "I know. You've got to go there and not be responsible, just observe. That's all."

Although reluctant Timms couldn't figure out an argument that would allow him to stay in the council offices and oversee the decorators.

Timms took a deep breath. "Okay. Let Sir Jeremiah know I'll be on my way day after tomorrow. There are a few forms I need to complete."

"I will, Steve."

Through gritted teeth, with his mouth pursed Timms added as pleasantly as he could; "Please thank Sir Jeremiah for this opportunity."

"I will be sure to, Steven."

Chapter 2

At the Basildon and District crematorium in Gowers Bifford, Stan Lord was on his tea break, feet atop the wooden table and leaning back in a chair reading the Daily Rimmor red-top.

He shook his head at the headline; "'**HIGH STREET CAPITALISM KILLING THE ELDERLY**' — *pre-Christmas sales force government created aged and poor to shop in sub-zero temperatures; fatalities rise whilst privately owned crematoria proprietors warm hands on increased profits.*"

Bloody government, he thought. *If they'd done more to make the bad weather better it wouldn't be so difficult for the poor people of Britain. Bloody government.*

A metallic *tringing* sound suddenly echoed around the crematory, the large empty room behind the incinerators. The noise-shock sent Stan flying backwards followed by a hot cup of tea and a sodden newspaper.

"Mr Farthington," Stan called out from his prone position. "The phone's ringing!"

Stan wasn't allowed to answer the phone due to numerous inappropriate statements made to prospective clients, whom, for one reason or another, had decided not to use the crem. afterwards.

"MR FARTHINGTON?" Stan yelled. But there was no response. The old-fashioned black Bakelite phone continued its incessant ring as it hung on the white-tiled wall of the crematorium's operations area.

Stan looked back over his shoulder. The phone rang again shaking its receiver's spiral cord. He sighed. He knew if the call was missed he'd get into trouble and he knew if he was caught answering the phone he'd get into trouble.

Stan flicked his long dyed-black hair from his face and scrambled to his feet, took one step towards the phone, put his foot into the remnants of his tea and slipped over, landing on his arse right back where he started.

To say the thin gangly Stan was clumsy doesn't quite convey Stan's unwanted skill. He was certainly fortunate to work mostly with dead people who couldn't be harmed by meeting him. Though there's nothing to say they didn't regret meeting him in any case.

Stan flicked his hair from his face and lifted the phone's receiver from its mount. "Hello?" he said.

A deep, dark and mysterious voice spoke as if coming from the depths of the throat; "This is OfSted.ED," the voice said, then broke into a rasping cough.

"Sorry?" Stan said. "Don't you mean OfSted?"

"NO!" the growling voice responded. "It's OfSted.ED," it managed to say before breaking into another round of phlegmy coughing.

"Okay," Stan replied. "I hope your cough gets better."

"It's not a cough," the voice said. "I don't normally talk like this!"

Stan held the receiver away from his ear for a few seconds until the third round of coughing had subsided. "How can I help?"

"We will be inspecting." This time there was no coughing, just the purr of a line disconnected.

Before Stan had a chance to replace the receiver the rotund and suited Mr Farthington came around the corner from the front of house. He pocketed his watch-chain.

"Lord, what are you doing?"

Stan stood there with receiver in hand not sure whether the proprietor was actually talking to him. Stan looked toward the ceiling.

"Don't be stupid, Lord. I'm talking to you. What are you doing with the phone?"

"Erm! Erm!... You had a call, Mr Farthington." Before Farthington could express his dismay that Stan had answered the phone, Stan continued. "They said it was OfSted.ED. Have you ever heard of them?"

Farthington paused considering this news. "Truly?" he said. "They said it was OfSted.ED?"

He started rubbing his hands together like he was washing them. Ebenezer Farthington was very worried, but he suspected his little payments may have paid dividends. "Wh... what did they say?" Farthington asked with an uncharacteristic stutter entering his voice.

Stan was curious. Especially as his boss seemed so worried. "Who are OfSted.ED?"

"Where have you been boy, these last three years?"

"Working for you, Mr Farthington!"

Farthington sighed. "I know that you fool. I meant... No matter. I will tell you. With all the government cut-backs, re-shuffles and consolidations, the Environment Agency has been disbanded and its roles distributed to other government agencies and departments. OfSted got Exhumations and Death, hence OfSted.ED, the Office for Standards in Education, Exhumations and Death. Now tell me; what did they want?"

"Between fits of coughing," Stan started. Farthington nodded to himself. *Must be a message from Deep Larynx*, he thought. "He said that 'we will be inspecting'!" Stan continued. "He didn't say what. Could be his navel as far as I can tell."

Farthington was silent for a long while. He impatiently waved a hand at Stan. "We've got to get this place sorted out. Disconnect the Hyper-Cin after you've stowed poor Mr De'Ath in the chiller."

Stan pushed the trolley with their latest customer on top, towards the cold-store. "But we've got so many bodies to toast this afternoon. We won't be able to do it without the Hyper-Cin."

"Stan, I wish you wouldn't call it that. I've told you many times."

"No one's listening."

"Ahem?" an elderly voice called from the doorway, trying not to interrupt but having every intention to do as much. It was the customer Farthington had been speaking to before he'd gone into the back to collect the album of caskets.

Farthington shook his head at Stan then turned to the person standing in the doorway. "I'll be with you in one minute, Mrs Penchant. I'm sure I've got just the right thing for Miss Tiggles. I'll bring it through in just a moment. Please bear with me. Staff problems, you know." *Work experience*, he mouthed to the elderly lady.

Mrs Penchant looked at Stan who was wearing his loose fitting pail grey-green long-sleeved tee-shirt with a huge picture of a skull on its front then back to Mr Farthington. She nodded. "I understand, Mr Farthington. But please don't forget I need Miss Tiggle's hair to look right, she's a long haired tabby after all."

"Why have we gotta disconnect the Hyper-Cin, Mr Farthington?"

Farthington made sure Mrs Penchant had left before he replied. "Have you not noticed the leaves on the trees during the summer, you clot?"

"Yeah. I thought that was a great idea, Mr Farthington. Making them all black 'n' all. Sort of goes well with the death 'n' stuff."

"Lord! That wasn't deliberate."

"Are you talking to me, Mr Farthington?"

"Yes! For God's sake. It's soot."

"SOOT! You mean...?"

Farthington nodded solemnly. "Yes. It's people."

"Coooool!"

Chapter 3

Steven Timms completed the risk assessment forms for his trip to the Basildon and District crematorium at Gowers Bifford. Making sure he followed the control measures to avoid paper-cuts, and the likelihood of blood poisoning then death, he pulled on his personal protection equipment, also known as gloves, and pushed the forms into their respective envelopes.

He nodded to himself. *Job well-done. Yet another start to a day without injury.* Little did he know what was about to happen in a less than two hours' time.

Timms eased his car out of the council office's car park and onto the dual carriageway. He looked into his rear view mirror and as soon as the offices were out of site he flicked a button on his dashboard and the well-known sound and site of a police siren and flashing lights started up. A maniacal grin crossed his face as he push the accelerator pedal to the floor.

Council Crème

Detective Inspector Richard Shaw hated his undercover persona as much, if not more so, than he hated all the health and safety twaddle. In his opinion there was no point working in a risk free country if you couldn't make a bean to live on.

However, the cover had been good and he'd been able to infiltrate the council as part of Operation Dissen Tree, a police effort to root out local government corruption associated with the management of death in the county.

It had come to the attention of the police that certain crematoria, undertakers and grave diggers were being favoured with preferential licenses and work whereas others were being blocked or delayed or even denied.

Someone in the council was getting a bung for this and Detective Inspector Shaw was going to uncover the perpetrator, or perpetrators. And now he was on his way to his first real break in the case; a crematorium that was exceeding the targets – very suspect indeed – how could they if all licenses and allowable advertisements were evenly distributed amongst the crematoria in the county?

*

"Lord! Will you get a move on? This place has to be cleared up before any inspection by OfSted.ED."

"Okay, Mr Farthington. I will, I will," Stan sulked.

"Thank you, Stan. I won't be long, I've just got to help Mrs Penchant pick out a casket for her cat."

Just before Farthington walked out the door to the front of shop he turned back to Stan. "Oh! One other thing. Can you get out of those damned awful clothes and remove that metal work from your face, put the uniform on, and come and collect Miss Tiggles?"

Stan harrumphed before acceding. "Okay, Mr Farthington," he said.

*

Nee-naw, nee-naw, nee-naw, D.I. Shaw thought as he sped along the A130 to the Gowers Bifford crem. He loved the high speed, he loved the sound and he loved not being Steven Timms. Life was good once again.

He could almost see the headlines in the Daily Rimmor; "'**D.I. SAVES THE AGED**' *— fanatical capitalist plot to rid the world of dead bodies, exposed. Crematorium proprietor charged.*"

*

Stan pulled on the black jacket, pulled his hair into a pony tail and made his way to the front of house to collect Miss Tiggles.

Sidling through the half opened door he caught his right foot on its base, stumbled forward and propelled the trolley with Miss Tiggles' cat basket and body atop through the front of the Chapel of Rest. The trolley stopped abruptly, its path halted by a chair, but the cat basket made an exit through the glass portion of the French windows.

It was fortunate that Stan hit his head on the corner of a mahogany table, a display of fresh flowers at its centre. The blood that spewed forth mitigating any animosity Mrs Penchant may have had with regards to her long-time friend and cat being fired, as if from a canon, through the establishment's outlook over its Gardens of Rest.

"Oh, my dear! Are you alright?" Mrs Penchant declared seeing the blood pour down Stan's face.

Stan was woozy. "I think so, Mummy. I'll be okay after I've had a bath. Can you wash my back tonight? I like it when you do that."

Mrs Penchant turned bright red.

"Mrs Penchant," Farthington started. "I am so sorry. Don't worry about him. You go home now. I'll make sure everything is perfect on the day."

"Thank you, Mr Farthington. I think I will. I'm sure it will come good."

"Rest assured it will, Mrs Penchant," Farthington said in consolatory tones as he walked Mrs Penchant to the car park and her car.

*

The Detective Inspector pulled off the main road and started down the long secluded gravel driveway to the front of the crematorium.

Farthington spied the new visitor and shuddered; he knew this was the inspector. Quickly about-facing he made his way back into the crematorium making sure to pick up the ejected cat basket and take it back inside.

"Stan, you blithering idiot."

Stan was dabbing his head with a handkerchief attempting to stem the flow of blood. "I'm sorry, Mr Farthington. It was an accident."

"You're so lucky that Mrs Penchant decided to keep her business here. Anyway there's no time for this. The health and safety inspector is on the driveway. He'll be here in a few minutes and you haven't done anything to sort out the back yet."

"I don't feel so good, Mr Farthington."

"Take some Paracetamol and then sort the back out. I'll try to keep the inspector out here as long as possible."

"Okay, Mr Farthington," Stan said as he got up from the chair he'd been sitting on and made his way out to the back of the crematorium.

"Don't forget the cat, Stan."

"Okay, Mr Farthington." Stan took the cat basket from his boss then disappeared out the back.

Chapter 4

The detective inspector got out of his car. The site was impressive. The Gardens of Rest were incredible, so carefully looked after. Rows of perfectly formed trees and shrubs. Bird song everywhere. The detective crushed the pang of guilt that had started to build. He was here to do a job.

D.I. Shaw spotted a man in a suit and waistcoat standing on the top step in the entrance to the building. He made his way towards the man.

Farthington nodded as the man approached. "How can I help in your time of need?" he said, feigning ignorance as to the man's purpose.

"Unfortunately, sir, I am here on official business. Not personal." D.I. Shaw reached out a hand and the two shook.

"With whom do I have the pleasure of speaking to?" Farthington queried.

"I am Detective Inspector Richard Shaw, but if you get to know me, which you won't, I'll let you call me Ric, for short."

Farthington nodded slowly. "Okay, er, Detective! How can I help you?" This was not the answer Farthington had been expecting. So this wasn't a health & safety inspection after all. Farthington wondered how *Deep Larynx* had managed to get it so wrong. Unless, of course, this hadn't been the upcoming inspection he'd spoken of. Or the idiot Lord had got the message completely wrong, which was another possibility.

"For the time being all I would like is to have a look around. Plus some questions, of course."

"That's it? Are you *sure?*"

"I've already told you my name and shown you my warrant card. YES! I am Detective Inspector Richard Shaw."

"No. I meant; is that all you need from me?"

"Oh! Yes, that's all."

"Would you like to view some caskets whilst you're here? I have a good selection. Is anyone in your immediate family going to die soon? I'm in a good position to help." Farthington was thinking of as many things as he could to keep the D.I. in the front of house so Stan could remove any evidence of the Hyper-Cin.

"Sir, I'm shocked at your suggestion that you can hasten the onset of death for members of my family. I have to ask; do you have any involvement with organised crime?"

"What? No! Of course not! Why d'you think that?"

D.I. Shaw referred to his notes. Then read them back. "'Death of immediate family, Farthington can help.'"

"What? I didn't say that!"

"The notes made are the gospel truth. That's why they're used in court."

Farthington was stunned.

"Can I have a look out the back?"

All the crematorium's proprietor could do was nod. Farthington lifted an arm and showed the D.I. the way.

*

Stan was rushing back and forth attempting to clear the broken crockery, move boxes containing the ashes of previously embodied people, and polish the stainless steel accoutrements. But still suffering from his head trauma he wasn't succeeding in any of the tasks.

"Stan," Farthington said, interrupting his employee's frantic clear up. "This is Detective Inspector Shaw. He needs to have a look around. Can I leave that with you as I have some paper work to finish?"

Stan stopped mid stride, holding a box of electronics associated with the partially dissembled Hyper-Cin. All Stan had managed to do was remove the safety button from the turbo charged incinerator. There'd been no time to do anything else.

"Er. Okay, Mr Farthington. No problem."

"You are?" D.I. Shaw asked the Goth.

"Er. Stan Lord. Honestly, I haven't done anything."

"Stan. Stan, calm down. I've no reason to suspect you of anything. I'm just looking around. Do you understand?"

Stan nodded.

"How did you cut your forehead?"

"It was an accident. I tripped over the door. That's all."

"Was the door lying on the floor?"

Stan's brow furrowed. He was puzzled as to why there would be a door on the floor. "Er... No. It was in the doorway."

"And you tripped over it?"

"Yes."

"Stan, it would be very foolish to lie to me."

"I did. I did. I tripped over it. Ask Mr Farthington."

D.I. Shaw raised a hand. "Okay. Don't worry, Stan. You're not in trouble. Okay?"

Stan nodded again.

The Detective Inspector looked towards the stainless steel hydraulic front loading doors. There were three of them. All or only one of these incinerators had produced the heavy soot that had been reported.

D.I. Shaw made his way to the incinerator nearest the exit to the front of shop. He pulled its steel lever and its door swung open, blocking the access to the front of shop. The inspector peered in at the brick-lined retort where the incineration occurred.

"Interesting!" D.I. Shaw said. "Stan, can you come over and explain the workings to me?"

"Of course," Stan said, still carrying the cardboard box; a cardboard box that concealed the floor from his view as he held it to his chest.

Unfortunately for Stan he hadn't had the chance to clear up the mess he'd made earlier with his tea and newspaper. It was something he was about to regret.

D.I. Shaw leant into the retort closely inspecting its workings. Stan made his way over and only after his fourth step towards the D.I. he plonked his foot dead centre of the remnants of his tea once more. Instead of falling base over apex, he glided forward like a professional ice skater performing the Bolero straight into the back of D.I. Shaw.

Shaw, thoroughly surprised and unsteadied, tumbled into the incinerator's brick-lined cell.

The machine now detecting it had been loaded, and with no fancy safety mechanism to stop it doing otherwise, swung its huge steel door closed behind the detective, sealing him in.

Stan span around on point and performed an almost perfect change-foot spin. As he moved his hand outwards to restore his balance he caught the 'start' button on the Hyper-Cin's control panel.

The rest of the mechanism kicked into action and the super-heated flames growled their wrath over the newly installed contents. Before the D.I. could describe his predicament as '*shite*' he had been caramelised and toasted.

Stan looked through the small heat resistant glass window. *Sorry*, he mouthed at the carbonised skeleton.

Stan was now, very probably, in deep trouble.

Chapter 5

Mr Farthington finished signing the relevant papers, opened his drawer and filed them. He then took an envelope from the stationary cupboard, folded the letter and placed it in the envelope. Once done he walked out the back to see how Stan was getting on with the Inspector.

Before Farthington could open his mouth to speak to his errant employee he noticed the trolleys.

"Lord! Why is Mr De'Ath still next to Miss Tiggles? He should be in the chiller by now."

"You told me to help the inspector."

"Of course, of course. Forgive me, Lord. Where is the inspector?" Farthington asked.

Stan didn't want to be in trouble and unlike most Goths he was quite the optimistic person. "He went to cover the grounds," Stan replied with the little white lie, avoiding telling his boss exactly how the D.I. had managed to do that.

"I see... I see. Don't know how much it'll help him, but I can understand it. When he gets back please inform Detective Inspector Shaw that I've gone to town on some business and should be back later this evening. Have you got that?" Ebenezer Farthington had to meet with Deep Larynx as soon as possible. Something about the detective inspector didn't smell right and had nothing to do with the recent cooking. Something Farthington was blissfully ignorant about.

"Er. Yes, Mr Farthington. You'll be back this evening?"

"Yes, exactly. And for the time being can you please try and reschedule the next few days' cremations. We're not going to be able to use the Hyper-Cin whilst the D.I. is inspecting. Okay?"

"Okay, Mr Farthington."

"And get this place tied up whilst I'm gone."

"Yes. Mr Farthington."

*

After Farthington left Stan decided to take a breather, get himself a coffee crème from the coffee machine, and figure out how to get himself out of the predicament he'd somehow got himself into.

He looked at the third incinerator, the one that was the Hyper-Cin — a Hyper-Cin without a safety mechanism — he shook his head.

Just as he was about to take a sip from his frothy coffee his hands started to shake. The most startling thought had flashed through his head. He had seen it on TV. With one cop dead the whole police department would be down on him like a tonne of bricks. They'd all want to bash his head in and after that the local SWAT would be waiting for him to make any move, like wipe a drop of sweat from his forehead, before opening fire. He was sure bits of his skull would decorate the crematory's white tiles with a smattering of red and pinky-grey. And as his body twitched on the floor they would take pot-shots at his limbs to make sure he couldn't get up and run for it.

Stan started to sweat but before he pulled a handkerchief from his pocket he checked the room to make sure he couldn't see any G36C assault rifle nozzles pointing at him. He wiped his forehead.

Stan really needed a way out of this situation and certainly before his boss arrived back at the crem. this evening.

Being a Goth one of Stan's major interests was death and especially the occult. This was the main reason he'd applied to work for the Basildon and District crematorium at Gowers Bifford. Stan remembered a book he'd downloaded onto his Kindle. It was an occult tome about convening with, and raising spirits thereof, the previously alive.

Stan swiped the surface of his mobile phone, launched the Kindle app. and swished through all the books he had; then he saw its comforting black and yellow colour scheme; '*Practical Reincarnation for Dummies*', the cover titled declared. He quickly flicked to the '*Recovering the Spirits of the Previously Alive*' chapter.

The specialist book told him to inscribe a circle on the floor with pieces from the person he was trying to resurrect. Stan looked at incinerator number three. Inside there would be some pieces of the former inspector he could use. They'd be pretty useful because soot usually was in these circumstances; it would almost be like sketching with charcoal. Within a few moments Stan had made his mind up and had retrieved some the soot of the D.I. and had sprinkled a circle on the floor of the back office area of the crematorium.

Next the black and yellow guide told Stan to write, around the circle of power he'd made, the names of powerful guiding forces. The first name he wrote was Ebenezer Farthington, he wasn't sure this was what the book meant, but he believed it to be so. The book named some examples to aid the process; Elohim, Edimiel, Bartzachhiaheschiel and then instructed him to add an equilateral triangle to encompass the circle. Stan did all these things.

He swiped the page on his Kindle app. If flicked over and described the next thing he had to do; that was to mark out pentacles at each point of the triangle he'd made using D.I. Shaw's ash.

Stan didn't like it but he opened the steel door once more and grabbed a hand-load of D.I. Shaw's ash once again. He trickled the powder out from the base of his clenched fist, but it didn't quite work. He retrieved what must have once been one of the D.I's finger bones and drew out three pentacles in the sootiest black ever construed.

Once done he consulted the practical guide further. It seemed that all he was required to do, now, was place candles at the centre of the pentacles he'd drawn out.

Candles were something the crem. could do. Very quickly he'd lit three candles and all were placed at each pentacles' centre point.

Stan checked the last part of the chapter in the guide. All that was now needed was for him to call the spirit of the former person back to the real world and the circle of power would channel them into the nearest body.

Stan started calling out. He was nervous, but he really needed the D.I. back if he wasn't going to get annihilated by the local SWAT team.

"D. D. Detective Shaw... I summon you to, to... return." Stan waited. Nothing happened.

"Detective Inspector Shaw," Stan stated more clearly. "I summon you to return. You have body. You can return... now! I summon you."

Stan looked around the crematory and listened. The entire place was silent. But the more he listened the more he could hear a far off scratching sounds.

Stan strained his ears. A rumbling got louder. The candles around the circle flickered. The electric lights in the crematory flickered then extinguished. The flames of the candles started flowing back and forth as if in a light tidal current.

From nowhere a moan echoed around Stan's darkened workplace. The steel gurneys upon which the bodies of Mr De'Ath and Miss Tiggles resided started to rattle and vibrate.

Stan wasn't happy. Although he knew what he'd started it wasn't really something he was pleased to experience. He covered his eyes and peaked out at the phenomena through parted fingers wishing it had never started. Within a moment of that thought entering his head everything stopped and the crematory descended into silence.

Stan looked around. The candles were still flickering in the odd manner but there was nothing until the lid of cat basket exploded upwards taking out the overhead fluorescent light strip.

The lid was followed by the rigid body of Miss Tiggles. Stan looked on gobsmacked. The lid crashed to the floor, skittering in Stan's direction. Miss Tiggles, however, landed on all fours.

When Mrs Penchant's cat hissed at him Stan realised that something had gone badly awry with his summoning of D.I. Shaw's spirit.

Now he had to figure out who he'd summoned and whether they really possessed the body of Miss Tiggles.

The cat made a bee-line for the front of shop taking on the rigidly sprung door as if its springs were made of nothing more than cotton thread.

Chapter 6

"JENKINS!" Sir Jeremiah Hoggs-Warch summoned his aide. "Get my driver to pick me up in five minutes." After a couple of deep breaths Sir Jeremiah broke into a chesty cough.

"Yes, of course, sir," Mike replied happy that the overblown, toffee-nosed, arrogant git was going to get out of his hair for a few hours. *I hope you've got tuberculosis*, Mike thought to himself as his boss left the room for the circular, faux-marble stairway, down to the council building's entrance.

Sir Jeremiah open the limo's door, stepped in and slammed it closed. "To the Victoria Shopping Mall, driver, and don't spare the horses."

"Sir, would that be at the speed limit?" the driver asked.

"Of course, you fool. Do you think I'm of the ilk that would ignore the law?"

The driver nodded. "No, Sir," he said.

Within minutes the limo pulled up at the entrance to the shopping mall, some three hundred yards from where the journey had started. Jeremiah got out and made his way to the meeting with Farthington in an anonymous Costa Coffee shop at the top of the town's high street, opposite its Odeon Cinema.

Jeremiah walked in and looked around. For a moment he considered he'd got the wrong Costa Coffee, but then, in the far corner, he noticed a pink Financial Times beckoning him over. Jeremiah nodded to himself. This must be Farthington he thought.

He queued for a coffee and very soon it was his turn to order. "I'll have a coffee," he said.

"Is that a Frappa-lappa-latté, or an American Dosy-Wosy-Danté, or a Skinny-winny-coolie, or a..."

"Speak English you ignorant twat. C.O.F.F.E.E, comprendre mi compadre?" Jeremiah didn't care that he'd commingled Spanish and French, nor that he'd just called the spotty faced herbert of a barista a Godfather. He felt the point had been made.

"Coffee with cream?" the barista said.

Jeremiah nodded. The simple response told him one thing; the youth really didn't have a clue about language and pretty much the supposedly different coffees were just a figment of some crazed American's deranged imagination.

Jeremiah walked to the end of the service bar and picked up his completely straightforward coffee, then wandered over to the huge pink Financial Times that seemed to be supporting itself on a table in the corner of the coffee shop.

Jeremiah sighed as he approached the table. Farthington was drawing attention to them just by hiding behind the luminous pink paper. He smashed his hand down on top of the paper and it crumpled. "What are you doing? Do you want everyone to notice us, Farthington?"

"I might not be Farthington," came the cool retort.

"We agreed we would meet in this damned coffee shop and that you would have a copy of the Financial Times with you. NOT THAT YOU WOULD MAKE A DAMNED TEEPEE OUT OF IT!" Jeremiah started coughing again. He knew he was going to have to drop the Deep Larynx persona. Perhaps there was a better way to communicate in secret. Perhaps the new-fangled simple messaging service he'd heard about, currently available on his mobile phone, could be used. He was certain his phone did something like that. He made a mental note to ask Jenkins about it when he got back to the office.

"Right. What's this about, Farthington?"

Farthington flushed turning from his regular pink to bright red and back again. With his head being so round the effect was like watching a chameleon, the shape of a snooker ball, attempt to decide which part of the table it was actually on, but fail.

"I think we have a problem, Deep Larynx."

"For a start you can call me Sir, or Sir Jeremiah – we don't need the cloak and dagger stuff now. Pray tell, what is this urgent problem?"

"Right, Sir Jeremiah. A man visited us today."

"What? Steven Timms, the health and safety officer?"

"No! Did you send him?"

"Yes. I'm sure my man Jenkins did. Don't worry Timms is an arse. He wouldn't involve himself in anything – it's the nature of being in Health and Safety, you know."

"That's not the person I met."

"What?" Jeremiah was a little confused.

"I met a guy calling himself D.I. Shaw. He was very interested in the crematory and especially the incinerators."

"What? D.I. Shaw?"

"I saw his warrant card."

"Did he have short blonde hair?"

"Yes."

"Did he have beady blue eyes?"

"Yep."

"Did he move about like he'd been a chicken in a previous life?"

"Can't be too sure about that, Sir Jeremiah."

Jeremiah Hoggs-Warch rested his chin on his palm as he placed his elbow on the table. "Hmmm... I think we could have a problem, Farthington."

"What do you mean, Sir Jeremiah?"

"I believe the council has been infiltrated."

"Oh my God!" Farthington was starting to feel sick. "What should I do?"

"I'm not sure yet. But I suspect you ought to disconnect any of those hyper-wossits you've installed."

Farthington nodded. He hoped the useless Lord had finished dismantling the Hyper-Cins without any interference from the inspector.

"OK. This meeting is closed," Sir Jeremiah stated as he got up to leave. "Don't call me again unless you have some good news. I'll find out about this inspector in the meantime."

Farthington looked at the tall person that was Sir Jeremiah as he made his way through the exit of the coffee shop. He checked his watch, it was late. For tonight he would go home and hope the work experience kid would actually complete the task he'd been set for the first time ever.

Just as Farthington was getting up to go his mobile phone rang out with its SMS message tone. He looked at the message, it said; "Manage it." The message was from Deep Larynx.

Chapter 7

Stan ran after the cat, though he was a bit worried by the fact it'd been able to push the door open with only its right paw. He tried to think back to recall whether the inspector had been right-handed or not.

Fortunately the broken French windows overlooking the Gardens of Rest had been temporarily fixed with plastic sheeting, so the cat could not have escaped and it still had to be somewhere in the building.

Stan tried calling out; "Here kitty, kitty, kitty." There was no response. Stan got on his hands and knees and started crawling around the floor amongst the wooden legs of the tables, display units and sideboards, trying to spot where the cat had hidden itself away.

Then he had an idea. "Here, D.I. Shaw, Shaw, Shaw," he said.

"Honestly. It was an accident," he added.

As Stan peaked around the base of a particularly nice display unit with a glazed front showing all the types of silver urn available to buy he felt his cheek split in multiple places. Blood streamed out of the five deep and linear cuts. The silhouetted figure of a cat, with apparent muscle fatigue, darted back through the door into the crematory.

Stan pulled the already blood-matted handkerchief from his pocket and started mopping at the mess of his right cheek. He shook his head. This was going to be a bit more difficult than he'd expected. However, the night had already had some benefits; once the deep scratches on his cheek had healed he'd have some excellent scars, ones that would look very cool.

Stan entered the side room and opened up the medical kit. Taking one of the large plasters from the box he pealed back the adhesive covering and stuck it to his face – not cool now, he reminded himself, but definitely cool later, given a few days.

After he'd patched his cheek he left building to retrieve his crash helmet from the carrier on the back of his moped. Within a few minutes, with his head appropriately protected by his crash helmet, he gently eased open the door to the crematory and poked his head through then peered into the darkened room beyond. For some reason the main lights were out again. The ones over the benches around the side walls flickered, intermittently spraying the room making shadows dance.

As he listened to the empty room he heard a peculiar noise. He held his breath and focused. The sound he heard froze the blood in his veins. It was almost a ripping of Velcro but with a more liquid undertone to it. Stan couldn't figure out what was causing it. That was, until he turned to look at the gurney he'd left Mr De'Ath's body on.

Stan quickly, but quietly, shut the door and took a deep breath. He couldn't believe what he'd just seen – it was the most horrific sight he'd ever laid eyes upon.

Shaking his head to clear the image, in case his eyes had been playing tricks on him, he opened the door once again and looked back into the crematory.

The same noise assaulted his ears as the same vision of horror presented itself. The cat, D.I. Shaw's new insane substitute identity, was standing over the face of the poor old and dead Mr De'Ath and that wasn't so bad. But the fact that it was pulling at the skin, ripping it away, and gulping it down with what appeared to be some relish, which was more to do with enjoyment rather than some savoury appetizer, made Stan's stomach spasm.

The Velcro-like noises continued as the cat caught pieces of flesh between its teeth relieving the dead body's facial musculature of its covering. And between times the cat purred; a deep rattling sound that reverberated around the crematory.

Stan felt sick to his stomach. He knew he'd brought this monstrosity into being and he should be the one to send it back. The question was; how?

He hadn't noticed any chapters in his book about 'unsummoning' the spirits of the previously alive.

Before he could think any more about his predicament a burning itch clawed its way up his forearm. He couldn't help himself and had to scratch. He was shocked at the result. The itch had dissipated but he'd left long and deep claw marks where he'd alleviated the annoying tickle. Stan made a mental note to cut his finger nails once he got home, if that was ever to transpire this evening. He still had the cat/D.I. Shaw to sort out.

Stan looked around for anything he could use as a baseball bat but there was nothing. A useful tool such as a baseball bat was not a normal piece of equipment to be found in a Crematorium. Stan need something else, a different method of defence. Then he recalled the knives Mr Farthington used to prepare the bodies for viewing before they were toasted.

He'd prefer not to get too close to the cat, but as a baton of any type was out of the question, knives would have to do. But the knives were in the back and Stan would have to make his way past the deranged flesh-eating animal to the room that housed Mr Farthington's mortician's toolkit, before he had any chance of sorting out the cat issue.

He had a lot to consider before he entered the crematory once more.

Chapter 8

Ebenezer Farthington tossed back and forth in his bed. He couldn't sleep. There were too many things going on. Even Mrs Farthington's 'don't worry dear' comments weren't helping. She was an exceptionally kind individual but had no idea of timing.

He recalled her thoughts from earlier in the evening when he'd been in the water closet contemplating how he should proceed, amongst other things.

Knock, knock, knock. Farthington had looked up from his newspaper. "What?" he'd said.

"Don't worry, dear," she'd responded.

Ebenezer had ground his teeth at that moment only to be asked what the strange noise had been. Mrs Farthington needed to stick to her Mrs Beeton's and that was it. Yes! Stick to her cooking and household management. Leave men to worry about men's work stuff and definitely don't disturb them whilst in the WC.

Farthington reached over and grabbed his wife's Valium prescription bottle from her bedside table, emptied a few into his hand, downed them and waited for sleep to invade.

★

Stan opened the door to the crematory and peeked in, his chin sagged at the view. The cat had finished its supper and was now paddling Mr De'Ath's stomach preparing for a siesta.

Each time the heavy cat pushed a paw down the cadaver belched. Experience had taught Stan that this was to be expected from the recently departed, barring the part where a dead cat, inhabited by the spirit of a dead police officer, was the cause; and as part of its relaxation regime had consumed half of the body's face to boot.

Stan decided to wait a while longer. Soon the zombie cat from Hell would be asleep, and he could retrieve Mr Farthington's knives.

A sudden thought struck Stan. *Do zombie cats sleep?* the thought asked. *Oh My God!* Stan subsequently thought. Then sighed with relief. The cat was paddling, preparing its bed. This zombie cat was surely going to sleep.

His mind was taken from the zombie cat sleeping issue when his forearms, yet again, started to itch madly. He pulled away from the door back into the chapel and sat down in its small alcove where the medical kit was stored.

He pulled his sleeve up to examine one of his irritated arms then pulled it back down as fast as he could, shaking his head. Although what he'd seen looked fairly cool to him. For a fact it wasn't normal.

The hair on his forearms was no longer of the usual titchy vestigial type. It was long and intermittently beige and black, with a few white strands thrown in here and there.

He rubbed his chin in thought, but no thoughts came. He had to remove his hand from his chin as it seemed the same hair growth was happening there as well.

He stood up, opened the medicine cabinet and looked into its mirror. Through the facial opening in the bike helmet what he saw was not the normal oval shape like an egg balanced on its pointy end, it'd become more like and egg lying on its side, as if on a chaise-lounge.

He pulled the helmet off, this had to be his imagination. But no! The view was clearer, not only had his head shape changed there were black dots either side of his nose, just above his upper lip but no higher. Out of those black dots wiry white whiskers had started to protrude.

Then he noticed the tell-tale sign. His eyebrows had migrated and were now above the bridge of his nose in the unmistakable shape of the letter 'M'.

*

With no apparent effect from his wife's Valium Farthington decided to get up and go to his crematorium to see if Stan had made any progress dissembling the Hyper-Cin.

He knew it was late and he didn't expect the kid to still be there, but at least he could look and rest his turmoiled mind, at least on this point.

Ebenezer slid his legs out of bed and looked back at his wife; she was still sound asleep. He pulled on his trousers and shirt and just before leaving the bedroom he leant over and kissed her cheek.

"Don't worry, dear," she murmured.

I would relish the day I didn't have anything to worry about, Mrs F., he thought to himself. He pressed the button to open the garage door, got into his silver Audi and started the engine. The journey to the crem. only took fifteen minutes. He would be there soon. And he hoped he wouldn't have to worry about its 'special' equipment – the work experience kid should have dealt with it all.

*

Stan slammed the cabinet door shut. He didn't need any further confirmation. It was plain to see; the fur, the itchy arms, the strangely shaped face.

There was no doubt about it, for whatever reason, whether it be by the scratches the weird zombie cat had dished out or whether it was just his time to change and his family had kept this a secret for eons, he didn't know. But it was happening. He was becoming a Weretabby, a hybrid between humankind and tabby-kind, namely cats.

One more check, he thought and opened the cabinet to gaze into the mirror one final time. He slammed it shut again. He knew he had to act quickly before his transformation completed.

He needed the knives that would give him the opportunity to kill the zombie cat and stop it from infecting any others that may come into contact with it and, possibly, reverse the changes he was experiencing. Or was that vampires? Stan couldn't quite remember.

He sneaked towards the door into the crematory.

Chapter 9

Farthington's Audi crunched along the gravel driveway up to the crematorium's entrance. He shook his head. The glaziers still hadn't been to fix the French windows.

As he walked into the Chapel of Rest spurts of light flicked beneath the door to the crematory. What on earth was going on he wondered, and strode towards the door. If there was one thing he was sure of, it was that he was going to find out what was going on in *his* Crematorium. And what that idiot of a work experience kid had done to the electrics.

*

Stan had made it past the insane cat without disturbing it. But that wasn't going to last long.

In the dark he made his way to the bench and Mr Farthington's mortician's knives. As he glanced back at Mr De'Ath's body and the sleeping zombie feline from Hell he reached for the knives and attempted to pick them up, without success. They clattered to the floor. The zombie cat was suddenly on all fours, tail vertical, hissing at the room in general.

Stan looked at his hands. *Ah*! he thought as he contemplated the things that were not hands any longer but quintessentially paws. *No opposable thumbs*, he thought further. There were more downsides to being a Weretabby than he'd considered. Not that he had any choice in the matter in any case.

*

Mr Farthington hesitated at the door. The crash of metal implements on the crematory's tiled floor had startled him, but not as much as the otherworldly hiss that had followed.

He started to feel relaxed and happy, though the situation didn't warrant it. He'd forgotten the Valium he'd taken. He chuckled to himself and wandered straight through the door into the crematory without a care.

Miss Tiggles jumped up and turned 180 degrees in the air to look at the man with a weird smile on his face, as he entered. Mr De'Ath belched as the cat touched down.

Inside the cat's head D.I. Shaw struggled to make his presence felt, the structure of the animal's mind was less nuanced and forming cohesive thoughts was difficult. But D.I. Shaw knew he needed to let Mr Farthington know what had transpired during the previous afternoon. How he'd been murdered and then resurrected as a cat. After a moment's consideration he decided he'd leave the bit about being resurrected into a cat for another time. He had to be credible if he was going to get Farthington to report the whole set of circumstances back to the police team dealing with corruption in local government.

Miss Tiggles leapt from the body of Mr De'Ath and attached herself to Mr Farthington's chest. Claws digging in, holding her fast.

"Look! I've been murdered," D.I. Shaw started. "And somewhere in this room is the murderer, your work experience kid. I'm certain it was pre-planned by someone in the council. They needed me off their case. Help! Please?"

All Farthington heard was; *Hiss, hiss, hiss. Spit, meow, hiss, meow, meow, meee-ow, hiss, spit, mee-ow.*

Farthington nodded. D.I. Shaw thought; *great*. And then Farthington burst into laughter. In his state, under the influence of Valium, this had been the funniest thing an animal attached to his chest had ever done.

D.I. Shaw was unimpressed and the more animalistic side of the being he inhabited exerted its presence.

From its position on Mr Farthington's chest Miss Tiggles lashed out, swiping at his face. Huge chunks of cheek were wiped away with the first contact of the zombie cat's vicious claws.

Farthington felt blood trickle down his neck and the cold of the crematory made the exposed flesh of his cheek sting, as the skin flapped about.

He burst out laughing. He didn't know why but the pain seemed very amusing. The blood from his cheek itched as it made its way beneath his collar. He laughed again. Mrs Farthington would be in despair with the stain on his shirt. As he considered her likely reaction, *'don't worry dear'*, he doubled over with amusement and cracked his forehead against Mr De'Ath's gurney.

*

At the back of the crematory Stan had figured out how to handle certain implements without the use of thumbs and had managed to lift the fire axe from its clasp on the wall.

Stan knew he had to eliminate the zombie cat that was once the beloved of Mrs Penchant.

As he peered out of the mortician's room he was aghast to see that his boss, with insane cat attached to his chest, was missing one cheek and laughing his head off. All Stan could construe in his mind was that his boss had been taking some serious drugs or something.

Anyway, Stan thought. This wasn't the question at hand. He had to get rid of the damned cat.

Moving from the area of darkness that was the mortician's room he grasped the fire axe and made his way across the crematory to his distressed boss.

Farthington's traumas were quickly forgotten when he saw the Weretabby come into the light – not that he knew he was looking at a Weretabby. As was usual, under the influence of some very strong Benzodiazepines, Farthington's mind gave up trying to make any sense of what he was seeing. He started to laugh even harder.

Stan stole himself for what he was going to do next. Although difficult he managed to swing the axe backward, making ready for an aim at the zombie cat.

Miss Tiggles seemed only concerned with hissing erratically at Mr Farthington in between cruel swipes at his boss's face.

Stan, the Weretabby, pulled back making ready for the maximum swing he could muster to destroy the cat from Hell. Then he let loose. The result was not what he had expected.

"Whoops!" Stan exclaimed as Mr Farthington's head plopped onto the floor, followed by spouting rich red arcs of arterial blood that left the air tinged with a faint metallic whiff. Miss Tiggles exited the room, slightly shaken, but one of the more animate dead all the same.

Chapter 10

At 9:15am on the dot Sir Jeremiah Hoggs-Warch entered the council offices hoping for a normal day at the office. He was beginning to regret his attempted misdirection as to who was behind the Gowers Bifford crematorium's success. There was no way on Earth he could have known that Steven Timms was, in fact, an undercover police officer.

"Sir. Sir?" Mike Jenkins called across the lobby.

Jeremiah rolled his eyes. *What does that idiot want?* he thought to himself. "Ah! Jenkins. What's so urgent at this time of the morning before I've had my coffee crème?"

"It's Steven Timms! He's gone missing!"

Excellent, Jeremiah thought. "How can you possibly know that?" He looked at his watch. "It's only 9:30 in the morning. He might be caught in traffic."

"Sir, he's usually here by eight and even if he's going to be one minute late he always calls in to notify Sarah. He says that there is too much a possibility of an accident if people start reacting inappropriately to a scenario that's not actually happening – the risk is too great."

"Who's Sarah?"

"Sarah Baskin. She's Mr Timms' second in command."

*

Jake Brushbins walked past the councillor and his aide as they chatted in the lobby. He smiled as he overheard the fact that the idiot Steven Timms was unlikely to be in today; perhaps he'd be able to finish quickly and line up some other decorating contracts as far away from this place as was possible.

*

Sir Jeremiah and Jenkins made their way towards their office as they discussed the missing Timms further.

"Well, Jenkins. What do you propose to do about our supposedly missing Mr Timms?"

"Erm! Perhaps… Perhaps we could send someone there?"

Jeremiah was about to berate his minion, as that's exactly what they had done to no effect, when it dawned on him that this may be the exactly right tack to take.

"Brilliant idea, Jenkins." Sir Jeremiah patted his assistant on the shoulder. Mike Jenkins nearly collapsed to the floor, the shock being so great that he had actually been complimented by his boss.

"Furthermore," Sir Jeremiah continued, "I will go in person." Jeremiah was certain something untoward had gone on. It *was* strange that the idiot Timms had not turned up at his usual time. Perhaps Farthington had taken care of the situation with the undercover officer and if this was so good old Ebenezer Farthington needed to have his hand shaken at the very least.

Mike Jenkins blinked and looked at his boss uncertain of what he was hearing. Not only had he been complimented his boss was offering to do some work as well.

"Some coffee crème, Jenkins. Then I'll be off to the crematorium to find out what's happened to our Mr Timms."

Mike felt a slight sense of relief as the old order of things started to be re-established. The feeling that too much change in one go was a bad thing, overcoming him. He scooted from Sir Jeremiah's office to the kitchen to make his boss' coffee. He felt today was going to be different somehow.

*

Light seeped through the crematory's fanlight windows and formed beams, one of which shone directly into Stan's eyes. Stan blinked and rubbed his eyes. Then stopped suddenly. It was probably the worst thing he could do, rubbing his eyes with fur covered paws, though cats seemed to manage it without getting hairs stuck to their eyeballs.

He stared at the things on the end of his arms and sighed with relief. He wouldn't have to go to the chemist and get some kind of eye balm; he had hands once again. He checked out his arms — they were normal. In fact it was apparent that he was back to his normal self, all over.

He didn't know how he had come to be on the floor but as he rolled to sit up he saw the decapitated torso of Mr Farthington and images from the previous night began to form in his mind's eye.

"Ah!" he said as he remembered the weird Miss Tiggles jumping onto his boss' chest. "Whoops," he said again as he remembered missing the cat with the fire axe and loping Mr Farthington's head off.

Stan looked around and realised there was only one thing he could do; put the Hyper-Cin back together and dispose of the evidence of last night's macabre events.

It was a couple of hours before the Hyper-Cin was ready but as soon as it was Stan heaved the body of Mr Farthington into the oven and put Mr De'Ath in there as well. Without Mr Farthington he didn't have the skills to fix Mr De'Ath's chewed face well enough for the old man's bereaved relatives not to notice.

*

"Summon my driver, Jenkins. I'm off to the Gowers Bifford crematorium." Sir Jeremiah got up and left his office taking the stairway down to the lobby. As he got to the mezzanine floor he saw Mr Timm's second in command, Sarah Baskin, having a heated discussion with a *buildery* type looking person.

"What do you mean I have to complete a risk assessment to enter the area where I was working just yesterday?" Jake Brushbins asked of the slight woman. His face was now beetroot.

"It's very simple," Sarah Baskin replied. "I have determined there to be an extra hazard, which must be risk assessed, before you can continue. This is the law, Mr Brushbins. Whether you like it or not."

"What is wrong with these?" Brushbins asked, lifting his left foot into the air.

"They are floppy and may cause and accident if they became loose for any reason."

Brushbins stamped his foot back down on the floor. "What you're saying are that my tied shoe laces are floppy and could cause an accident?" Brushbins was not only bright red but sweating profusely now. "This is utterly ridiculous. How can there be a new hazard when there wasn't one yesterday, Ms Baskin?"

"It could be that the original assessment were incorrectly made, Mr Brushbins. But that is not the point of the matter. I have determined there to be a risk with your footwear and this has to be addressed. I'm afraid you cannot not continue until the appropriate assessments have been made and the correct forms completed."

"I'm only painting the walls you daft, bureaucratic nonsense of a person!"

"Now, now, Mr Brushbins. There's no need to be offensive about this. I don't make the rules you know."

Just as Sir Jeremiah was about to push the rotating door of the council building to exit and get into his awaiting car he heard a dull thud come from the mezzanine. He turned back to see the *buildery* type person flat on his back twitching with foam spewing from his mouth. Jeremiah quickly retrieved his mobile phone and called Jenkins.

"Jenkins, I think there's something you need to look at on the mezzanine. Be a good chap." Sir Jeremiah snapped the phone closed and left the building.

Chapter 11

Within twenty minutes Sir Jeremiah's driver had pulled off the main road and started down the gravel driveway that led to the front of the crematorium and its Chapel of Rest.

During the journey to the crem. Jeremiah had wondered what had happened to Mr Timms, aka Detective Inspector Richard Shaw, and his man on the ground, Mr Ebenezer Farthington. It was strange that both had gone silent; especially the cop.

But his thoughts were interrupted by the strange pallor of the leaves on the trees that lined either side of the gravel driveway. He wound down his window and stuck his head out. His cheeks flapped in the stern wind and he shouted over the breeze for his driver to slow down so he could get a better look.

As the car got nearer to the crem's parking area the darker the leaves seem to become. What a superb idea, he thought. He nodded an acknowledgement to what was obviously Farthington's design skills. The nearer you got to the crem. the deeper the acknowledgment of mourning and hence the blacker the leaves. Genius!

Sir Jeremiah's driver pulled up opposite the steps up to the Chapel of Rest's entrance. Jeremiah waited for his chauffeur to open the door before he got out.

*

As Stan was looking around to make sure he'd cleaned up the crematory he heard a car crunch across the gravel and kill its engine. Someone had turned up. He hoped it wasn't Mr De'Ath's family. He wasn't sure how he could explain their relative's missing body.

"Ebenezer, it's Sir Jeremiah, are you about somewhere?" a voice called out. There was a slight pause before another question emanated from the chapel. "What happened to your windows?" The voice carried on; "It's a bit of a mess out here. What have you been up to?"

Stan considered his options but before he could think of anything the door into the crematory swung open and Sir Jeremiah entered. He looked at the young lad.

"Who might you be my young and tatty Goth?"

"I'm Stan..." Before Stan could finish Sir Jeremiah finished his sentence for him.

"Stan Lord. I know. Ebenezer has spoken of you. Where is my dear friend?"

"Er! He's gone away," Stan said trying to keep to the truth as much as he could.

Sir Jeremiah nodded. He felt there was something the lad was not telling him. "I see. Anywhere in particular?"

Stan hadn't thought this far, but recalled his boss' previous journey to town the night before. "To town, on business," Stan answered.

"I see, Mr Lord. And you'd have no reason to lie to me would you?"

"No! Of course not, Sir," Stan lied.

Jeremiah looked around the crematory and spotted a dark ball in the corner next to a stainless steel preparation table. He squinted and then nodded to himself.

"And what might that be, Stan?" Jeremiah pointed towards the football-like shape hidden in the shadows of the crematory.

Stan looked at the shaped then gulped. In a timid voice he said; "I... I'm not sure, Sir."

"I think you do know, Stan. Please bring it to me."

Stan wandered over to the corner and retrieved the round object, it was partially covered in some viscous fluid. Stan walked back to Sir Jeremiah with object in hand.

"Thank you, Stan. What would you say this is?" Jeremiah grabbed Stan's wrist and raised his hand to bring the object to eye-level.

Stan knew exactly what it was. With everything going on in his head to make the crematory right and clean, he'd missed this significant part of the mess he should have tidied away. Stan was at a loss as to what he ought to do next. He felt he ought to run, but he didn't have any idea as to where. What remained was answering Sir Jeremiah question.

"Er! It's..., er!... it's, ... it's..."

"Say it boy," Sir Jeremiah demanded.

"It's a head." As Stan finally admitted the truth of the matter he cringed away from Jeremiah.

"It is certainly that, Stan. And whose head exactly?" Jeremiah wanted Stan to understand, completely, who was in charge. And there was no better way than being the inquisitor – a lesson learned from history.

Stan thought his time was up, the way he was being interrogated. But he knew he'd no choice but to answer. "It's Mr Farthington's!" Stan finally said.

"Thank you, Stan. It certainly is my good friend's head. But don't worry. I'm not going to ask you about the rest of the body, nor how this came to be. In fact you have done me a great favour. Mr Farthington was becoming a liability."

Stan couldn't believe what he was hearing. He questioned his own interpretation – was he being told he'd actually done something right?

Before he could think any further Sir Jeremiah asked another question. "Do you know anything about Detective Inspector Richard Shaw? Don't muck me about lad, be honest."

"T. . ., toast!" was all Stan could manage.

"In there?" Jeremiah pointed to the retorts.

Stan nodded.

"Well done, my lad. You do not know how much grief you have saved me."

Stan decided it was a good idea not to mention the fact that he'd managed to resurrect the detective's life-force into a cat's body that had been ready for cremation, and also not mention the particular cat had escaped to somewhere or another.

Sir Jeremiah put his arm around Stan's shoulder. "I think we can do some business," the councillor said. "How do you feel about becoming the owner of this crem?"

Stan couldn't believe his luck. Immediately he nodded. Sir Jeremiah reached out and grabbed Stan's hand shaking it generously.

Epilogue

Stan ended up becoming the proprietor of the Gowers Bifford county crematorium and some nights in the area, when there is no rain, strange and loud cat-like meowings can be heard echoing around the Gardens of Rest.

Sir Jeremiah Hoggs-Warch sent a letter to Mrs Farthington, purportedly from her husband, stating that he had gone away because he couldn't cope with his administrative mix-up that had allowed Mr De'Ath's body to be cremated before the family could say their goodbyes.

Mrs Penchant apparently found a stray that looked exactly like Miss Tiggles. Though from time to time the cat's demeanour bears no resemblance to that of Miss Tiggles, with constant meowing, hissing and spitting. Mrs Penchant puts up with this, mostly, because she feels she's got her Miss Tiggles back.

Finally, the police denied any knowledge of Operation Dissen Tree and any undercover operative going by the pseudonym of Stephen Timms; they claimed the paperwork had accidently got shredded and there was no way to follow up.

The crematorium is doing very well and the local council continues to operate in the way it has always done barring one change; health and safety inspectors, prior to being employed/deployed are hazard assessed and a full risk assessment is made of those inspectors in order to avoid the sad circumstances around Mr Brushbins' demise happening once again.

Struggling in Matters of Love

By Elliot Thorpe

Without love I struggle
Forced unto a life of solitude
The loneliness takes hold and I gasp
Nowhere to go but down

Tunnel vision: no left, no right
Only noise of despair
Hissing, scratching, howling
A banshee on the cusp of frenzy

But then, as the nightmare takes hold
As the river of abandonment takes me under
You arrive and take my heart
Giving me strength and breadth and time

Time to heal, to seal over the wounds
No more pain in my chest
I smile again! Facing the very outside
That I hid from so easily

Air fills my lungs as you hold me
You need me! You want me! You love me?
My soul sings like a new life
I exist again, whole, wanted, adored

And then you're gone
As quick as a rainstorm

Grave Matters

Leaving me distraught and fighting for breath
Without love I struggle

Why have you done this to me?
What have I done to deserve such torment?
When did you know you were breaking my heart?
How could you do this to the mate of your soul?

So back down I go!
Nowhere else is left for me
I gasp, the liquid filling my nose
The back of my throat tightens

And I die

My last sight of your sad face
As you regret your choice
To end it

To end me.

Wrong Options

By David Shaer

Chapter 1

All my life, I have been confronted by choices. My ability to select a solution has always been suspect, sometimes with far reaching consequences. It goes back as far as eating with my left hand or right hand. Kicking a ball, punching an adversary. Choosing friends, partners, lovers. I am allowed to say this because I know when I have made a mistake, usually within seconds.

For other people to come to the same conclusion about me needs them to take a step back before they advise me of their views. Occasionally, they don't and it ends in tears. Sometimes theirs but rarely mine.

However, there is always the exception that proves the rule and, about twenty five years ago, my respected oldest cousin stepped over that line. He was about seventeen at the time, and I was only fifteen. It wasn't the words, it was the deeds, and his anger emanated from our different backgrounds. He was a country lad from a small village in Wiltshire. I wasn't. This rattled him and he viewed me as a pompous and arrogant townie.

Conversely, I hero worshipped him, because he was funny, relaxed and full of adventure. I had none of these and, in fact, a complex about my sheltered town life. I once punched the young guest of a neighbour because he upset my sister. It hurt. Not the neighbour's guest – me. My hand felt as though it was broken, but the neighbour's guest ran off crying. Many years later he became the Member of Parliament for Maldon in Essex, albeit with an ugly broken nose, which was a direct consequence of my intervention, which he never let me forget.

But the problem was my cousin. He had other cousins from his diverse family and, ironically, one was the future Member of Parliament mentioned above. They didn't like each other and my cousin was over the moon when he discovered my misdemeanour. In fact, he became obsessed with his own form of hero worship, but only because he wanted me to do it again, but with much greater force. In fact, he became so obsessed that he was boring and constantly trying to come up with ideas for me to inflict further pain on his behalf. The problem was two-fold. One, I had no reason to do it again and two, I had become a coward.

So, being a naïve townie, I failed to spot an exocet weapon being lined up against me by my cousin, who was trying to back me into a corner to inflict his evil wishes against this future MP. In all innocence, I was party to a devious plan which would inflict pain and humiliation.

Measuring the height of a railway bridge from the track below was the sort of thing that young boys did. Using a brick and a long piece of string seemed a logical way to do it. Hearing a shriek and not noticing the rapid departure of my cousin on his bicycle as the village policemen slapped his hand on my shoulder, was just carelessness on my part but giving out the name and address of somebody else, as advised earlier by my cousin, just seemed like a way of keeping out of trouble.

The following day, my school holiday was over and I returned to my townie existence none the wiser.

What I was unaware of was the fact that a train had been derailed at that bridge some months earlier, having struck a loose railway sleeper placed on the track. Investigations had faltered until that moment when I gave a false name and address and promptly disappeared. Sadly the village policemen had more or less accepted my explanation of measuring the bridge height because I was only very young and had simply filed the report with "my name and address" on record.

Of course, I was unaware that years later my moment of stupidity would affect the career of an MP, albeit coupled with a few of his own moments of weakness.

My cousin, of course, has 'dined out' on the story for many years, albeit with certain modified 'facts'.

Chapter 2

One of the further problems that arose as a direct consequence of the above story was that there was a further distraction when a dead sheep was hit one night at the same bridge. Sadly the dead sheep had been lowered on a piece of rope from the bridge and hit the driver's cab, inflicting much damage and no small amount of personal injury. The sheep was not local, having been rustled earlier in the day from over fifty miles away, along with over a hundred other sheep. After much investigation, it was decided that the sheep had been left as a spoof to arouse attention in the village, thereby drawing attention away from the remainder of the unpleasant process.

Inevitably, this was merely leading up to something much larger and one of the local gentry was found hanging from the same bridge. His fate had been sealed over the compulsory purchase of some farm grazing land for brownfield development that benefited the family of the hung man.

Predictably, in years to come, the MP for Maldon was again called to task for failing to declare an interest in this very brownfield project.

But worse was to come when I found myself based in Swindon for a couple of years working on an innocent audit. Swindon, a dead railway city a mere twenty odd miles from my cousins' village, was so dead and uninspiring after 5pm that I took to staying with my cousins during the week and relaxing with them and their friends.

My townie naiveté was going to get me in trouble again before long and, of course, it did.

First we decided one evening to go into Trowbridge to a 'gig.' I had no idea that a 'gig' in this area was a euphemism for a bottle fight. Apparently I looked at someone's girl, but then I did speak with a strange accent, so they may not have understood what I was saying. My cousin gave my name again, because I had a split lip and couldn't talk. He also gave my address. How was I to know it would come back and haunt the MP for Maldon in years to come?

Then "I" punched a car driver on the A4 near Bath. As "I" started to walk away, "I" saw it was a left hand drive car and "I" had punched the front seat passenger. Apparently, "I" apologised profusely and game him a business card printed with "my" name and address on it.

There were at least five or six other similar incidents over the forthcoming years and my cousin was very generous with "my" name and address.

But his final neat little side-step surpassed even his high standards.

Chapter 3

The MP for Maldon had been invited to Shanghai on a secretly guarded tour selling the production licences for a UK designed, and constructed, civil airliner. The BAC 1-11 would change the relationship between England and China.

Sadly, so would my cousin's similarly timed trip with a group of his buddies, during which time they would be unbelievably well entertained by some of the finest ladies of the night in Shanghai. Following a mysterious tip-off, the evening party was interrupted by a visiting group of frustrated locals, who started something similar to the Battle of The Somme. After the police had waited long enough for some of the old scores to be settled, their intervention was amazingly efficient and all of the out of town visitors left their names and addresses, pleading diplomatic immunity. It was painfully obvious that my cousin and his buddies did not have any such immunity, except they all gave "my" name and address, albeit all in different sequences of words.

Thus the MP for Maldon had his Party Whip withdrawn, despite his being ever present in Shanghai at the time with our own Prime Minister. Everything was kept low key until their return to the UK, when a Federal Enquiry was implemented.

It was not possible to refute each individual charge because apparently, to the Chinese witnesses, we all look alike but, needless to say, the MP for Maldon's reputation had become shabby.

Now I know that there is naïveté and naïveté, but it was outrageously obvious that the MP could not possibly have been in as many bad places as seems possible all at the same time.

So I was arrested on holiday in France and carted off to prison in Shanghai under the terms of some strange extradition order. It appeared that some old retired local village policeman in Wiltshire had added two and two together and worked out that my cousin needed help – either that or he owed the policeman money. It was obviously my own fault, because the Labrador dog in the Fox and Hounds pub in the village was known as 'Pernod' which sounds very unusual with a Wiltshire accent. It had recently sired some puppies of the Village policeman's bitch and they all smelled of aniseed. He had suddenly remembered my liking for the product when I was working in Swindon and my fate was cast.

I had anticipated that my days were numbered and had produced some amazing examples of alibis that proved that I could not possibly have been anywhere near the various scenes of crime.

But the world was closing in on my cousin when he suddenly produced his 'ace up the sleeve.' His case for the defence was that he was but a pure country bumpkin and I had been running the scam all the way along, also stitching up his other townie cousin, who would ultimately become the MP for Maldon in Essex. Apparently that all stemmed back to that incident many years earlier when the MP and I fought bitterly over the hand of a sweet maiden.

The fact that she was my seven year old sister somehow escaped disclosure, along with the fact that she had been insulted and her big brother was protecting her. After many months, a small element of sense crept in and we were both deported, on condition that we were banned for life from China.

Suited me, albeit the MP would have to find a way around the problem, which he seemed to achieve easily enough. It hadn't dawned on me that he actually had diplomatic immunity, regardless.

Despite our ancient fisticuffs, we travelled home together and the MP began a severe character assassination of my cousin. They obviously knew each other intimately and some of the revelations were totally eye-opening. By the time we reached Brize Norton, the MP, whom we shall call Patrick, because it's not his name, had worked out a strategy. My cousin would soon be 'dead meat.'

He was no longer a hero for me – he was a mental defective who needed help. But, despite being family, he would find no help coming from me. Patrick, the MP, had devious plans afoot.

Initially I went along with his plans but could see that he was evil beyond belief and the plans would involve my cousin ending up in jail for most of the rest of his life. In the meantime, I began to lose sleep realising that this whole project was becoming blinkered and vindictive. In fact, Patrick wanted only to inflict the greatest pain possible so that he could walk away laughing, conscience free. But as I thought more, I began to realise that Patrick wasn't quite as nice and innocent as he made himself out to be.

During our long RAF flight home, in a battered old C130 (none of your luxury VC10s for us), he had drunk the lion's share of a litre bottle of Bells Whisky and several bottles of good red wine. His conversation had become repetitive and boring, mostly incomprehensible. The volume needed turning down badly but Patrick was intent on telling everybody what a good bloke Patrick was. Most other people on the flight were either military or government and even they were getting hacked off by Patrick's whinging and droning, consistently at high decibels.

The more I thought back to the flight, the more I realised that other passengers kept backing off and wandering to far ends of the aircraft. In fact, whenever we stopped to re-fuel, Patrick and I were always left alone and our fellow passengers were very hard to find when the flight was due to depart. It was as though they were going out for a very long cigarette at every opportunity.

When we reached our final fuel stop before the UK, at Amiens Military Barracks, not far from Paris, several of the other passengers disappeared completely but, regardless, Patrick excelled himself for the last leg. By now he was delivering his discourse standing up and waving his arms around. From memory, I had turned off and just wasn't listening. I may have nodded from time to time but it wasn't with approval – it was more like I was trying to fall asleep.

Over the Channel, the flight became choppy and Patrick suddenly changed colour. As his pallor shifted rapidly from deathly white to 'vomity' green, I remember his trying to stagger to his seat but missing and ending up as a heap on the ground. Nobody moved a muscle, other than to raise the odd eyebrow or offer a slight snort. He lay there in a slumber-bound mess until we started our descent into Brize Norton, when a couple of burly soldiers grouped him into a piece of messy tarpaulin and hoisted him onto the top of a small storage cupboard. They tied him there with a few strands of rope, then disappeared smartly into the cockpit.

The landing could have been smoother but everybody was prepared. Patrick, however, was thrown with a resounding crack onto the floor of the aircraft, causing several people to wince and suck in breath, but only as they all turned their backs on him.

After some particularly bumpy taxi-ing, the aircraft drew up and switched off the engines, leaving all passengers free to disembark.

Unless your name was Patrick or you were a friend of his.

Apparently, the deportation order didn't give us freedom. We had to await the re-appearance of the burly soldiers, who came in like auditors to bayonet the wounded. Patrick got a discrete kicking and I was hauled up and out. By the time Patrick caught me up, he had obviously 'walked into a door handle' or two. He was going to be very sore in the morning but probably wouldn't remember much, which was for the better. I even remembered the pleasure I had gained, despite the pain, by teaching him how to control himself all those years before.

Chapter 4

Patrick and I finally left the Wootton Bassett police station having seen nobody because it was Tuesday and, therefore, closed. Our two burly soldiers obviously had failed to check that beforehand but I doubt it was their responsibility. However, it made them less than gracious towards us and, in particular, Patrick. His 'door handle' marks, were looking ugly and pronounced and he may also have 'fallen down some stairs'.

But their duties were over and we were taken to Swindon railway station and abandoned. Not so much as a pat on the head, a kick in the butt or even a travel warrant were given to us, so we were forced to fend for ourselves.

The obvious solution was to call my cousin, who lived not an hour away, and to rely upon his mercy.

Big mistake.

We both felt unsure how we would greeted over the phone but neither of us really expected ridicule and dismissal. Perhaps we were both being naïve but for different reasons.

I had assumed that he would be sympathetic to my detention caused by his usual practical joking. I expected the issue to be with Patrick who would ultimately very angry for the lying and deception and its effect on his political career. I expected my cousin to be full of remorse and embarrassed.

But outrageous laughter followed by a blunt "Sod off" and the slamming down of the phone, surprised us both.

I controlled my feeling of hurt but Patrick's incandescent rage shook me rigid. We were standing in a public phone box in the entrance to Swindon station in a fairly public spot. Patrick smashed the bottom panel of side glass, first with his boot, then with the telephone receiver which he had wrenched off its stand. His anger was far from satiated and he started work on the other side panel.

Being a natural coward, I escaped onto the concourse and looked for assistance, although I had no idea of what sort. My options were limited to a twelve year old community support officer or an eighty year old ticket vendor. Maybe I had misjudged their ages but I had misjudged everything else so far so I didn't even consider them to be appropriate.

Second mistake.

The CSO heard the sound of smashing glass and bounded across the concourse, unintentionally felling Patrick as he failed to stop himself on arrival. With the two of them lying in a heap of body, glass and blood, I was able to turn and walk away.

Wrong Options

"Not so fast, Sunbeam," came an instruction from nowhere. I scanned around rapidly but failed to find the source. To my horror, the voice repeated its message but added, "Yes, you!"

I spun round again to see that the ticket vendor had been replaced by a Fat Controller character who was already on the phone, probably summoning support. I had nowhere to run to or hide and raised my arms in submission. I shuffled towards the ticket office where the big guy said, "Wait there," and came barrelling out to greet me.

"What the hell's going on?" he asked, pointing directly into my face.

"Don't ask me," I replied. "He's the guy with the anger management problem," I added, pointing at Patrick, who was beginning to hack me off totally. Thinking rapidly, I realised neither my cousin nor Patrick were going to be of any use to me, and the time had come to defend myself.

"In fact, would you mind calling the police, please? I have had to put up with anger, stupidity and self-centred people who don't give a damn about anybody else other than themselves. Beware, the pillock kicking the phone-box in is a person who should know better and is supposed to set an example to society. I've had it up to here with him and the time has come to call a halt to all of this crap.

"Do you want to be famous, enhance your reputation? That pratt is a senior MP and needs a good seeing to."

"Looks to me like he's already had one," said the Fat Controller, smiling. "But if you want me to look the other way for a few minutes, feel free."

The temptation was there but I could feel my hand hurt from the last time I had punched him and thought better of it. Apart from which, I could hear the wail of sirens coming towards us. With my luck, I would be caught at just the wrong moment. But I need not have worried, because at that second, Patrick took a wild swing at the CSO but missed. The CSO didn't but neither the Fat Controller nor I was looking at the time. By the time we did focus, Patrick was on the floor again with stars coming out of his head.

"He fell," said the CSO to the arriving policeman, "and I can smell drink on his breath."

"Don't worry, son, leave him with us," said the policeman, looking at Patrick, the glass, the blood and adding two and two together. "He can call his solicitor later – much later. Right now, we'll just check for any ID and let him sleep it off. Well done, lad."

The policeman turned to the Fat Controller and me and said, "I don't suppose either of you two gents saw anything, eh?" and winked a smile.

We both shook our heads independently and watched as the police lifted Patrick into a station wheelchair and took him out to their van, still away with the pixies.

The Fat Controller turned to me and said, "Would you like a cup of tea, sir?" and gave a similar smiling wink. I nodded and was led through an open barrier into the station café, where two teas were already on their way to us. The Controller sat at a table and beckoned me to sit opposite. He discreetly tapped the side of his nose and leant forward to me.

"I remember that guy from about two years ago. He's been here before and he was pissed and aggressive then. What is it with these guys? They think they're above the law, the law that they control. Good riddance, I say," and sipped his tea noisily. "Now I presume your ticket got damaged in the scuffle, eh?

Leave it with me, I'll issue a replacement. I'll just need a little signature. Any name in particular? Roy Best?"

Ironically I once knew somebody of that name but I wasn't going to be allowed to give 'no' as an answer, so I just nodded and smiled.

"To where were you going, Mr Best?" asked the winking Controller.

"Chalkwell would be good," I started, only to be interrupted by the Controller, who said, "Did you say Shoeburyness, Mr Best?"

"Of course," I replied, "thank you very much."

"The least I can do for your inconvenience, sir," and he beckoned over the eighty year old ticket vendor, giving him a scribbled note on a very small piece of paper, which mysteriously re-appeared moments later attached to a single ticket. The note got detached instantly, scrumpled up and dropped into bottom of a half finished cup of tea at the next table.

The Controller stood up, proffered his hand and said, "The 09.37 will be in shortly, sir, if you get a move on. Takes just an hour to Paddington. Have a nice day, Mr Best, and please give my regards to Mrs Best." With a rapid handshake and almost a bow, he whisked himself away and left me speechless, but somehow smiling at the experience and my renewed faith in mankind.

As I watched the 09.37 braking its way into the platform next to me, I suddenly realised that I had not seen a suitcase since we had boarded the aircraft, and my stomach pitched. But then I smiled and thought, "What the hell? I'm free and out of here. What's a few clothes and toothbrush anyway?"

By 11.00 a.m. I was on the Circle Line round to Aldgate and couldn't give a damn about anything. At Fenchurch Street I realised I was ravenously hungry but still had only my passport in my pocket and no money or access to money. I would have to get home to eat. But the hunger was intense. I looked in the passport and was amazed to see that my name wasn't Roy Best at all, but, of course, I already knew that.

The early edition of the Evening Standard was being delivered into the boxes at the entrance to Fenchurch Street station and I picked one up. As I looked at the headlines, I was horrified to see below them a picture of a very dishevelled Patrick, with a sub-heading of "MP arrested after running battle with police."

I mounted the escalator up to the platforms and was relieved to see nobody I knew and slipped onto the 11.40 slow train, where I found plenty of space. By the time the train pulled out, my mouth had dropped open as I read about Patrick being evicted from a shabby night club, when he had taken a swipe at a policeman on duty outside the Trowbridge Club that I hadn't seen since that bottle fight many years before. How ironic was that? But it did go to show that you should never believe everything you read in newspapers.

As the train pulled into Chalkwell, I stood and walked towards the doors. A young mother with two children was struggling to get them all in the right position by the doors and I thought I would offer her a hand.

The smaller of the children turned towards me and I watched her face shrivel in horror as she looked up. She turned to her mother and shrieked, "Mummy, that man's all dirty and's got blood on his face!"

I turned to the mother expecting something but I wasn't sure what. What I didn't expect was her even louder scream. "Oh, my God," she screeched, clutching her hands to her face, as she fainted into a heap. The children turned away in disgust and started to sob with tears.

As the train stopped, I opened the doors and called out for help. An elderly couple turned towards me and suddenly the colour drained from their cheeks. The woman collapsed and the man was torn between stopping her from hitting the deck and staring at me, open mouthed. Suddenly I felt the cold blast of sea air hit my face and raised my hand to my cheek to discover a bloody mess.

The fallen mother below me started to come to and shouted, "Get off, children. Look the other way!" and started to struggle onto her knees with her backside towards me. "Help," she called out to anybody on the platform. Straight away people started to gather and stare, mostly with abject terror.

"You animal!" someone shouted, pointing at me. "Quick – someone get the police – he's been eating his face!"

And the whole world went soft and dark.

The Predator

By Sandra Maynard

Where evil lurks and shadows play,
on the minds of the worthy.
The ghost of the night prowls dimly lit streets,
Seeking out unsuspecting prey.
Watch every corner, nook and cranny,
You really don't want to dwell.
Beware the Predator looking to vent
his hatred on the world.
A murderous glint, a flash of a smile,
A knife that is hidden from view.
Don't be a victim, don't be a fool,
Don't let him sneak up on you.
A cat's sharp hiss,
A warning for sure,
That the Predator is near.
Searching for more.
Bloodthirsty lust, urges him on.
Protected by the darkness of the night.
Don't walk alone, please stay at home,
Keep out of the Predator's sight.

The Unquenchable Fire

By Elliot Thorpe

Father had gotten angry with the sales guy. An overbearing chimp in a suit, he called him, all because he wouldn't buy our truck.

But it was pretty beat-up, to be honest, so I wasn't surprised that no one wanted it. As Father navigated it out of the car lot onto the shimmering road, its engine wheezed unhappily.

"Look around you, boy," Father said, chewing on a stub of gum. "Lowlifes, scroungers, every one."

I looked and saw people, ordinary folk who probably were a bit on the hard done by side of things, but who likely didn't really warrant Father's sweeping moniker.

He was the sort of man who believed we're all responsible for our actions and those who expected hand-outs were the dregs of society.

Self-sufficient we were, Father, Ma, my sisters and me.

We didn't go to school. Father taught us all we needed to know and Ma ran the home.

Father had a job; at least he called it a job. He went and made stuff, furniture mainly, then sold it door to door. But he'd not sold anything for a good few weeks and Ma was getting worried that money was running out. She said it was the image he was projecting – him and the state of the pick-up.

They argued about it, Father insisting that homespun was what attracted people – not the smooth, corporate look with its flat-packed furniture and salesmen that reeked of cologne.

Father always won the arguments. I reckon it was because Ma didn't have the strength to argue back but we didn't know that at the time.

We lived in Newport, Arkansas. I was happy there for a while, but my sisters left when they were old enough.

Ma much preferred Little Rock, about an hour and a half south on Route 167. It was probably because she loved Marilyn Monroe.

Father hated TV, hated movies and had little patience with the radio, so we never got to see what other people saw or heard. In fact I don't even remember seeing a newspaper in the house, so how Father could criticise the world around him when he and us were so far removed from it I never knew. He did read though. Read and read. He devoured books. Kerouac was his favourite and another called Burroughs, but not the one who wrote the Tarzan stories. He said their work reflected humanity back on itself and it was about time that they started introducing them into the schools.

But as we'd never set foot in a school they could have very well been on the curriculum for all we knew.

The stop sign flashed up and the pick-up's brakes squeaked as we shuddered to a halt.

A big Cadillac hummed across our path and Father tutted, the gum at his lips amplifying the sound of disapproval but I could see in his eyes beneath his cap a brief flash of envy.

"Don't you like it, Pa?" I ventured.

"It's a statement, Josh," Father growled. "Showing off is unhealthy."

He was full of contradictions, my Father. Hated the poor, dismissed the rich. But as I looked at my jeans with their holes in both knees and Father's baggy t-shirt that I always saw him in, I wondered where we fitted in.

Perhaps we didn't. Perhaps that was why he always seemed so angry.

The light changed to green and Father cranked the truck into gear, pulling away.

A red Chevy came hurtling at us from the left, jumping its own set of lights.

Father wrenched at the wheel and braked. We careened wildly over the cross-roads but luckily Father regained control and we carried on our way.

"Fucking asshole!" Father screamed out of the window, giving the disappearing Chevy the middle finger. "You okay?"

I nodded. A little shaken but I was fine. I'd struck my knee against the dash. It only hurt for a bit and by the time we reached the hardware store, I'd forgotten about it.

One of Father's chisels had snapped last week and he found he couldn't repair it. He'd not bought a set of tools for as long as I could remember and he wasn't happy about it. I think the set he used was his Father's, so some form of sentiment – an emotion I had never seen in him – had surfaced but was subdued as quickly as it had appeared when the store manager emerged behind the counter.

As he and my Father talked about tools and drill bits, I wandered around the shop for a while, poking and prodding at all the stuff stacked on shelves or thrown in dump-bins. Fluorescent orange labels with black marker pen words told me what it all was and how much I could pay for it. But Father had not yet taught us the value of money.

The spinning ceiling fan was erratic and I couldn't feel its benefit in the stuffy, sweaty shop so I decided to wait outside.

The little bell jangled as the door opened and closed and I leant against the cool window, watching the traffic go by, wondering where it was all going. Everyone was going *somewhere*, I figured, and that there was always a destination. Father told us it wasn't where you ended up, it was how you got there.

That never worked for me. I could see my Ma and the sad look on her face whenever she walked by the bus station and saw the ads on the ticket office's walls for holidays in far off places. Father would never take her away and as far as I knew, they hadn't even had a honeymoon – and they'd been married for twenty-odd years. None of us had a passport anyway so it was a bit pointless to hope.

The same red Chevy that had cut us up at the lights pulled up next to our truck and two men got out: a black guy and one who looked Hispanic. They both wore long coats, which I thought was strange in this heat. The Spanish man said something to me but I didn't understand what it was, but by his expression it wasn't friendly.

I stared at him, not sure what to say back and as he went to say something more, his companion called him over and they whispered to each other, sometimes looking in my direction but mainly looking up and down the street.

I peered in through the shop window. Father was still at the counter, most likely arguing over the price of things. As I turned back to face the street, the two men entered the store, quite quickly I thought. I guessed they were in a rush and my thoughts turned to them getting frustrated waiting for Father to finish haggling before they could be served.

I found a little stone at my flip-flopped feet and spent the next few minutes negotiating its journey from the sidewalk to between my right foot's toes. It felt funny against my skin, sort of sharp but round at the same time. I flicked it back out and it hit the men's Chevy.

I hoped they wouldn't notice. It hadn't made a mark but all the same I took a quick look in through the window to see if they'd been watching.

I couldn't see Father at first but the men were at the counter and there was lots of arms waving. The man who owned the shop didn't seem too happy but he put his hands up for some reason.

I tapped on the window as I saw Father wander back to the counter. He'd picked up some sandpaper and was busy reading the pack's rear.

He looked up at me and then I saw one of the men swing around to face him. A loud crack and a flash and Father fell to the floor.

I couldn't make out what had happened for a few moments but then, as the two men barged past me and into the Chevy, wheels skidding in the dust as they sped away, it dawned on me.

A coldness enveloped my face and neck as I stood there, rooted to the spot. I tried to shout through the window but I couldn't find my voice.

I could only watch as the store keeper used his telephone, hang up then crouch next to Father's body.

Something triggered me into moving finally and I entered the shop.

There was a darkness I hadn't noticed before, a pallor hanging low amidst the hardware.

The distance between the door and the counter could have been miles for the effort it took to cross. It was as if my feet were encased in clay.

"Out! Out!" the man said, waving at me.

I tried to say that it was my father lying there but still I had no voice. Instead I resolutely moved closer. Then the man recognised me from earlier.

"I'm so sorry, son..." he said but the apology didn't really wash with me. Why couldn't he have just sold Father what he wanted at the price Father wanted to pay and then he wouldn't have still been in there to have gotten shot.

I noticed the blood then. Pools of it collecting around Father's body.

Father himself was still, his skin ghostly white. Eyes staring up at the ceiling. He was still wearing his little gold-rimmed specs. His cap was on the floor behind him.

I knew he was dead. The sandpaper was still in his hand and the chisel he had chosen was on the counter.

I knelt at his head and looked at the hole in his chest.

I didn't know what I felt. Was it rage? Was it despair?

I knew that the one person who I considered to be my best friend was laying there before me, devoid of any life, taken cruelly and swiftly from this world by two men who were violent opportunists. The scum that Father detested.

I cried in the days and weeks after, not even being able to face going to his funeral. Ma had been so upset at that, adding to her grief and hopelessness, the cancer that she had been hiding so well from all of us, even Father, took advantage of her weakened state and only took a matter of months to finally kill her.

I did attend Ma's funeral, using the time to finally say goodbye to Father too.

The Unquenchable Fire

And as I stood there, looking at the double grave, my sisters next to me, I realised that those two men had taken *both* our parents from us. And they had never been found.

I could drive (Father having taught me when I was ten) so I took the pick-up and roamed the streets for days, focusing all the efforts that the police didn't have the time, inclination or resource to do to track the men down and exact my revenge.

I did find them. Of course I did. Even though it took me a while.

They didn't remember me, didn't remember gunning Father down in cold blood. That in itself told me Father was not the only one they had done it to. So I reminded them, told them how they had ripped my family apart, how they had caused my mother to die, how they had taken my childhood from me when I had so much more to learn and want from my parents. How they had made my sisters in to what they were today. How they had made me like them.

They begged me for their lives at the end. But I wouldn't give them the opportunity. Father had no choice so why should they have had that luxury? The cancer may have taken Ma anyway but I knew that it had taken her sooner than was due.

The two men died in their own piss and I was glad – the Chevy burnt like a beacon - but it didn't make me feel better because I didn't get back what I had lost.

So now Death Row wants me. But I'm not about to let it catch me. *I* will find death in my own time, when I am good and ready. It don't scare me because I know it's coming. One day. Father will be waiting for me. And Ma too. And that's what keeps me going.

Is There Anyone Out There?

By Colin Butler

It's the year twenty twenty-five,
A strange dehumanised world.
No-one celebrates the joy of being alive
In the absence of human contact

Gone are the corner shops with helpful staff
Replaced by self-service supermarkets
The internet has written their epitaph,
And on-line shopping certainly safer.

Phones are answered by robotic voices
Accompanied by musak Mozart.
Listing numbers to decide your choices
Everywhere robots replacing real people.

"Is there anyone out there?" I cried
But an eerie silence was the only reply
That seems to reverberate around the nation,
As people long for human friendship.

People live behind electrified fences
Just like animals in their secured cages
Residents protected by alarms and other defences
So afraid to leave their secure houses.

People transfixed by their multi-media TV sets,
Afraid to attend shows and sports events.

Grave Matters

Circling overhead are the police patrol jets,
Even Hospitals barricaded like fortresses.

The streets are strangely quiet,
But bullet-proof cars built like tanks,
Law enforcers seeking to prevent a riot
Relentlessly patrol the highways

Criminal gangs roam the streets,
Whilst feral serial killers proliferate,
Lurking in the sinister no-go beats,
As the world slowly descends to chaos.

Suicide rates continue to escalate,
As lonely people suffer severe depression,
Feeling so utterly lonely and desolate,
Cut off from even their closest neighbours.

The figure stands on the rooftop ledge
Tearfully shouts "Is anyone out there?"
Before he slowly creeps to the edge
And plummets to earth with a sickening thud.

About the Authors

Paul Bunn

I have worked for more years than I care to remember for a telecoms company in a number of different roles. I became interested in writing when in my 30's, which led me to complete a creative writing course.

That gave me the writing bug and as a result I joined a new writing group "Writers Anonymous" to help fulfil my dream of being published.

I get a great deal of pride knowing I have contributed to all the books WA have published to date and will continue to do so in the future.

Colin Butler

Born in Tottenham, but an avid Arsenal supporter, he is married with 2 sons and 6 grandchildren and currently lives in Thorpe Bay.

After retiring from a career in Local Government, he took a creative writing course and re-joined Writers Anonymous in June 2007 and has had a number of poems published. Recently he had a collection of poems published under the title "Views from the Estuary."

He is also a keen photographer and bowler.

Sandra Maynard

Aside from my family, writing is my main passion. One of the modules in my Open University degree was 'Creative Writing' and since then I haven't put my pen down! I love creating dark, macabre stories with a twist and was thrilled to be invited to join 'Writers Anonymous'. I am looking forward to sharing my sinister thoughts and inspirations.

David Shaer

A numerically challenged chartered accountant, my main ambition was to get past writing unpublishable letters to The Times. I played rugby during five decades but was only ever going to be the player most likely to be lent to the opposition if they were short. I also need a large atlas when driving, but only to see over the steering wheel. I was starting to get a complex about life when I was ejected from French evening classes, so I joined a creative writing course and now I shall let you judge whether I should go back and start again.

Elliot Thorpe

I'd always been told since school that I had a flair for writing and I never quite believed it until, after years upon years of countless short stories and false starts, I was finally commissioned to write the BBC-licensed full-cast audio drama Doctor Who – Cryptobiosis starring Colin Baker and Nicola Bryant. I have previously worked for Starlog and written for the sites Den of Geek, Shadowlocked and Doctor Who TV as well as for Encore, the magazine for the theatre professional and the Dean Martin Association, Dino's first official fan club. As well as being part of this illustrious and creatively rewarding Writers Anonymous collective, I also write for the site www.cultbritannia.com and work with the West End stage production The Definitive Rat Pack.

My first novel, Cold Runs the Blood, was published in 2013.
– Website:
http://coldrunstheblood.wix.com/elliot-thorpe-author.
My Twitter account is: @elliot1701

Simon Woodward

After working consistently in I.T. for 27 years I decided it was time to forego the strictly logical world of computing and take up writing in my spare time. I don't think I'll ever truly get to grips with this literary world but I'm certainly having great fun finding out about it, though I think my wife, Yve, is not so enamoured by my frequent requests asking 'what do you think of this?'

That said, without my wife, I don't think my three children's books would have ever seen the light of day and I wouldn't have enough stuff to be able to have my very own website created — http://www.srwoodward.co.uk

Other Anthologies

Sinister
Bedside Manner
Sinister Too
East Scythe
Toxic Legacy
Dead Letters
Coffee Break 200
Coffee Break 350
Halloween & Hot Chocolate

www.writersanonymous.org.uk

33113865R00169

Made in the USA
Charleston, SC
04 September 2014